CELEBRITEENS

Break the Rules

CELEBRITEENS

Break the Rules

Joanna Philbin

MSCHOLASTIC

Scholastic Children's Books
An imprint of Scholastic Ltd
Euston House, 24 Eversholt Street
London, NW1 1DB, UK
Registered office: Westfield Road, Southam, Warwickshire, CV47 0RA
SCHOLASTIC and associated logos are trademarks and/or registered
trademarks of Scholastic Inc.

First published in the US by Poppy, an imprint of Little, Brown and Company, 2011
This edition published in the UK by Scholastic Ltd, 2012

Text copyright © Joanna Philbin, 2011

The right of Joanna Philbin to be identified as the author
of this work has been asserted by her.

ISBN 978 1 407 12118 5

A CIP catalogue record for this book is available from the British Library.

Printed and bound by CPI Group (UK) Ltd, Croydon, CR0 4YY
Papers used by Scholastic Children's Books are made from wood grown
in sustainable forests.

1 3 5 7 9 10 8 6 4 2

www.scholastic.co.uk/zone

7 of JJ

We,
CELIBRITEENS,

have formed the following rules and guidelines for
optimum happiness and drama-free living:

1. Never read tabloids or surf the celebrity gossip sites.
   But if you have to, try not to look at the stuff about
   your parents.

2. All friends are good, but only one of us knows
   what your life is really like. Bond with as many as
   possible.

3. Friends are always more important than guys.
   Always.

4. Be nice to everyone, and if people *still* say you're
   conceited, the just let it go.

5. If you need to discuss parental drama, only do so with
   each other. (See rule #2.)

6. Never talk to the press about your parents. Especially
   when they're hanging out in front of your house and
   yelling at you to say stuff.

7. Always date a guy for at least a month before taking him to a red-carpet event. The same goes for taking him on your plane, bringing him on tour, etc.

8. If you see another daughter of someone famous being criticized on a blog, always write a post sticking up for her, even if you don't know her.

9. When meeting new people, only give them one name – your first one.

10. You are not your parents, and your parents aren't you. No matter how well-known – or mortifying – they are.

Chapter 1

Carina Jurgensen squeezed the rubber stress ball over and over, looking out of the tinted window as their car sped across town. Her dad's black Mercedes raced west on Forty-second Street, gliding over potholes and swerving past taxis, as sleek and fast as the Batmobile. They seemed to be headed straight towards the Lincoln Tunnel, which could only mean one thing: they were leaving Manhattan. As they blew past the glittering marquees of Times Square, Carina got the feeling that she was leaving for good.

Beside her in the back seat, her father, Karl Jurgensen, tapped on his BlackBerry with his thumbs, his brows knitted in fierce concentration. From the moment they'd got in the car together, he hadn't said a word, not even to their driver, Max. This, she knew, was a bad sign. Wherever they were headed, it was clear that her dad had already made all the arrangements.

And he could do anything. That was the thing about having billions of dollars – nothing was impossible. If you wanted to whisk your only child out of New York City on an ordinary November night and make sure she was never seen or heard from again, you could do that. Nobody would stop you.

Carina's best friends, Lizzie and Hudson, were probably just reaching her building right now. She'd texted them minutes before she left, and now the doorman would tell them that she'd just walked out with her dad and a duffel bag, into a waiting car, and they'd panic. They'd been warning her about something like this for weeks. Carina pictured them in her lobby. Hudson would do that frenzied-pacing thing, and Lizzie would stare off into the distance and pull at her red curls, trying to figure out just how serious this was. Of course they'd start firing off texts and phone calls, but she wouldn't get any of them. Her iPhone was in her bag, which was locked up in the boot and completely out of reach. But she wouldn't be able to talk to them anyway, not with her dad sitting so close to her, emitting a kind of cold rage she'd never felt from him before.

"Where are we going?" she finally asked, daring to turn and look at him.

Karl kept his eyes on his BlackBerry. From this angle, in the dim light of the back seat, Carina thought her forty-two-year-old dad could almost pass for a college kid. It helped that he still had a head of thick brown hair, albeit sprinkled with salt-and-pepper grey, and a strong, movie star's jaw. His days in the rowing team at Harvard had given him a lean, broad-shouldered physique, which he maintained with the help of a personal trainer and strict instructions to his chef.

"Dad?" she asked again. "Can you just tell me?"

Without bothering to look up, he shook his head. "You've lost the privilege of more information," he said flatly, still typing.

Carina felt her throat tighten with dread. She'd had plenty of fights with her dad over the years, but this was different. She was in serious trouble – the kind of trouble that could possibly alter her life for ever, and not in a good way.

It had all started in September, two months ago. They'd been in the middle of another silent dinner at the twenty-seat dining room table – he at one end, reading a stack of daily status reports on his company and emailing his minions on his ever-present BlackBerry; she at the other, doing her geometry homework and texting Lizzie and Hudson – when suddenly he'd said, "Put that away for a second. I'd like to speak with you."

She looked up to see his stern face, and a prickly sense of foreboding ran along her skin. The Jurg (as she and her friends called him) had no time for chitchat. His kind of talk usually fell into two categories: announcements and orders. Whatever he had to say sounded like both.

"I'd like you to start coming into the office," he said, his brown eyes boring into her like lasers from across the table. "Three days a week. Wednesdays and Fridays after school, and all day on Saturday. We'll start from there."

"Come into your *office*?" Her voice bounced off the wood-panelled walls and floated up to the car-size crystal chandelier. "What for?"

The Jurg steepled his hands. "You're my sole heir, Carina. It's time you learned about the world you're going to inherit."

That world was Metronome Media, his empire of newspapers, magazines, cable television stations and social networking websites. He'd started the company with one weekly newspaper when he was still at Harvard and twenty years later, it had become the largest media conglomerate in the Western Hemisphere. One in three people read a Metronome publication or visited a Metronome-owned website every day. And all of this success had made the Jurg one of the richest men in the world. He owned five homes, a collection of vintage Jaguars, a fifty-foot yacht, a helicopter, a Gulfstream jet and a collection of late twentieth-century art that rivalled the Guggenheim Museum's. Celebrities, socialites, kings of small countries and even the president called him on his private line. He'd even toyed with running for mayor once or twice and then backed out at the last minute, much to Carina's relief.

"Dad, I know all about your world," Carina said, looking him straight in the eye. "And I don't want to inherit it."

The Jurg gave her a grave stare. "Isn't it a little too soon to know that already? You're fourteen. You don't know what you want. And honestly, this is better than having you come into the business when you're twenty-two," he said. "By the time you're out of Wharton you'll be completely prepared."

"I'm going to *Wharton*?" she asked.

"You used to love to come into my office when you were a little girl," he continued, slicing into his steak. "Don't you remember? Sitting in my chair? Pretending to hold a meeting in the conference room?"

"I was eight. I liked playing with Barbie dolls, too."

"Carina, I was your age when I had my first job," he said, more seriously. "Delivering newspapers. Now, I'm not asking you to have a paper route. What I'm asking for is a few hours a week."

"But I have other stuff going on," she said, sitting up straight in her chair. "I'm the captain of the Junior Varsity soccer team this year. Did you know that? And I already signed up for Model UN. And what about going to Montauk on the weekends? What about surfing? What about hanging out with my friends?"

Her father put down his fork and a faint, exasperated sigh escaped his lips. "Carina, soccer and Model UN are extra-curriculars," he said. "They're not your future."

Before she could respond, the door to the kitchen swung open and Marco walked in. He was dressed in the khakis and polo shirt that the Jurg made all of his help wear, and his sneakers barely made a sound on the wood floor.

"You have a phone call, sir," he said in his quiet, deferential voice. "Tokyo."

The Jurg took one last sip of his iced tea – he never drank alcohol – and stood up, dropping his silk napkin on the table. "You'll start next week," he said decisively, and walked out.

Carina sat for a moment in the empty dining room, and then pushed her heavy wood chair back from the table. So it was finally official, she realized. Her dad had no clue who she was.

For the past four years, ever since her parents' divorce, she and the Jurg had lived together like room-mates who were determined not to be friends. They avoided each other in the halls, made polite conversation when they had to, and generally pretended the other person wasn't living there. Even though they had dinner together at least twice a week, it was usually silent, with both of them texting or emailing in between every mouthful. Carina learned to stick to "her" parts of the three-storey penthouse: the den, the kitchen and her bedroom. There was one obvious perk to all this: most of the time, she could come and go as she pleased, with only Otto, the security guard at the front door, keeping tabs on her. Unlike her friends Lizzie and Hudson, whose parents were sometimes *too* involved in their daughters' lives.

But sometimes the distance between her and the Jurg was depressing. He didn't know a thing about her, and he didn't ask. Weren't fathers supposed to know certain things about their kids, or at least *want* to know? For instance, he had no idea how much she loved to surf the waves at Honolua Bay, or how she couldn't wait to turn eighteen so she could go on Outward Bound's Patagonia trip, or how she had recurring dreams of finally beating Sacred Heart in the soccer championships and being hoisted on the shoulders of her teammates like in some corny sports movie.

But the Jurg had no time for details like this. He marched through the apartment always on his way to something else: the office, a meeting, a workout. He lived his life on a schedule. And there were no slots for her.

And now the fact that he wanted her to "learn the business" only proved how little he knew about her. True, she didn't exactly have a specific life plan yet, aside from taking a year off before college to surf Fiji and then become a certified Outward Bound instructor. But she did know one thing: she would never be a business-person. She couldn't care less about making money. Or money, in general. And the idea of being around her cold, preoccupied, money-obsessed dad every day for the rest of her life was not an option.

In the days that followed, she pretended to forget their dinner-time talk. It wasn't like her dad was going to *make* her work for him. But she knew from experience that when the Jurg said that he wanted something to happen, there was little besides a bomb or an act of God that could actually stop it. After a few more stony looks across the dining room table and unsubtle hints – like having his assistant call her to arrange an ID card – she gave up her spot on the soccer team, withdrew from Model UN and went to his office.

As she expected, the work was mind-numbingly boring. All she did was Xerox status reports, memos and charts of sales figures, none of which made sense. Just like at home, her dad was nowhere to be seen. Instead he'd stuck her with his chief operating officer, Ed Bracken, whom she'd nicknamed the Anteater and Creepy Manservant. Creepy Manservant was in his fifties and had greasy thinning hair, a clammy handshake and a shuffling walk. He sucked up to the Jurg so much that Carina couldn't believe her eyes half the time. She thought her dad would have been better off with a twenty-five-year-old super-hot MBA grad, or at least a guy who didn't still live with his mother. But Creepy Manservant was by the Jurg's side twenty-four seven, and now she had to answer to him. It was awful.

But even worse than the boredom and Ed Bracken was the sense that her future was slowly closing in around her. As she sat in a small office in her dad's sterile, glass-walled skyscraper, forty floors above Times Square, she felt as trapped as if she were in a stuck elevator. Nothing she wanted to do or learn or try would ever matter. Her entire life was already mapped out, and she was marching in a straight line towards one, and only one, end point: to be her father's Mini-Me.

And then one quiet Saturday morning at the end of September, she came across the memo that changed everything.

It was about Jurgensenland, her father's annual charity event. Every Labour Day weekend, he turned the grounds of his Montauk estate into an amusement park, complete with spinning teacups, a Ferris wheel, an underwater submarine ride in one of his lakes and a huge ball at night that cost ten thousand dollars a ticket. All of the proceeds went to Oxfam, the charity devoted to solving poverty and hunger. The Jurg had grown up poor in rural Pennsylvania and knew what it was like to go hungry. Whenever Carina worried that her dad had turned into a shameless money-making machine, she always took comfort in his charity work. Finding a solution had become one of his causes. When she saw *Re: Jurgensenland* in the subject line, she picked up the memo from the tray on Ed Bracken's desk. It was from her dad's accountant. It explained that the most recent event had raised three million dollars, but then she read:

> Of this, $2M will go directly to the aforementioned charity. The remaining $1M will be diverted as discussed for Karl Jurgensen's other use.

Other use. She read the words over and over again. At first she didn't understand what they meant. And then it began to sink in.

He's keeping the money, she realized as a chill went over her. *He's cheating the charity.*

The more she thought about it, it began to make sense. It wouldn't be the first time her dad had cheated. While her mom had never told her that he'd been with another woman, she'd pieced enough together to explain their divorce. As she stood there in Ed's office with the memo in her hand, her thoughts

9

flashed back to a night when she was ten years old, listening to her parents behind the closed bedroom door, her mother sobbing, her father yelling at the top of his lungs that *I can do whatever I damn well want; you deserve it if you're going to be so selfish.*

She looked behind her, out of the door to Ed's office. His assistant had stepped away from her desk. She knew that she didn't have much time.

Quickly she walked the memo down to the photocopy room. Without stopping to think about it, she placed it on the glass, shut the top cover and pressed Start. The copy spat out of the machine. A few seconds later she snuck the original back into the file folder and put it in the tray on Ed's desk. Then she folded the copy and stuck it in her bag.

For the next six weeks, she kept the memo in the desk in her bedroom, hidden under her passport and her certification from scuba school. But she thought about it constantly. She talked about it with Lizzie and Hudson. And each night she lay in bed, wondering what would happen if she let it slip out into the world – say, over the Internet. She could always do that if things got really bad.

And then at the beginning of November, things got really bad.

"Ed says that you're not applying yourself," her father said one night after he called her into his office. He leaned back and forth in his swivel chair, stony-faced, and tapped his index finger on his lips, which was code for I've Had It. "He says that

10

most of the time you're there, you're shopping on the Internet. Or that you skulk around, looking bored. And one time he found you asleep on the couch in your office."

She grabbed a rubber stress ball from his desk and started squeezing it. "It's not my fault if there isn't a lot for me to do," she said defensively.

"Then you *find* something to do," the Jurg snapped. "You walk around. You sit in on meetings. Damn it, Carina, you have to *apply* yourself. I can't do everything for you. You're supposed to be learning something here."

"Well, if you're so concerned about me learning something then why is your creepy manservant the one in charge of me?" she snapped back, feeling the sting of tears in her eyes.

"Because I have a company to run." He looked down at the stack of papers in front of him and shook his head. "This isn't a joke. I thought you were mature enough to know how to behave. This is my *company*. I guess I overestimated you."

Something that felt painful lodged itself in her throat. She was only trying to please him with this dumb internship, she thought. And now she was being criticized? It wasn't fair.

"Just don't embarrass me," he added, giving her a hard stare. "You're my daughter. Remember that." He uncapped his pen and returned to his work. "You can go now."

She wheeled around and stalked out of the room, too furious to cry. So it wasn't enough that she'd given up everything she loved to do. It wasn't enough that she'd

11

sacrificed her Saturdays – and her social life. Now he was going to yell at her, too?

When she got to her room, she ran to her desk and opened the drawer. If she'd had any scruples about sending the Jurgensenland memo into cyberspace, they were gone now. Her dad was anything but a do-gooder. He was a jerk and a cheat, and she didn't care if the entire world knew it.

The next day, she scanned the memo into one of the Macs in the Chadwick School computer room and then wrote a sinister email:

> To Whom It May Concern:
> I have reason to believe that Karl Jurgensen, net worth
> $225 billion, may not be handing over all the money
> he raised from his last Jurgensenland charity event.
> Please see the attached document for proof. Thank you
> so much.

She created a fake email address, using just her first initial and her middle name as ID. And then with one click, she sent it right to the Smoking Gun, a website known for breaking news stories – and exposing the secrets of the rich and famous. She left the computer room and headed to Spanish, feeling very calm and satisfied, as though she'd had a great run. Finally, she'd gotten back at him.

When she got home from school a few hours later, she checked the website on her MacBook Air. The story was already up. A headline in big fire engine-red letters made her gulp: DO-GOODING BILLIONAIRE A THIEF? SEE THE DOCUMENT THAT MAY PROVE IT. Below it was the memo. Beside it, a caption called it a "scathing indictment" from an "unnamed source" within Karl Jurgensen's "inner circle". The words *Karl Jurgensen's other use* were highlighted and blown up, just in case people missed it.

Carina sat on her bed, staring at the screen of her laptop, her mouth open. She felt an immediate need to take it back. But she couldn't. She'd done it. There was no going back. Now it was up there, for the whole world to see...

She jumped as her bedroom door burst open. There, in the doorway, out of breath and red-faced, stood her dad. His jacket was off, the knot of his navy-blue-and-white-striped tie was askew, and his normally slicked-back hair was hanging in pieces over his forehead. He looked like he'd just run forty blocks. She'd never seen him look this upset before. He knew.

"Get your things," he said, still panting. "We're leaving. You have ten minutes."

"Where ... where are we going?" she managed to ask. She was almost too stunned to talk.

"Ten minutes," he repeated, and then stormed out, leaving her door wide open as he disappeared down the hall.

She grabbed her iPhone. She had to text Lizzie and Hudson. With her fingers trembling, she typed,

OMG! Come to my house ASAP!!!!

But as she touched send, she knew it was pointless. They'd never get there in time. When the Jurg said ten minutes, he always meant eight.

She yanked out a duffel bag from underneath her bed as her mind raced in circles. How did he know she'd done it? And where were they going? Their apartment in Paris? Was he so mortified that he had to leave the country? Was he going to ship her off to Hawaii to live with her mother? For a time she'd wanted to go live with her mom, but she'd got over that by now. Maui was a twelve-hour plane ride and four time zones away. She'd never see her friends again.

"Carina?" her father yelled from downstairs. "Let's go!"

She threw whatever she could reach into the bag – a few pairs of her Stella McCartney underwear, her purple suede Pumas, her worn-in Cheap Monday skinny jeans, her MacBook. At the last moment, she grabbed the purple stress ball from her desk. She had a feeling she was going to need it.

She ran down the three flights of stairs, and then speed walked down the beige-carpeted hallway towards the front door. The walls were lined with part of her dad's art collection and Carina said a silent goodbye to all of the paintings as she walked by: *Good-bye, Jasper Johns. Goodbye, Jackson Pollock.* Just next to the Andy Warhol soup can stood the staff. They were in their usual bon voyage huddle, ready to see them off, except this time they were looking at her like she wasn't coming back. Maia, the petite, sad-eyed housekeeper, gave her a teary smile. Nikita, still in her chef's apron, slipped her a bag of freshly baked chocolate chip cookies. Marco gave her a small, official-looking nod. Even Otto, the serious security guard, gave her a brave smile. "Good luck, kid," he whispered as she walked past, as if she were headed into mortal combat.

Just before she reached the front door, she craned her head to look at her dad's Basquiat one last time. It was simply a black crown against a sea of white paint, but it had always spoken to her, even though she didn't quite know what it meant. For all she knew, this would be the last time she'd ever see it. A tear blurred her vision, and then she blinked it away.

"Carina, come on!" her father shouted.

She walked out of the front door and saw them waiting in the elevator: her father in his Burberry wool coat, staring coldly past her, and beside him, holding his garment bag and a small valise like it was his life's only purpose, Creepy Manservant himself, Ed Bracken. It was hard to believe, but his comb-over looked even thinner and greasier than usual.

"Hello, Carina," Ed said, giving her one of his typical smirks as she walked into the elevator.

And that's when it hit her. Ed had told her father on her. Somehow, he'd found out that she'd copied the memo and leaked it online. All he'd said was hello, but she knew this with as much certainty as she knew anything. As the elevator dropped down to the lobby, she promised herself that no matter what happened to her, she'd make Ed Bracken pay for this.

Out on the street, Max and the black Mercedes were already waiting for them. Ed handed Max her father's things and then took Carina's duffel bag off her shoulder. "There'll be more room for it in here," he said snidely, dropping it in the boot. Carina got in the car on the other side from her dad and watched Ed practically salute him as they drove off. *Ugh*, she thought. Of course it had been him.

Now Carina watched as the Mercedes hung a left on Ninth Avenue and barrelled straight into the mouth of the Lincoln Tunnel. Her heartbeat sped up into double time. She was definitely leaving New York.

"For your information, I didn't steal that money," her dad suddenly said, making her jump in the back seat. "I put it in a foundation. Do you know what a foundation is?"

She looked over at him. He'd put his BlackBerry away and was staring out of the window at the blur of white tile inside the Lincoln Tunnel.

"Sort of," she murmured.

"It's for tax purposes," he said slowly. "That extra million is *still* going to the charity, but through the foundation instead of me. If you'd just asked me, you would have known that. Instead, you went ahead and formed your own conclusions." He turned towards her, and his eyes blazed at her in the dim light. "How could you think I would actually do such a thing?"

Easily, she wanted to say. But she just swallowed and looked away from him.

"Well, this is all going to go away very fast," the Jurg said briskly, turning back to the window. "Tomorrow morning, I'm releasing a statement that every dime is going to charity, and it's going to run in every newspaper I own and all the ones I don't. By the end of tomorrow, nobody'll even remember this. It'll be swallowed up by ten more important stories. But that still leaves the problem of what to do with you."

Carina felt the golf ball in her throat come back. It stretched upwards towards her eyes, where it swelled dangerously to the brink of tears. She squeezed her stress ball.

"You've had a reckless streak since you were a little girl," he went on, tapping his steepled fingers on the car door. "You got it from your mother. And I stupidly thought you'd grow out of it." He shook his head and gave a rueful chuckle. "It's only gotten worse."

They emerged from the tunnel into the wide-open darkness of New Jersey. As they took the curve of the New Jersey Expressway, Carina could see the skyline of the city west across the Hudson, already so far away it looked like a painting.

"So where are you sending me?" she asked.

"California," he said crisply. "There's a school a few hours north of LA, near Big Sur."

Carina was silent. California: it was almost as far as Hawaii. "Is it a military school or something?"

"Not quite," her father said. "But close."

"And why are you coming?"

"To make sure that you actually enroll. I can't trust you to do that on your own. I wish I could, but I can't."

The car turned off the expressway and on to a deserted two-lane highway, and then they finally turned on to a gravel drive, past a sign that read TETERBORO AIRPORT. A chain-link fence opened for them like magic, and they drove into the airport. There, on the tarmac, under the ghostly white lights, was her father's Gulfstream jet, its tiny door flipped open and waiting to ferry her across the country.

"But when will I come back?" she asked, trying to keep her voice even. "When will I come back to New York?"

"June," he said.

"What about Christmas?" she asked more desperately. "Will I come home then?"

"You'll spend that with your mother," he said. "In Hawaii."

The car finally coasted to a stop a few feet from the plane. Carina heard the boot pop open. Her heart was racing. She needed to get to her phone. She needed to let Lizzie and Hudson know what was happening before she got on that plane.

Someone opened the door on her right, letting in the near-freezing air. The roar of the plane's engine was deafening. "Hello, Miss Jurgensen," yelled the airport manager. "Welcome to Teterboro."

She leaped past him and ran around to the back of the car. An airport technician with bright orange headphones was lifting her bag out of the boot.

"I'll take that!" she yelled and grabbed it out of his hand. *Spoiled brat*, she could practically hear him think, but she didn't care right now.

Her father was already striding towards the plane, the airport manager trotting after him, carrying his things. She didn't have much time. She crouched down to the ground, unzipped the bag, and felt around frantically for her iPhone. At last she felt its glassy, cold surface under her clothes. She swiped the screen with her finger and went to her email.

HELP! Jurg shipping me off to CALI!

she wrote, tapping the screen as quickly as she could.

"Carina!" Her father yelled from where he stood on the bottom stair. "Let's go!"

She threw her phone in her bag and zipped it back up. With the bag over her shoulder, she hurried to the plane, sweat beading her hairline, her heart beating so fast that she thought it might explode. From this moment on, all she had was herself. Her friends couldn't save her. Her old life was gone. But no matter what, she refused to cry. She would never cry in front of her dad. Not ever.

Chapter 2

"Welcome back to the Four Seasons Hotel Los Angeles, sir," said the blond, tanned hotel manager, clearing his throat as he slid the key card through the slot and pressed the elevator button to the top floor. "I trust you had a good trip?"

"It was very nice, thank you," the Jurg replied to his shoes.

"Glad to hear it, sir," the manager said, standing stiffly against the wall with his hands behind his back. "And I know you've stayed with us before, but may I remind you of our twenty-four-hour bottle service? I mean, butler service?" he quickly added.

Chill out, Carina wanted to say from where she was slumped in the corner, duffel bag over her shoulder. She'd seen this kind of thing so many times before. The nervous smiles, the strained formality, the unnecessary information. People always got so weird around her dad. Waiters forgot the specials, busboys dropped forks, and women automatically leaned forward to show off their cleavage. She called it the Cha-Ching Effect. Nothing had a more powerful – and embarrassing – effect on people than a billionaire.

"Here we are," the manager said too loudly when the elevator coasted to a stop.

They stepped out on to the hushed floor and walked down a long, thickly carpeted hall. Finally, they reached the doors at the very end. A gold placard on the wall read PRESIDENTIAL SUITE.

"You'll see we took your advice about the flat screen, Mr Jurgensen," the manager said earnestly as he unlocked the doors with another swipe of the key card. "We've hung it on the wall without the glare from the window this time."

The manager held the doors open and they walked into a black marble foyer. Beyond it Carina could see a palatial, high-ceilinged living room. A baby grand piano stood near a pair of French doors. On the sleek glass coffee table was the usual stunning arrangement of white roses, and next to it stood a gift basket that she knew would be stuffed with Vosges chocolate bars and rare French cheeses.

"Are you familiar with our Scotch selection, sir?" the manager asked. "We have a variety of ten-year-old malts…"

Carina veered to the left and straight out of the room, eager to skip the spiel. She needed to be alone.

She walked past the dining room and the kitchen and around the corner into a spacious, light beige bedroom with a canopied king bed. She dropped her bag on the floor, flopped on to the bed, and yawned into the silk bedspread. She was completely exhausted. For the entire six-hour flight, they'd stayed on opposite ends of the plane and hadn't spoken a word. Ignoring someone on a Gulfstream wasn't easy to do, after all. The Jurg sat up near the front reading the *Economist* while she lay on a couch in the back, keeping an eye on the screen that monitored their trip. With every state they crossed, she felt her throat tighten a little more. Even Marsha, their ever-chipper flight attendant, sensed her anxiety. "Everything OK?" she asked Carina brightly as she set down a Diet Coke and her favourite grilled artichoke.

"Fine!" Carina had said, tearing off an artichoke leaf with a fake smile.

Now it felt good to be alone. She hopped off the bed and padded towards the marble bathroom. But when she flipped on the light, she almost didn't recognize herself in the mirror. She'd done and undone her ponytail so many times that her blonde, chin-length hair looked dark and greasy, and pieces of it fell in chunks around her face. Her brown eyes were bloodshot, and underneath them were dark purplish circles. Her tanned and normally freckled skin looked sallow. She looked like a prisoner of war, and this was only the beginning. For the next eight months she'd be held captive in some quasi military school on the coast. Of course her friends had been right. Releasing that memo had been a huge mistake.

But maybe this was a weird blessing in disguise, she thought, as she splashed some cold water on her face. She'd been miserable living with her dad. Not in a conscious way, but in a low-grade, just-under-the-surface way. He didn't care about her – he didn't even *know* her. And she'd figured out long ago that the only reason he'd wanted her to live with him was just so her mother couldn't have her. So maybe being shipped off was a good thing. If only she could get used to the idea of never seeing Lizzie and Hudson again.

She left the bathroom and went back to her bag. It was time to hear her friends' messages. She knelt on the floor and pulled out her iPhone. There were ten voicemails.

"C? We're standing in your lobby. The doorman said you left. We don't know what's going on. Call us!" Even though Lizzie almost sounded mad, Carina felt a pang of sadness at hearing her voice.

"Carina? Oh my God ... Carina? Where are you? We know what happened. We know you sent out that Smoking Gun thing. Oh C, why'd you do it? Did you really have to? Oh C, where are you?" Hudson always sounded like an exasperated, terrified mom, but Carina missed her so much she almost wanted to cry.

Then she scrolled through their texts.

WHERE R U?!!

We <3 u, C!

U ok?

23

The last text was from Lizzie, sent at ten p.m. New York time.

Hold on. Think yer gonna b fine. Stay tuned…

Carina looked at this one in disbelief. Lizzie wasn't usually this optimistic. And how, exactly, was she going to be fine?

It was the middle of the night in New York right now, so she couldn't call them back. She thought of her mom in Hawaii. It was only ten o'clock there.

She dialled her mom's number and listened to the phone ring once, twice, three times. Finally her voicemail came on.

"Hi, you've reached Mimi … Leave me some love." *BEEP*.

Carina slid her finger across the screen and hung up. She could leave a message, but she had no idea when, and if, her mom would return it. Mimi was a little flaky when it came to messages. When her parents had first got divorced, she and her mom had been in constant touch, scheduling phone calls between New York and Maui and IMing with each other at night. But over the past couple of years, their contact had dwindled to a weekly phone call and an occasional text. Carina suspected her dad had something to do with that. He hadn't even wanted Carina to be in touch with her mom at all when they'd first split up.

Carina yawned again, feeling her eyelids start to droop. She'd write to her friends in the morning and try her mom again later in the day. Right now, she just needed to sleep.

Without even bothering to get undressed, she pulled back the covers and climbed into bed. She pulled the thick, soft sheets over her, breathing in their powdery hotel scent, and felt a small measure of comfort. She'd done something terrible, but there was one thing she was proud of.

At least he didn't see me cry, she thought, just before she drifted off to sleep.

"Carina?"

She opened her eyes halfway. Even though she'd forgotten to close the curtains before falling asleep, the room was still dark.

"The car'll be here in fifteen minutes. Time to get up."

At first she could barely make out the slim, tall figure of her dad in the doorway. But as her eyes adjusted to the darkness she saw that he was already dressed in a suit and had the newspaper in his hand.

"Fifteen minutes," he repeated. "Let's go."

After he left, Carina propped herself up on her elbows. Her head felt enormous and heavy, like a bowling ball filled with concrete. The clock on the bedside table said six a.m. Leave it to her dad to keep the torture coming.

She dragged herself to the bathroom, where she showered and brushed her teeth with the complimentary toothbrush and paste. She pulled out a Splendid tee and a pair of skinny jeans. Finally she dressed, went to her bag and picked up her iPhone. There were already two more texts from her friends, sent before she'd woken up.

WHERE R U??

R U ALIVE????

Carina glanced at her watch. It was almost nine-thirty in New York. Lizzie would be in honours English and Hudson would be in Spanish. It was time to let them know what was going on.

Except how could she begin to tell them what she needed to in a text? She had to call them. But who first? Lizzie or Hudson?

"Carina?" her father called out to her from the dining room. "Breakfast!"

She tossed her iPhone back in her bag and headed into the dining room. The longer she held off on telling her friends about this, the longer she could pretend that it wasn't happening.

The Jurg sat at the head of the long mahogany table, reading the *Wall Street Journal*. "Eat," he said, nodding at the lavish spread of eggs, bacon, fruit, croissants and orange juice he'd ordered. Clearly, he didn't know that she only ate oatmeal for breakfast. "We only have a few minutes until the car's here. And it's a long drive." He fluttered his paper and went back to it, as if she weren't even there.

She looked out of the French windows to the balcony. The sky was just beginning to turn an indigo blue and the palm tree-lined streets of Beverly Hills below looked deserted. It was going to be a long day and it hadn't even started yet. Suddenly the idea of being trapped with her dad in a town car for hours as they drove up the coast was unbearable.

"You don't have to come with me," she said, speaking to him for the first time. "I can go by myself, it's not a big deal."

"The plane's picking me up in Monterey," he said, turning the page.

"Dad." Carina walked up to one of the hard-backed chairs and held on to it to steady herself. She'd been trying to think of the best way to say this since last night. She had to be careful. She was so tired that anything was liable to tumble out of her mouth. "I'm sorry. I really am. I just want you to know that."

He kept his eyes on the paper. "It's a little late for that," he said.

"But I'm *apologizing*," she pointed out.

He folded the paper noisily and turned the full force of his disapproving stare on her. "I don't understand, Carina. I think I've been a pretty decent parent to you. Even a good parent. I've denied you nothing, for starters. I give you anything you want. And this is how you act?"

"Dad—" she attempted.

He threw the paper down on his empty plate. "Don't I send you to the best school in the city? Don't I pay your credit card bills? Don't I send you on every mountain climbing trip under the sun?"

"Yeah, but..." Her mind whirled around, struggling to come up with an argument. "Is that all that being a father means to you? *Paying* for stuff?"

She knew as soon as she said it that it had been a mistake. The Jurg didn't blink but his right eyebrow twitched, the way it always did when he was about to really get furious.

Ding-dong.

Both turned their heads towards the front door. The doorbell rang again.

"I'll get it," she said, thrilled at the chance to leave the room. It was probably another overeager room service waiter, checking to see whether they were done with breakfast.

She ran out to the foyer and threw open the heavy front door. Instead of a room service waiter it was a short, slim woman sporting a black suit, fuchsia lipstick and tightly curled black hair. In her right hand she held a shiny caramel leather attaché case with aged clasps, the kind that held ticking bombs and spy secrets in the movies.

"I'm Erica Straker," the woman said abruptly, thrusting out her hand. "Carina, right?"

Carina shook her hand loosely. She wasn't used to adults addressing her by name. "Uh, yes," she said.

"I'm with the law firm of Cantwell and Schrum, here in Century City," she said briskly. "Is your father here?"

"Can I help you?" said the Jurg. He'd come to stand behind Carina.

"Erica Straker. We've met before," she said brusquely. This time she didn't offer her hand. "I represent your ex-wife."

The Jurg didn't move and without waiting for an invitation Erica Straker stepped right into the room.

"What's this about, Ms Straker?" the Jurg asked, straining to sound polite.

"My client's been notified about your plan to send Carina away to boarding school," she said matter-of-factly as she lifted her attaché case and placed it on a glass credenza by the door. "And the custody agreement you and my client signed says you are not to change your daughter's living arrangements without my client's permission." She popped the case and took out a thick, stapled document that seemed to be hundreds of pages. She hefted it out of the case and handed it to the Jurg. "Maybe you forgot that clause?" she asked, cocking her head, as if she didn't already know the answer.

The Jurg swiped the document out of her hands. "These plans came up very quickly," he muttered. "And as you probably know, she's not the easiest person to reach."

Ms Straker smiled, showing her coffee-stained teeth. "Well, my client understands that you may have forgotten the agreement, so she wanted me to come by and remind you. Of course she'd like Carina to stay in New York. And if you do choose to disregard her wishes," she went on, "she'll have ample grounds to sue you for custody. And she knows how much you'd hate that."

Carina looked down at the gold and crimson Persian rug, aware that her eyes were bugging out of her head. *Lizzie,* she thought. This was why she'd sent her that text saying that everything was going to be fine. Lizzie and Hudson had told her mom. They'd saved her.

The Jurg cleared his throat. "All right then. Tell your client I'm impressed by her quick response. I didn't think she'd have the time. What with her tight yoga schedule and her meditation commitments and all."

With the smugness of someone who knows they've just beaten their opponent – badly – Erica clicked her attaché case shut and pulled it off the table. "Have a nice trip back east, Mr Jurgensen. And you take care, Carina," she said, winking. Then she walked out of the door.

As soon as the door shut, the Jurg tossed the agreement into the trash. "I suppose you had nothing to do with this," he said. His cheeks had turned a dark shade of pink. Karl Jurgensen was not used to being foiled in his plans, much less in front of his daughter.

"I didn't," she said. "I didn't even call her—"

"Don't think for a minute I'm going to forget about this," he interrupted. "Now get your things. We're leaving."

"Ten minutes?" she asked sarcastically. She couldn't help it.

The Jurg turned around and glared at her. "*Now*," he said.

Carina rushed back into her room and grabbed her iPhone. Now she knew exactly what to say to her friends.

I'M COMING HOME!! she tapped out as the California sun slowly lit up the sky.

Chapter 3

"You can pull over here!" Carina yelled from the back seat. "Thanks, Max!"

Max dutifully pulled the black Range Rover over to the kerb as Carina unclicked her seat belt. Up the block she could see Lizzie and Hudson turn into the doors of the Chadwick School. She'd arrived home too late from California to call them the night before, and now she couldn't wait to see them.

"Oh my God, *stop*," she said as Max opened his car door. "My dad can make you drive me to school, but he can't make you open the door for me."

"Have a good day, C," Max said, smiling at her in the rearview mirror. "Glad you're back."

"So am I," she said before she slammed the door. She took off in a wild run up the block, bounded through the doors and attacked her best friends in the lobby with a bear hug that practically knocked them down. "Hey guys!" she yelled.

"Oh my God, *hi*!!!" Lizzie yelled back, squeezing Carina so hard that she almost couldn't breathe. At nearly six feet tall, with huge hazel eyes, full lips and red curls, Lizzie was the most unique-looking girl Carina had ever seen. But Lizzie had always been uncomfortable with her unruly and unusual looks, especially because her mom was Katia Summers, the supermodel. Over the past couple of months though, Lizzie had been "discovered" – first by a photographer and then by the whole fashion world – and been dubbed the "new face of beauty." Carina hadn't been the least bit surprised. Whenever Lizzie walked into a room, people always noticed her – and Carina often wished that she had the same effect on people.

"Yay! You made it!" Hudson cried, her sea green eyes lighting up as she threw her arms around Carina. Hudson was just a little bit taller than Carina but more petite and more delicate, with wavy, shoulder-length black hair and flawless French toast-coloured skin. Most of the time Carina felt like a mess just standing next to Hudson, who was always wearing something from either the most avant-garde boutiques in TriBeCa or the coolest vintage stores in the East Village. Her look was bohemian, which meant lots of floaty tunic dresses in metallic fabrics, futuristic necklaces, huge hoop earrings and floppy hats. Carina loved accessories, too, but generally stuck to gold and silver earrings and bracelets. Hudson's ability to mix beads, gold and gun metal was completely beyond her.

"Oh my God, you guys *saved my life*," Carina gushed. "You should have seen my dad's face when that lawyer showed up. It was the first time in his life he'd heard the word *no*. I almost wanted to record it on my iPhone."

"It was Hudson's idea," Lizzie said proudly, using her long legs to take the steps to the Upper School two at a time. "She remembered that time when we were talking about boarding school and you said your mom would need to sign off on it."

"But Lizzie was the one who actually *called* your mom," Hudson said, pulling off her gloves. "She talked to her for, like, an hour."

"You did?" Carina asked. "How'd you get her on the phone?"

"I don't know, she just picked up," Lizzie said, shrugging. "And get this: she'd seen my picture in *Rayon*. She knew about the whole modelling thing. I couldn't believe it. I'd forgotten how cool she was."

"Yeah," Carina said wistfully. Mimi Jurgensen was really cool. Much cooler than the man she'd married. It was never quite clear to Carina what had drawn her parents together. The Jurg was a tense workaholic who cared only about making money, and her mom was a free-spirited Sarah Lawrence grad who couldn't have cared less about belonging to the right country club or driving a vintage Jaguar. "So ... was she really upset when you told her what was happening?" Carina asked.

"Oh yeah," said Lizzie. "Completely. How'd she sound when *you* talked to her?"

"I didn't, I mean, I haven't yet," Carina replied, feeling a little uncomfortable. When she'd got off the plane in New York, she'd thought there'd be a voicemail from her mom on her phone, but there was only a text.

Glad to hear things worked out. I miss you! Love, Mom.

Her mom now ran a yoga studio in Maui. From what she could tell, that's all people really did there, besides surf.

"So how are things with your dad now?" Hudson asked, unknotting her cashmere scarf. "Is he still totally furious?"

"I have no idea. We've managed to not speak to each other since the whole lawyer stand-off. Which I'm totally fine with, by the way."

Lizzie opened the swinging door that led to the Upper School and they joined the streams of people walking up and down the halls.

"He got the story taken down from the site and put out a press release saying it was a lie and everything," Carina added, breaking into a smile as she waved at people. "So I think it's totally over. Thank God."

"You sure about that?" Lizzie asked sceptically.

"Well, he did say he wasn't going to forget about it or something like that, but I apologized," Carina said. "And it wasn't like I said he was definitely stealing."

Lizzie and Hudson both gave Carina a look.

"What?" she asked them.

34

"You basically said that your dad was a *thief*," Lizzie pointed out. "That's libel. People go to jail for that."

"But he didn't do it. And have you guys forgotten what he did to *me*?" Carina asked hotly. "If I didn't do something now, he'd have had me working for him full-time in two years. I probably wouldn't have even graduated!" Carina pulled her blonde hair back into a ponytail, which always calmed her down. "Look, if he's got some huge horrible punishment coming my way, then fine. I know I screwed up. But I had to do something. And I really *did* think that he was doing something wrong."

"I want to know how he caught you," Hudson put in. "Did you ever find out?"

"Oh, this is the best: Creepy Manservant."

"No way!" Hudson shrieked.

"Are you sure it was him?" Lizzie asked.

"Totally. He was in the apartment when it all went down. And he gave me this really smug smile when my dad was yelling at me. But don't worry. I'm getting him back. I have a plan for revenge."

"Oh no, not more revenge," Lizzie groaned.

"No, this is awesome." Carina took a page out of her bag. "Look at this." She handed the page to Lizzie and Hudson.

"'If I never feel you in my arms again,'" Lizzie read out loud. "'If I never feel your tender kiss again, if I never hear "I love you" now and then...'" Lizzie stopped and looked up with a confused squint. "Isn't this a song?" she asked.

35

"Yeah," Carina said. "Look at the bottom."

Lizzie and Hudson both glanced down at the words scrawled in huge letters at the bottom of the page.

I WANT YOU.

"I don't get it," Hudson said.

"I'm gonna make him think he has a secret admirer!" Carina cried.

"*That's* revenge?" Lizzie asked.

"Come on, he's the saddest, grossest, unsexiest guy on the face of the earth and he's probably never had a girl be into him, *ever*," Carina said. She tossed the letter back into her bag. "When he realizes it's a joke, he'll be totally humiliated. It's the least I can do."

"Well, good luck with that," Lizzie said, patting Carina's shoulder.

They were just about to walk into homeroom when Carina heard the unmistakable *clip-clop* of kitten heels coming down the hall behind her. She instantly knew who it was.

"Oh no," Lizzie said under her breath. "Incoming."

"Oh please, God, no," Hudson whispered. "No."

"Hey guys!" a familiar voice called out.

The three of them turned around.

Ava Elting was walking straight towards them in short, determined steps, wearing a newly whitened smile and the largest distressed-leather Kooba bag that Carina had ever seen.

"Hold up!" she called out, waving a perfectly manicured hand. "I need you guys!"

"She *needs* us?" Carina said out of the side of her mouth.

"I'm *sure*," Hudson griped.

Five days after her notorious break-up with Todd Piedmont, the reigning queen of Chadwick's social elite looked more perfectly groomed than ever. Her auburn curls were pulled back from her face with the usual jewelled barrette, and the diamond A on her necklace glinted in the hollow of her collarbone. Her oxford – Ava never wore turtlenecks, not even in November – was unbuttoned just low enough to show off a hint of lace-trimmed camisole against her artificially tanned skin. There was no indication that she'd been a crying, lying wreck just a few days ago, when Todd Piedmont had finally come to his senses and broken up with her. Afterwards, to save face, Ava spread a ridiculous story about him cheating on her. *Only Ava Elting can do that,* Carina thought, *and waltz into school a few days later like it never happened.*

"So hey, you guys," Ava said in an overly friendly tone. "I just wanted to ask you all a really quick question."

"Go ahead," Carina mumbled, speaking for the group. Lizzie, Todd's new girlfriend, was respectfully silent and Hudson was just being shy, as usual.

"So I think I told you guys that I'm the chair of the Silver Snowflake Ball this year?" Ava said excitedly, letting her voice turn up into a question. "I'm soooo psyched. The charity we're raising money for is amazing. It's the Make New York Beautiful Foundation."

"The what?" Carina asked.

"It gives free cosmetic surgery to the underprivileged. And the dance is shaping up to be an *amaaaazing* event. So amazing I'm pretty sure it's gonna make it into the *New York Times*."

"Really?" Lizzie asked, trying not to laugh.

"Well, the style section," Ava clarified, wrinkling her nose. "You know how they mention all the great parties of the week on Sunday? That's sort of my goal with this."

"Oh," Carina said. *Reach for the skies,* she thought.

"Which r*eminds* me," Ava went on, flashing another blindingly white smile at Lizzie and Hudson. "I think I asked you guys a few weeks ago if your moms had anything they could donate? To the raffle? Do you guys remember?"

Lizzie and Hudson studied the shiny wood floor.

"I was thinking tickets to your mom's concert?" Ava said to Hudson. "Or dinner with her after?"

Carina almost laughed out loud. Holla Jones, Hudson's pop star mom, would rather die than eat dinner with two strangers.

"And maybe your mom has some awesome vintage Alaïa dress," Ava said to Lizzie. "Or she could donate some lingerie from her line."

Lizzie turned even paler than usual as she hid behind her massive red curls. Katia had just started her own lingerie line and Lizzie was still mortified by it. "I can try," Lizzie hedged, eyeing the wooden floor.

"And you," Ava said to Carina, narrowing her eyes as she played with her diamond A necklace. "I was going to ask if *you* wanted to be on the Executive Planning Committee."

"You were?" Carina asked, too surprised to laugh. "What is that?"

"It's a bunch of people who meet a few times and talk about the event," Ava said. "But it's mostly having your name on the invitation. Anyway, it's an honour. We only ask the most socially viable people to be on it."

Ugh, Carina thought. The only reason Ava thought she was socially viable was because she had money. It didn't matter that Carina had never once gone to the polo matches out in Bridgehampton, or done cotillion in fifth grade, or been to any other fancy, two-hundred-dollar-a-ticket dance, or anything else that Ava would consider "social". It was just the Cha-Ching Effect, plain and simple. She was cool in Ava's opinion simply because her dad was rich.

"No thanks," Carina said. "It's not really my thing."

Ava raised one of her expertly arched brows. "OK, fine," she said, sounding a little offended. "And you guys can let me know about that other stuff," she said to Lizzie and Hudson, raising her voice a little as if they couldn't hear her. "See ya."

Once Ava had sauntered away down the hall, Lizzie clapped her hand over her nose. "Oh my God. Is it me or does she *shower* in Marc Jacobs Daisy?"

"Executive Committee?" Carina cried. "More like the Crazy Committee. Even the Lower School knows how she lied about Todd."

"And socially *viable*?" Hudson asked, her green eyes wide with disgust. "What does that even mean?"

"I guess it's just being able to have your name on an invitation," Lizzie said, rolling her eyes.

"At least she's being honest about how lame it is," Hudson pointed out. "I guess it was nice of her to ask you."

"Yeah, well, I'd rather have my eyeballs poked out than be involved with her stupid dance," Carina said as they walked into homeroom.

Carina realized that Lizzie was making a beeline to the back of the room, and then she saw why: Todd sat in the back row next to three empty desks that he'd claimed for them. He looked adorable as usual, with his floppy brown hair and baby-deer-like blue eyes.

"So are you guys officially going out now?" Carina whispered to Lizzie as they approached him. She'd heard about their epic kissing moment in Washington Square Park.

"I think so," Lizzie whispered into her curls. "But don't say anything."

"No problem." Inside, Carina felt a small twinge of something. Not jealousy. Nobody deserved an adoring boyfriend more than Lizzie. But as long as the three of them had been friends (which had been since they were having nap time), none of them had ever had a serious boyfriend. Now, it seemed, Todd would be joining their trio. And as much as she liked him, Carina wasn't sure if she loved that idea.

Carina pushed the thought out of her mind as she sat down next to Lizzie and waved to Todd. After all, Todd's dad was going to be charged with some pretty heavy stuff after he was caught stealing from his company. The least she could do was let him sit next to them in homeroom.

"Hey, Todd," she said as she slid into a desk. "What's up?"

Todd returned Carina's high five. "Not much. Good to have you back."

"Thanks," Carina said.

"How are you?" he asked Lizzie, turning to her.

He reached out and grabbed her hand under their desks. Carina turned away. Of course she was happy for her friend, but PDA this early in the morning wasn't her thing, either.

Chapter 4

"So I have to say, I've never really appreciated New York so much as I have today," Carina announced, just before she bit into her favourite meal at the diner: a turkey burger topped with Swiss cheese and cranberry sauce. "I bet they don't have burgers like this in California."

"If they do, you wouldn't be allowed to eat the fries," Lizzie said, stealing some of Carina's from across the table.

Next to her, Hudson put down her fork and let out a long, noisy yawn. "Sorry, guys," she said. "This album's kicking my butt."

"You're still not done recording?" Carina asked.

"We had to start all over, remember?" Hudson said, trying to spear a cherry tomato in her salad. "We had to move to another studio, redo all the songs, change musicians. All because my mom thinks I need to be less

Starbucks easy listening and more Christina Aguilera," she said wryly.

"But the song we saw you doing that day in the studio was so beautiful," Lizzie said. "What happened?"

"My mom thought it was boring," Hudson replied. "Welcome to my world."

Pop icon Holla Jones had very definite opinions about turning her only child into a star. With her soulful voice, incredible songwriting skills, and intense presence, Hudson had everything it took to be a cross between Joss Stone and Nina Simone. But Holla wanted Hudson to be a frothy pop star with top forty hits, just like herself. Lizzie and Carina were starting to wonder if that was something that Hudson actually wanted.

"Is your producer at least on your side?" Lizzie said.

"Not any more," she said, sipping her iced tea. "We started out on the same page. You know, no samples, no fake beats, no synthesizers. Just something low-fi and rootsy. Now it's like that never happened. He does everything my mom says. It's really annoying."

"Sounds like he and Creepy Manservant should go on a man date," Carina said, taking another bite of burger. "The way that he kisses my dad's butt is shocking."

"Maybe your producer's just afraid of your mom," Lizzie offered.

"Speaking of being afraid of people, what's the latest with Martin Meloy?" Carina asked Lizzie.

43

Lizzie made a face as she slurped some of her chicken noodle soup. "After I walked out of the shoot he told *Women's Wear Daily* that he had another 'vision' for his new line," she said, using finger quotes. "But at least I got to keep his new bag." She picked up the bag he'd dubbed "The Lizzie," made of white leather covered with silver buckles. "I'm wondering how much I could get for it on eBay."

"Oh, don't sell it, keep it as a souvenir," Hudson said. "And you're always going to be a model. Who cares about Martin Meloy?"

"Andrea's so much cooler anyway and I'm doing those portraits for her show at the Gagosian," Lizzie said. "But right now I'm just trying to get back into my writing. And my relationship."

"I can't believe you just said *relationship*," Carina teased. Lizzie blushed.

"I think it's cute," Hudson said. "I swear to God, Todd just gets hotter every day. I'm really happy for you, Lizbutt."

"Yeah, me too," Carina said, a little less enthusiastically.

"Thanks, you guys," Lizzie said, letting out a nervous giggle. "And Hudson, don't look now, but I think your stalker is on her way over."

Carina looked up from her turkey burger to see Hillary Crumple, Hudson's biggest eighth-grade fan, manoeuvring her way through the room. Her thin brown hair had mostly escaped her ponytail, but her square pink-and-blue backpack was firmly strapped to both shoulders. Today she wore a magenta sweater embroidered with one giant heart edged with sequins and an enormous kilt that hit the middle of her shins. Carina almost respected Hillary for being such an unapologetic dork, but she didn't like the way Hillary followed Hudson around school trying desperately to be her friend. Last week Hudson had got a call on her mobile from a celebrity tabloid, just days after Hillary had practically forced Hudson to give up her number at the Chadwick dance. As she watched Hillary trudge over to their table, Carina got another prickly feeling along her skin. Hillary Crumple was bad news.

"Are you still getting those calls from the tabloids?" Carina asked Hudson.

Hudson nodded but put her hand on Carina's arm. "*Don't* say anything, OK? I really don't think Hillary Crumple is selling my number."

"No, she just has a shrine to you in her bedroom," Carina joked.

Hudson gave her a look. "I'm serious, C. *Don't* say anything. I can hold her off."

Carina nodded, but she shot Hillary a suspicious glare as she reached their table, just in case.

"Hi, Hudson," Hillary chirped, her yellow-green eyes fixed on her idol. "Those are really cool earrings."

"Thanks," Hudson said, touching her gold leaf drops.

"I need to find earrings like that," Hillary said in her rapid-fire voice. "Maybe in silver. My mom says silver looks better on me than gold. Maybe we could go shopping for earrings this weekend? Are you around? Maybe down in SoHo? Or NoLIta?"

Lizzie and Carina nudged Hudson's shin under the table.

"I would love to, Hillary, but I'm gonna be in the studio this weekend," Hudson said sweetly.

"That's OK," Hillary said, still in rapid-fire mode. "I can come down there and hang out with you. If you need company. Or just someone to play Xbox with. I heard that recording studios have Xbox. Does yours have Xbox?"

Hudson looked pained. Carina and Lizzie nudged her under the table again.

"You didn't give Hudson's number out to anyone, did you?" Carina asked, unable to help herself. Under the table, she felt Hudson give her a swift kick right back.

"*Me?*" Hillary turned to look at Carina for the first time. "No way. Who would I have given it to?"

The three friends exchanged a look. "No one, just forget it," Hudson said quickly.

"Then I'll give you a call this weekend," Hillary said brightly, stepping away from the table. "That cool?"

"Great," Hudson said, forcing a smile. "See you this weekend."

"Oh, and I'm awesome at *Rock Band*," Hillary added just as she turned around and almost bodychecked a waiter with her boxy backpack.

"Are you *crazy*?" Carina yelled as soon as Hillary was gone. "Now she's never gonna leave you alone."

46

"What was I supposed to do? Tell her she can't call me?"

"*Yes!*" Lizzie and Carina both said at once. "Or at least change your number," Carina added.

"I'm not going to change my number because of a couple of weird calls," said Hudson.

"Remember that when you end up in the *National Enquirer*," Carina said, taking another bite of her burger. "You are way, *way* too nice. If you don't start channelling your inner bee-yatch sometime soon, you're gonna regret it."

Hudson shrugged and went back to her salad. Carina sipped her Diet Coke. She knew that she could be bossy sometimes, but someone had to toughen Hudson up. If only to help her deal with Holla.

Just as she was about to take another delicious bite, Carina looked out of the window at the street and froze. There, only a few feet away, was Carter McLean. He was standing on the sidewalk, talking to his friends as he ate a slice of takeaway pizza from the place on Ninety-first Street. The edges of his brown curly hair lifted in the wind. As he laughed at something someone said, his green eyes glinted in the sun. Carina felt her heart do a bungee jump right into her stomach. Thank God she hadn't been sent to boarding school. *Thank God.*

Carter was a sophomore, a track star and one of the hottest guys in the city. She'd worshipped him from afar ever since he'd smiled at her in line for popcorn at the East Hampton cinema. She'd realized that it was purely an accident, but then last week at Ilona's party, Carina had caught him staring at her. Now she couldn't get him out of her mind. He hung out with the coolest crowd at Chadwick – a group of super-rich, super-independent kids who travelled in a pack to each other's houses all over the world. Nobody seemed to have parents, or if they did, nobody seemed to bother running plans past them. Crazy rumours flew about their adventures clubbing in South Beach and chilling at celebrity parties in Malibu. Carter was the unquestioned leader of the group, as famous for being a daredevil as he was for breaking girls' hearts. She knew that of all the guys at Chadwick he was her boyfriend, just waiting to happen.

Now, almost as if he could read her mind, Carter turned and looked through the window, right at her. Her heart stopped. His green eyes locked on hers, a playful smile curled around the edges of his mouth, and Carina gulped. She had to look away before she threw up her burger.

"C, what's wrong with you?" Lizzie asked, squinting at her. "Are you sick?"

"Carter McLean just looked at me again," she whispered, nodding towards the window. "Don't look."

Lizzie and Hudson both craned their necks to take a quick look, but Carter was back to talking to his super-cool friends, Laetitia and Anton. Laetitia Dunn was a tall, rangy blonde sophomore whose chilly, bored look said she'd done it all, seen it all and had nothing to say about any of it. She was supposedly dating a twenty-five-year-old male model who lived in Paris.

Anton West had dark hair and piercing brown eyes and never smiled. Carina found them both pretty intimidating.

"That's the second time in a week," Hudson said, impressed. "He's really checking you out, C."

"OK," Carina said, wiping her hands on a napkin. "I'm gonna go talk to him." She stood up.

"*Now?*" Hudson asked.

"Yeah, why not? I mean, he obviously wants me to."

"I don't know," Lizzie said. "I get a weird vibe from him. And his friends."

"I'm not gonna talk to his friends," Carina argued.

"He seems kind of full of himself," Lizzie added.

"He's *confident*," Carina corrected.

"He'd have to be," Hudson added. "Didn't he just climb Kilimanjaro or something?"

"I heard it was hang-gliding over the Sahara," Carina put in, wrapping her scarf around her neck.

"Well, go work your Carina magic," Lizzie said, with a patient smile. "We'll just sit here and watch."

As she set off past the tables towards the door, Carina felt the adrenaline start to kick in. She loved making the first move with guys, even though sometimes her friends didn't approve. She knew that guys were usually just too scared to talk to her first, and nine times out of ten, if she started the conversation, they eventually asked for her number.

But that's when she usually stopped liking them. She didn't really know why. Her friends said it was because she only wanted a challenge. "It's like you want to *climb* a guy instead of go out with him," Lizzie liked to say.

But Carter McLean, she knew, was different. She would never, ever get tired of looking at the cleft in his chin, or soaking in his laid-back, effortlessly cool vibe. Plus, Carter wasn't the kind of guy who would fall all over her. He would always be a little out of reach. Which was just what she liked about him.

She pushed her way through the door and stepped on to Madison Avenue. Carter had finished his pizza but was still talking with Laetitia and Anton. As soon as Carina walked out, he turned to look at her.

"Hey," she said, waving slightly as she walked down the street. "You need anything from the candy place?" She was so nervous that her voice almost caught. She could feel Laetitia and Anton staring at her.

"Huh?" he asked.

"I'm going to get candy," she said, nodding her head in the direction of Sweet Nothings down the street. "You need some, too?"

He plunged his hands into his coat pockets and took a step towards her. Fortunately, Laetitia and Anton started talking to each other.

"Nah, but I'll go with you if you need some help," he said, giving her a smile that seemed to say that he knew just what she was up to.

"Great," she flirted back and they started walking to the store.

They walked into the Sweet Nothings boutique on Madison. Carina stopped in here most days after school because they had all the hard-to-find European goodies. She grabbed a plastic bag and made her way to the tubs of candy by the pound. Carter trailed behind her. Suddenly she realized that this was a little awkward. She'd got him to come in here with her, and now she needed to say something.

"Smells like snow," she said as she opened the tub of dark chocolate Bavarian truffles and scooped some into her bag. "I can't wait to do some boarding. You snowboard, right?"

"Definitely, but not around here," he said in his less-is-more voice. "East Coast sucks."

"Well, yeah," Carina said. "Aspen's so much better."

"No, that sucks, too," he said. "You ever been to the Alps?"

"No," Carina said, tying her bag of truffles into a knot. "But I've heard it's incredible." Being this close to Carter was giving her butterfingers.

"The powder there makes Vail look like the Catskills," Carter said, toying with one of the plastic scoops on a chain. "My uncle has a place in Chamonix. A bunch of us are going over Christmas break."

"Really?" she said, almost unable to look at his sexy green eyes.

"His place is right on the mountain, with amazing views of the whole valley," he said, shaking the curls out of his eyes.

51

"It's got a hot tub, this huuuge kitchen. And the clubs there are off the hook." A smile crawled across his face. "You want to come?"

She almost dropped her plastic bag. "Uh ... what?" she asked.

"A whole bunch of us are going for ten days over New Year's," he said, opening a tub of chocolate malt balls and popping a few in his mouth. "Laetitia, Anton, all those guys. I figured since you like to snowboard..." He swallowed and grinned at her, showing her his perfect white teeth. "You should come."

A vision flashed through her head: she and Carter on their boards, carving their way down a mountain together, and kissing when they reached the bottom as a pink and gold sunset lit up a picture-perfect Swiss valley...

"Sure!" she said, a little too loudly. "Count me in."

"Cool," he said, stepping away from her. "I'll let you know how much lift tickets are. And a bunch of us already have our flights on Swissair. Laetitia's got all the details. She's sending around some group email."

Of course she knew that other people would be there, but the prospect of hanging out with Carter for ten days – ten days straight – was almost too much to absorb.

"Sounds good," she said, struggling to sound casual as she handed the woman behind the till a twenty-dollar bill. "Oh, and I hope you're not all talk. 'Cause I am gonna kick your butt on that mountain."

"That's what you think," Carter said, flashing a grin. "I look forward to it." They left the store and Carina watched him walk back to Laetitia and Anton.

When she glided back into the diner, she was smiling so hard that Lizzie almost choked on her hot chocolate.

"Oh my God, *what* happened?" she asked.

"You'll never believe it," Carina said, sliding back into the booth. "I'm going with him to the Alps for Christmas break. To go snowboarding." She dumped her candy bag on the table with a dramatic thump. "Isn't that cool?"

"You're gonna go away with him *alone*?" Hudson asked, her sea green eyes becoming as big as silver dollars.

"No, his friends are going, too," she said casually.

"Wait – you're gonna go on a trip with *those* guys?" Lizzie asked, looking back at Laetitia and Anton. "Are you sure you want to do that?"

"They're not serial killers or anything," Carina said defensively. "And he asked me if I wanted to go."

"As a *friend*," Lizzie clarified.

"Yeah, but it's definitely the beginning of something," she argued. "What's wrong with that?"

"Nothing," Lizzie said. "It's just not really our crowd, that's all."

"Well, it's gonna be amazing," Hudson said. "What's his sign again?"

"I'll find out," Carina said, tearing open the plastic bag. "Did I tell you his uncle has a *hot tub*?"

"Man, C," Hudson said, looking down at her plate and shaking her head. "You should teach a seminar or something."

"There's nothing to it," Carina said, grinning as she popped a chocolate into her mouth.

Chapter 5

Carina twisted this way and that, singing along to the pounding music as she checked herself out in the mirror. The Catherine Malandrino halter top was perfect. The bright yellow brought out the buttery highlights in her hair, the straps showed off her toned, lightly freckled shoulders and the fluttery silk fell to just the right place above her hips. *Done*, she thought. Odds were that Carter would ask her out before they left for Chamonix and this was exactly what she wanted to wear on their first date. Plus, at two hundred and eighty bucks, it was practically a steal.

"How're you doing in there?" asked the bubbly salesgirl through the fitting room curtain.

"Great!" Carina yelled, unzipping the top and whipping it over her head. She held it and her platinum Amex card through the side of the curtain. "I'm gonna take it."

"Nice!" chirped the salesgirl as she grabbed the goods. "I'll go ring you up!"

Carina pulled her turtleneck over her head and winced. Diana, her personal trainer, had put her through a killer series of press-ups and planks earlier to make up for the two days she'd spent sitting on her dad's plane and now she could barely lift her arms. She couldn't wait to get home and take a hot bath, except there was a good chance she'd run into her dad. She'd managed to avoid him ever since they'd come back from California and she was in no hurry to end her winning streak. She checked her watch. Six thirty. Hopefully he was out at some cocktail party or another highly publicized, paparazzi-infested waste of time.

Carina pushed aside the curtain and walked to the till, where the salesgirl was wrapping the top in delicate pink tissue paper. She looked like all the other salesgirls at Intermix: tall, so skinny that her chest was practically concave, and with her copper-coloured hair in a messy knot that said "I don't even have to try to look beautiful".

"This is soooo cute," she cooed, lovingly putting a sticker on the paper to hold it together. "What's it for?"

"A date," Carina said matter-of-factly as she fingered a pair of gold drop earrings.

"Oooh, he's gonna *love* it," the salesgirl assured her with one of those conspiratorial grins that always bugged her. She looked down at Carina's Amex card. "Are you related to *Karl* Jurgensen?"

"Yeah. He's my dad."

The salesgirl blinked with surprise. "Then you should give us your email," she said. "So you know when we get in new stuff, have sales, that kind of thing. We do that for all our preferred customers."

Cha-ching, Carina thought. "Um, OK," she said.

The salesgirl swiped her credit card. There was an annoying beep.

"Huh," she said, frowning at the machine. "It's saying this card's cancelled."

"What?" Carina looked at the silver card in the girl's hand. "Are you sure? Is it past the expiration date?"

The salesgirl looked back down at the card. "No. It expires next year." She swiped it again. The till gave the same small but decisive beep. "Huh. It still won't go through."

"That's weird," Carina said, opening her wallet. "This should work, try this," she said, handing her Visa debit card to the salesgirl.

The salesgirl swiped again. This time, the beep sounded more like an irritated squawk.

"This one's saying you don't have adequate funds," the salesgirl said. She grimaced at Carina in a friendly, we're-in-this-together way. "You want to try another one?"

"Um, sure." Carina felt her cheeks start to get hot. She pulled out her emergencies-only MasterCard, the one with the fifty-thousand-dollar credit limit. "Try this one."

The salesgirl took it without a smile and swiped again. The machine beeped again.

"Hmmm," the salesgirl said, pretending to be completely mystified. "This one's not working either. If you want, I can hold the top for you till you get things figured out."

"No, that's OK," Carina said.

The salesgirl handed back the MasterCard. "You sure?" she asked nicely.

"Yep, it's cool," Carina said, dropping the card right into the pocket of her bag. "Something must be screwy with my account."

"I'm sure," said the salesgirl hopefully.

She broke the seal on the tissue paper and pulled the top out. Carina stared at it longingly.

"Sure you don't want me to hold it for you?" the girl asked.

"Yep," Carina said, aware that her cheeks were fully ablaze. She needed to get out of here. "Thanks for everything." She hoisted her gym bag up on to her shoulder, whirled around, and hurried to the exit.

Out on Madison Avenue, Carina could still feel the salesgirl looking at her as she hailed a cab. Luckily, one pulled up right away.

"Fifty-seventh and Lex," she told the driver, and she slammed the car door.

As the cab turned on to Park Avenue, Carina unzipped the front pocket of her bag, took out her wallet, and dumped all of her cards into her lap. They lay there, useless and flimsy-looking. Something was terribly wrong. Ever since her dad had given her a MasterCard for her twelfth birthday, she'd never been declined, not even when she'd checked herself into the swanky St Julien hotel in Boulder when she was done with Outward Bound or bought the Helmut Lang jumpsuit that was totally overpriced. Even more unsettling was that her debit card hadn't worked either. She wasn't quite sure who took care of her actual account, but now it looked like she'd have to have a conversation with her dad whether she wanted to or not.

At the corner of Fifty-seventh and Lex she pressed a ten into the driver's hand without asking for change and got out of the cab. She waved a quick hello to the three doormen behind the concierge stand, sidestepped the elderly woman walking three pugs, and skipped down the hall to the elevator. The Jurgensens had their own elevator, which went straight up to the penthouse on the sixty-second floor.

Inside the elevator, she leaned back against the wall and let her bags drop to her feet. Her stomach grumbled as she wondered what Nikita had made for dinner. And she still needed that bath, she thought, as the doors began to close...

BANG!

A hand reached in between the doors to push them aside, and suddenly her father stepped into the tiny space, elegant and slightly menacing in his single-breasted midnight blue suit and tie. The doors rumbled shut. She was trapped. For the next sixty-two stories.

"Hello, Carina," he said smoothly, pushing the PH button even though she'd already pushed it. "Good to see you."

"Hi," she said coldly.

The elevator thrummed as they rose up, up, up. Carina stared at the diamond-patterned carpet, wanting to cringe. The awkwardness was so thick she could taste it.

"I've been thinking quite a bit about what you said to me yesterday morning," the Jurg said in an eerily calm voice.

"What I said?" she asked. She was dying to ask him about her bank account and credit cards but sensed that this might not be a good time.

"How you said that giving you things was my idea of being a father," he said. She looked up to see him staring at her, right in the eyes, and she thought that she could see the faint beginnings of a smile on his stern, handsome face. "I decided that you were right. So I'm going to stop."

"Stop what?" Her stomach grumbled louder. She hoped that Nikita had made gnocchi in pink sauce.

The elevator doors opened and they stepped out into a small vestibule.

Karl stopped at the titanium-enhanced front door, pressed the ten-digit security code – *gamechange* – and the door clicked open. They walked into the softly lit entry hall lined with paintings. At his bank of security cameras, Otto gave her father a curt nod.

Her dad still hadn't answered her, which she took as a cue to follow him down the hall. They walked past the Basquiat and the Campbell's Soup can and the canvas of broken plates and turned into his office. Through the window behind his desk, the northern half of Manhattan glittered like a collection of diamonds.

"So, stop what?" she asked again.

The Jurg flicked on his desk lamp, throwing shadows on his chiselled face. "The money I give you," he said simply. "No more credit cards, no bank account. No unlimited funds. Because you're right. I've been much, much too generous with you."

"Wait – you're cutting me off?" she asked, tightening her grip on her gym bag.

"No shopping, no hair appointments, no trainer," he went on, sitting down and touching his laptop gently awake. "No gym membership. No fancy trips. No iPhone."

"You're taking away my *phone*?" she cried.

"Not exactly. I've gotten you something a little more affordable." He opened his desk and took out something so ancient-looking that it might have been made before the turn of the century. "This should be more than adequate," he said coldly as he handed it to her.

She stared at the squat, thick, silver device in her palm. "Are you *kidding* me?" she asked.

"And Max will no longer be taking you to school. You can use this." He picked up a thin yellow card from his desk. The Metropolitan Transit Authority logo was clearly marked on the front. "This should get you everywhere you need to go. If it's late, I can call you a car."

61

He put the MetroCard on top of the phone in her hand. "Is this a joke?" she asked.

"Oh, and I almost forgot," he said, frowning as he took out his wallet from his jacket pocket. "Your allowance."

Carina took a breath as he reached into his wallet. So her dad hadn't completely lost his mind. Thank God.

He pulled out a crisp bill and laid it on top of the other two items. "You'll get that every week."

She looked down and sucked in her breath. It was a twenty.

She stood there, blinking, unable to move. Twenty dollars a week – in New York City? Was he insane? He might as well have given her nothing.

"*Twenty* dollars?" she burst out. "How am I supposed to live on that?"

He shrugged in an exaggerated way. "You're not living on it, it's your allowance, to spend on things you *want* – not that you need," he said calmly. "You have clothes to wear, food to eat and your school is paid for. What else do you need, Carina?"

Her mouth moved but no sound came out. "Wha – what?" she sputtered. "Why are you doing this? Do you think I'm just some trust fund kid who wants to go shopping all the time?"

"I get your bills, Carina," the Jurg said coolly, leaning back in his swivel chair and steepling his hands. "I think I know who you are better than you do."

Anger rose up in her throat, bitter and hot. "So of course

this is what you do to punish me," she said thickly. "Just because you're obsessed with money, you think that everyone else is."

"This was *your* idea, Carina," he said. "You're the one who said that I gave you too many things. Remember?"

She wanted to keep yelling but she knew it was pointless. The only thing she could do, the only thing that could possibly save her dignity right now, was to leave.

"Whatever," she spat, and then turned and ran out of the room. She took the stairs two at a time, even though her legs were already sore, and slammed the door to her room so hard that she hoped one of his precious paintings crashed right to the floor.

"Aghh!" she yelled, pounding the door behind her with her fist. The twenty, the MetroCard and the phone all fell out of her hand and on to the carpet with a soft thud.

She needed to talk to her mom. It was only twelve thirty in the afternoon. Her mom would be furious at him. She'd hopefully be around. She picked up the vintage phone, flipped it open and pressed the red power button. There was an ear-splitting chime, and then a digital panda started crawling across the black and white screen. A panda? Nobody – *nobody* – could ever see her with this.

She dialled her mom's number and listened to it ring. Finally the voicemail clicked on.

"Hi, you've reached Mimi—"

She flipped the phone closed and tossed it across the

room. What could her mom say or do anyway? How could she help her this time? Depriving their daughter of her credit cards wasn't really against their custody agreement.

She hated her dad, *hated* him, she thought, flinging herself on to her bed. This was all so unfair – she didn't even *care* about clothes and hair and make-up. Of course she liked to buy nice things once in a while – who didn't? But that wasn't the real her. The real her could go for six weeks on the side of a mountain with just a shovel and a toilet roll. But of course he didn't know that. How could he? And could *he* last on top of a mountain? If he had to go a day without using his Kiehl's Silk Groom it would be a national emergency.

She grabbed the purple stress ball from her bedside table and kneaded it in her hands, until a sudden thought made her sit right up. He thought she was a spoiled brat? Then she was going to prove him wrong – starting now. If he wanted her to live on twenty dollars a week – which in New York was basically impossible – then that's *exactly* what she was going to do. And hopefully, after a couple of weeks, he'd see that she'd learned whatever lesson he wanted her to and he'd drop this ridiculous exercise.

Maybe it won't be so hard, she thought, glancing at the crumpled-up bill on her floor. It was just money. And it wasn't like she was Ava Elting, who'd probably go into withdrawal if she couldn't buy an eight-thousand-dollar bag.

He'd see that she was just fine, that he hadn't done anything at all to change her life. That he could *never* change her life. That he had no control over her – no matter how much he thought he did. She was still Carina, after all. And no matter how much money she had, *that* was never going to change.

Chapter 6

"So your dad did it just like *that*?" Hudson asked, snapping her fingers with a jingle of her mom's vintage enamel bangles from Fiorucci. "He just cancelled everything without even telling you first?"

"It's not like he's going to OK it with her," Lizzie said, stretching out her long, pale legs under the tiny homeroom desk. "It's all about the element of surprise. Like what they talk about in *The Art of War*," she said, dropping her bag on to the empty desk next to her. "You know, that book all businessmen are required to read."

"He wasn't taking over a rival cable station, he was just supposed to be grounding me," Carina grumbled. "And by the way, did he ever even *hear* of grounding?" She unwrapped her scarf and wiped her brow with the back of her hand. At first taking the subway had been fun, but then the train had been held up for what seemed like hours and she'd had to run from the station to school.

"Well, you did publicly humiliate him in front of thousands, if not millions, of people," Lizzie pointed out. "I'm just saying."

"Let me get you the Catherine Malandrino top," Hudson said, placing a hand on Carina's wrist. "You can pay me back later."

"That's sweet but no, thanks," Carina said, taking out a piece of paper from her bag. "This really isn't the end of the world, you guys. It's not like I'm a shopaholic or anything."

She glanced up to see Hudson and Lizzie looking at her sceptically.

"You *guys*. I'm not."

"Really, C?" Hudson gave Carina the hardest look she could. "Have you *ever* had to live on just twenty dollars a week?"

"No, but you're missing the point," Carina said. "I'm not obsessed with money. And the fact that my dad thinks I am is kind of offensive."

"You might not be obsessed with it, but you do like to *spend* it," Lizzie clarified, pulling a red curl straight between her fingers.

"So what? Everybody does. And I can stop," Carina said. "It's not a big deal."

"But what about the Carter trip?" Hudson asked, chewing her pouty bottom lip.

"I'm sure my dad will have stopped the madness by then," she muttered. *But maybe he won't*, a little voice said inside of her. Like something out of a sci-fi movie, those visions of her and Carter carving their way down an Alpine mountain were starting to get fainter and fainter. "And even if he hasn't, I'm sure I can find a cheap flight to Switzerland."

"For twenty bucks?" Lizzie asked.

"I'll figure it out," Carina said, kicking her backpack on the ground. "This is so not a big deal. OK?"

She looked down at the page she'd taken out from her bag. It was a another song that she'd printed out as soon as she'd got to school.

My first love, you're every breath that I take
You're every step I take

Underneath it she scrawled in red pen:

ED, YOU ARE MY ENDLESS LOVE.

She folded it up again and stowed it in her earth science notebook. At least these love letters were still making her laugh.

"Todd just texted that he's going to be running late," said Lizzie, checking her phone. "He wants us to save him a seat."

"Is he gonna sit with us every morning?" Carina asked, realizing too late that she'd actually spoken this out loud.

"Yeah," Lizzie said, sounding hurt. "Is that OK?"

"Yeah, it's fine, fine," Carina said, pretending to doodle.

When Todd arrived a few minutes later and headed straight towards Lizzie's saved seat, Carina made sure to give him a broad smile and a wave. Even though her question seemed to hang in the air between her and Lizzie like a storm cloud.

For the rest of the morning, Carina sat in class, thinking about her twenty dollars. She'd always been good at disciplining herself to reach a goal, whether it was running a six-minute mile or doing fifty boy press-ups in a row. Now the goal was to keep that bill in her wallet for as long as possible. Starting now, she would only spend that money when and if she absolutely needed it. The Jurg was right, as much as she hated to admit it. She had clothes. She had transportation. She had food. What else could she need?

"Who wants to go to the diner?" she asked Lizzie and Hudson at their lockers at the beginning of lunch, as another wave of hunger pangs clenched her stomach.

"Um . . . can you afford that?" Hudson asked warily.

Carina rolled her eyes. "I'm not *penniless*. And I kind of forgot to pack myself something."

"Maybe you should just get a toasted bagel from the deli," Lizzie suggested. "The diner can get pricey."

"One little burger isn't going to break me," she assured them. "Come on."

At the diner, Carina scarfed down her turkey burger, scooping up all the extra cranberry sauce with her sweet potato fries. Everything tasted so good. *Maybe being broke makes you appreciate yummy food more,* she thought.

"Want some?" she asked her friends.

Hudson shook her head, chewing her plain grilled cheese.

"No thanks," Lizzie said, taking a bite of her toasted bagel.

When the waiter dropped the bill down on their table, Carina snatched it up. "I'm sure I owe the most," she said blithely, scanning the numbers.

Her gaze stopped at the figure next to her burger and fries. She owed ten dollars. Ten dollars. *Half* her allowance. Which meant she had only ten more dollars for the next six days.

"C? You OK?" Hudson asked.

"Yeah, yeah, no problem," she said, taking out her wallet. "I need to break this baby anyway."

She laid her lone twenty on the top of the cash pile very carefully, like something to be sacrificed.

"Carina?" Lizzie asked gently, darting her huge hazel eyes at Hudson. "Let me pay for this."

"No, no, I got it," she protested, trying to smile. "Hey, it was worth it."

But when the unsmiling waiter came by and scooped up their money, it was all she could do not to yell for him to come back.

Later that afternoon, in earth science, Carina jerked herself awake. The burger and fries may have been amazing, but they had done nothing for keeping her alert. At the front of the room, Sophie Duncan and Jill Rau were giving a very boring, very nap-friendly presentation on greenhouse gases. Carina felt her eyelids start to shut. This was something she could definitely miss.

At last she heard Sophie say, "Which brings us to our conclusion..."

Carina fluttered her eyes open.

"We'd like to collect donations for the Carbon Emissions Fund," Sophie announced, pushing her glasses higher on her nose. "All of the proceeds will go to buying carbon offsets to keep our air cleaner. So anything anyone can give would be welcome."

Carina froze. Donations meant money. She watched as Sophie and Jill each dropped a bill into the basket. And then people started unzipping their bags. The sound of wallets being opened and crinkled money being taken out was suddenly deafening. Carina began to panic. She was going to have to put *something* in the basket – she couldn't *not* donate money, especially for cleaner air. But all she had was her last ten-dollar bill.

Jill was already walking the basket over to Carina's table. She didn't have much time.

"Hey, Will," she whispered to the boy sitting next to her.

Will McArdle gave her a suspicious look. They hadn't spoken in a few weeks, ever since she'd accused him of cheating during their test on the periodic table.

"Do you have change?" she asked him cheerily, holding out her ten.

71

Glaring at her, Will took her ten, and from the impressive stack in his wallet peeled off two fives. "Here," he huffed, handing her the money.

She'd really wanted a five and five singles, but she was too embarrassed to quibble about it. "Thanks!" she chirped.

As the basket passed in front of her, she threw in a five-dollar bill. Then she looked at the other five in her hand. That was all she had left now. For the next six days.

What had just happened? In three hours, she had spent two-thirds of her allowance on a turkey burger and cleaner air. But she hadn't had a choice. She'd had to eat lunch, and she couldn't be too cheap to donate money to a worthy cause.

Right?

Now she wasn't sure. Trying to save money turned out to be exhausting, like trying to figure out an impossible algebra equation. She shoved the five into her wallet. She wouldn't think about this any more. At least not until she absolutely had to.

At the end of the day, she, Lizzie and Hudson walked out of school and right into Carter and Laetitia and Anton hanging out in front of the gelato place on the corner.

"Hey, Jurgensen," Carter called out. "Want to get some ice cream?"

After her tense day of thinking about money, easing back into flirt mode felt like a relief. "Sure," she said, walking towards him as her heart started to beat in triple time. Carina looked back at her friends, silently urging them to follow her inside. Lizzie and Hudson followed.

Inside, Carina manoeuvred herself up near Carter at the counter, surveying the flavours. "So I take it you like to be cold?" she asked him playfully.

"Only when you're around to warm me up," he said, smiling.

Carina felt a shiver go down her back. Suddenly she couldn't think straight.

"OK, what does everyone want?" asked the grouchy woman behind the counter, brandishing the metal scoop in her hand like a sword.

Carina suddenly remembered that she had to order something. She glanced at the list of prices above the counter. A small gelato was three fifty. She had five dollars left. The panic she'd felt in earth science began to course through her body again. It had been a dumb move to come in here, but now she had to order something. Otherwise Carter would think she'd only come in here to flirt with him. Which was basically the truth.

"Sour cherry," Carter said. "A large."

"Small mint chocolate chip," Hudson ordered.

"Small pumpkin," Lizzie said.

Carina kept looking at the flavours, paralysed.

The woman tapped her fingers on the glass. "And you?" she asked.

"Uh, small pumpkin, too," she finally said.

73

That was it. She had a dollar fifty left now. Carina bit her lip as she watched the woman scoop up a bunch of pumpkin gelato she didn't even want and smash it into a paper cup. The woman handed Carina her cup of gelato, and she handed her the five-dollar bill with gritted teeth.

After the woman had rung everyone up, Carter leaned in close enough to her that she could feel his arm against hers. "Hey, we're going to Serafina tonight for pizza," he said. "The one on Seventy-ninth and Madison. Want to come?"

Yes! she wanted to say. "Oh, I can't," she fibbed as her heart sank. "I'm going to Montauk tonight. But maybe some other time?"

"Sure," Carter said coolly.

"And I'm still really looking forward to the Alps," she said, smiling.

"People are starting to get their lift tickets," Carter said, spooning gelato into his mouth. "I think they're, like, two hundred bucks. Isn't that what I said?" he asked Laetitia, who nodded in a bored way.

"Just give Carter or me a cheque as soon as you can," she said in her usual blasé tone. "And we're all taking this flight from Kennedy to Zurich on the night of the twenty-sixth. On Swissair. I can get you the rest of the info later."

"Great!" Carina chirped. She needed to get out of here. "Have a good weekend!" With one yank she pulled Lizzie with her towards the door and Hudson followed.

74

"Is everything OK?" Hudson asked as they stepped into the freezing wind.

"My house – *now*," Carina said, steering them both to the corner.

"Actually, can it be my house?" Lizzie asked. "I'm grounded, remember?"

"Fine," Carina said as Lizzie hailed a cab.

A few minutes later, Carina paced Lizzie's carpet as a wad of Bubble Yum made her jaws work overtime. Every few seconds she wheeled around on the balls of her feet and paced in the opposite direction.

"Calm down, C," Lizzie said from behind her computer. "It's stressing me out just looking at you."

"I refuse – *refuse* – to let this happen," Carina said, wheeling around once more. "He can cut me off, he can give me a phone that's twenty years old, but he cannot, can*not* ruin my love life!" She stopped and blew a bubble until it popped with a satisfying *thwock*. "I can't believe it. Carter McLean finally asks me out and I can't go."

"C, let's put this in perspective," Hudson said, stroking the furry white head of Lizzie's cat, Sid Vicious. "He invited you to go to Serafina's with a bunch of people. It wasn't a date."

"But it *could* have been," Carina said, pointing at Hudson. "I mean, we could have ended up at his place – or my place, and then people might have gone home, and we would have been alone, and watching TV, and he could have kissed me,

75

and then it would *definitely* have been a date. And now *none* of that's gonna happen."

Her friends were staring at her like she'd just sprouted another head. "And no one will ever love you," Lizzie supplied.

Carina gave Lizzie a sour look.

"OK then, here," Hudson said, leaning over the bed to reach into her bag. "Go out tonight. Have a good time. Pay me back on Monday."

Carina stared at the twenty in Hudson's hand and shook her head. "That's totally sweet of you, H, but I'm not going to take your money. I'm gonna figure this out on my own. I have to. Even though I have exactly a dollar and fifty cents."

"But you only got lunch and gelato," Lizzie pointed out, twisting her hair into a knot and securing it with a pencil.

"Sophie and Jill asked everyone to make a donation in earth science," Carina said.

"You gave money to Sophie and Jill?" Lizzie asked.

"It was for cleaner air!" Carina cried. "I had to give something!"

"Well, let's look at these flights," Lizzie said wearily, turning back to the computer monitor. "Yeesh. The one that everyone's taking from Kennedy to Zurich looks like it's eleven hundred bucks."

"Oh great," Carina muttered.

"But here's something," Lizzie said quickly, peering at the screen. "There's a flight on BudgetAir. It stops in London.

And in Frankfurt. And in Zurich, where you get on a puddle jumper—"

"How much is it?" Carina demanded.

"Seven hundred bucks," Lizzie said. "Economy class. And they can't guarantee an actual seat."

"Seven hundred bucks, plus two hundred for a lift ticket, is nine hundred," Carina recited. "And then I'm gonna need money for a cab from the airport, and to go out at night, and eat during the day…" She sat down on the edge of Lizzie's bed, lost in thought. "That's at least a thousand bucks." Her mind was racing in circles, and she was getting a headache.

"Maybe you should just tell Carter you can't make it," Hudson suggested, touching Carina's wrist.

"Yeah, C," Lizzie said, flopping on to the bed. "It's not like this is the only chance you're going to have to hang out with Carter McLean the rest of your life. And have you even asked your dad if you can go?"

Carina snorted. "I don't need his permission. And he'd probably be thrilled to get rid of me for a few weeks anyway."

"Personally I think you should save yourself the stress," Lizzie said. "This trip really isn't that important."

"No, it *is*," she said slowly, trying to keep her voice even. "If I don't go, then it's like proving the Jurg right. That he has complete control over my life."

"Well, he kind of does," Lizzie said gently, toying with a dog-eared cover of *The Great Gatsby*. "My parents control me with money. It's what parents do."

"Yeah, me too," Hudson murmured.

Carina and Lizzie gave their friend a look.

"What?" Hudson asked innocently.

"Once your album comes out, you're never gonna have to worry about an allowance again," Carina said tartly. She sighed and stared at the sky blue wall. "Let's face it, people. I'm screwed."

"What if you get a job?" Lizzie asked, propping herself up on her forearms. "Isn't that the obvious way out of this?"

"Yeah, a job!" Hudson chimed in, so excited that Sid Vicious leaped out of her lap. "You already have experience!"

"At my dad's company?" Carina asked, watching Sid settle himself into a white fluffball at the foot of the bed. "Please. He's not gonna hire me again. Much less pay me."

"I was thinking more like the Gap," Hudson said.

"Or Old Navy," Lizzie suggested.

"They don't hire people under sixteen," Carina fired back. She'd already thought of that.

"Well, there has to be someone out there who needs help for Christmas and would hire someone a teensy bit underage," Hudson said cheerfully, winding a strand of black hair around her thumb. "What about all those tiny little shops on the Upper East Side, right near school? What about the candy store?"

"Maybe," Carina said. It wasn't a bad idea. She stood up and grabbed her bag. "I'll look into that. Who wants to get together tomorrow and ride the subway?"

"Hang in there, C," Lizzie said, standing and giving her a hug. "We're always here."

"And Carter's not going anywhere," Hudson added, confidently shaking her head. "Besides, staying home tonight makes you more mysterious."

As Carina hugged her friends goodbye, she wondered if they were right. Maybe she needed to give up on Carter McLean and her dreams of a fabulous Alpine romance. But right now that felt like the same thing as giving up on herself.

Chapter 7

That night Carina lay on the leather couch in the downstairs den just off the Jurg's office and watched a marathon of *The Real Housewives of New Jersey*. Every few minutes she told herself that she was being mysterious. It wasn't working. Every cell in her body wanted to be at Serafina's right now, sitting next to Carter, laughing and joking with him as they split a pizza margherita and some tiramisu. She could just picture how much fun everyone was having, how they'd be talking about the ski trip, how cute Carter probably looked with a little gel in his hair and in a wrinkled blue-checked shirt...

She reached for her MacBook Air and touched the keyboard. Carter's Facebook page shot up on to the screen. Holding her breath, she moved the cursor over to the "Add Carter as a friend" box, but just before she clicked, she stopped herself. After all, she wasn't desperate, she thought, putting the laptop back on the floor. Lizzie was right. She'd have *many* other chances to hang out with him. She hoped.

"Carina? Nikita give you dinner?"

The Jurg stood in the doorway in his shirtsleeves and tie, his hair still wet from his post-game shower. On the Friday nights that they didn't go out to Montauk because he had a late meeting, he liked to play squash at the Union Club with other Masters of the Universe. As if he didn't get enough pleasure out of being an alpha male during the workday.

"Yeah, I had some pasta," she said listlessly. It was the first time she'd seen him since her dramatic exit the night before and she didn't want to be too friendly.

"How was your day?" he asked. He actually sounded interested.

"Fine," she said, her eyes on the flat screen. *Go away*, she thought. *Just leave.*

"Good," he said awkwardly, leaning against the doorway. "Did Marco tell you that I'm going to London later tonight?"

"Uh-huh," she said, keeping her eyes on the TV.

"Be back on Monday."

"Awesome," she muttered.

"And what we talked about last night," he said, stepping into the room. "Carina? Would you mind looking at me, please?"

She flicked her eyes away from the TV. *Maybe he's about to apologize,* she thought. Maybe he wanted to tell her this would just be for a few days, until she learned her lesson.

"That MetroCard I gave you was just for a week," he said,

reaching into his back pocket. "This one is for an entire month." He pulled out another yellow card and placed it on the wooden credenza inside the door. "At the end of the month, just come speak to me and we can get you another one."

She sat perfectly still on the sofa, too stunned to say anything. Another one? For the next *month*?

"Uh, fine," she said, turning back to the TV. She was so angry that she felt like her blood might actually boil.

"Carina," he said more urgently, coming to stand in front of the couch. "I just want you to know that this is for your own—"

"I got it," she snapped, cutting him off. "Have a good—"

She was cut off by the sound of ringing. It was the Jurg's BlackBerry. He pulled it out of his jacket pocket and answered it. "Yes?" he said curtly, pivoting around towards the door. "No. Tell him to wait. I'll be there in the morning."

He walked out of the den and a moment later she could hear him climbing the stairs. She reached for one of the mocha-coloured suede throw pillows under her head and threw it at the door. It hit a framed photograph of the Jurg and Richard Branson instead. With a clatter, the photograph fell to the ground.

So this wasn't going to be a weekly experiment. This was going to be a *till-the-end-of-the-year* experiment. Which meant that if she wanted to have any shot at blissful love with Carter McLean, she'd need to get a job, stat.

Just then an ear-splitting chime rang through the room. It

was her panda phone, lying on the floor near the computer. The number on the screen had an 808 area code. Hawaii. Her mom. She reached for it.

"Hello?" she answered.

"Hi, honey, it's me," came her mom's soothing, honeyed voice over the crackle of static. "I saw that you called me a few days ago and I've been meaning to call you back … How are you, sweetie?"

Where do I even begin? she thought. "I'm OK. Things have been pretty crazy this week. Dad and I had kind of a fight—"

"I heard, but I thought that was taken care of," her mom said. "Didn't that lawyer come pay you a visit?"

"Yeah, she did, that was great, it's just that afterwards, something happened—"

There was a faint clicking sound on the line.

"Oh sweetie, I'm so sorry but I have to get that, it's this reporter from *Condé Nast Traveller* and they're doing a story on the yoga studio. Can I call you back later?"

"Sure," Carina said, twisting a piece of hair around her finger. "No prob'm."

"Actually, it's late there. I'll try you tomorrow. Get some sleep tonight, honey. I wish I were there to tuck you in."

"Me too," Carina said, suppressing a swiftly forming lump in her throat.

"Bye, honey."

"Bye," she said.

She tossed the phone away from her. Hot tears welled in

her eyes but she swallowed them away. So her mom didn't have all the time in the world to talk to her. So what? It wasn't her fault that some magazine wanted to interview her.

But that old feeling swept through her again. That feeling she'd had on and off since she was ten, when her chest would get tight and her mouth would get dry and she'd feel a terrible sense of homesickness, like walking through a ghost town of a place she used to know. Talking to her mom did that to her sometimes. Whenever this feeling came over her, she needed to distract herself from it as soon as possible, so she reached for the stress ball on the coffee table and worked it in her palm as she thought.

She needed a job. That was all that mattered right now. And tomorrow, she'd get one.

Chapter 8

"But have you ever worked as a barista *before*?"

The college-age girl with pink hair squinted at Carina from behind the counter, her pierced eyebrow already raised in serious doubt. Behind her, Carina could feel the line of customers getting restless.

"Well, not exactly," Carina finally said. "But I think watching you guys counts and I have lots of experience doing that. And I'm sure once I actually got behind the counter I'd just pick it right up."

The pink-haired girl looked at the tattooed guy hovering over the milk steamer and sighed.

"Hold on," she said, utterly defeated. "I'll get the manager." Then she leaned past Carina to address the next person in line. "Can I get something started for you?"

Carina stepped out of the way and positioned herself

near a display of chocolate-covered espresso beans. Her feet were killing her, the tip of her nose was still numb from the cold and her stomach was growling. So far her job search had been a complete bust. First she'd tried a tiny bookstore on the corner of Seventy-fifth and Lexington, where the manager had laughed in her face when she'd asked whether he was hiring. Then she'd tried a clothing boutique across the street, where the woman at the till just shook her head and went back to talking on her mobile phone. Lastly, she'd wandered into a toy store, where the hordes of screaming kids and their miserable-looking parents had made her run right back on to the street.

Java Mama didn't look so promising, either. The pink-haired girl seemed worn out and harried, and the tattooed guy with the perma-frown seemed to take milk steaming very, very seriously. And just looking at the line of tense yoga moms attached to gigantic pushchairs and ordering half-caf skinny lattes made her tired. Almost every woman had a designer-made leather changing bag hanging from her shoulder. How did everyone afford this stuff? And why had she never noticed how wealthy everyone was in this neighbourhood?

After a few more minutes of watching the pink-haired girl continue to take orders, she decided that she'd done enough job searching for one day. Her dad's couch was calling her name, and so was his fridge.

She'd barely reached the door when a girl her age barged inside and almost knocked her down with the help of three enormous shopping bags from Scoop. As soon as Carina saw the auburn curls, the silver Searle Postcard coat and the knit cap with devil horns, her mood sank even lower. It was Ava.

"Oh, sorry!" Ava said, gathering her bags. When she saw who she'd bumped into, her smile faded. "Oh, hi," she said coldly, straightening her hat. "Sorry 'bout that. What's up?"

"Not much. How's everything going with the event?" Carina stepped closer to Ava to make room for a mom with a pushchair and almost choked on Daisy perfume.

"Great," Ava replied. "We just had one of our committee meetings. It was sooo fun," she said pointedly. "It's too bad you didn't want to join." She took off her devil cap and shook out her lush curls with a dramatic, shampoo-commercial toss of the head. "So aren't you getting something?"

"What?" Carina asked.

"To drink," Ava said.

"Hey!"

Carina whipped around to see the pink-haired girl at the counter, standing with a stocky, balding man wearing an apron.

"Did you still want to speak to the manager?" she asked, jerking a thumb in his direction.

"No, that's OK!" Carina yelled back.

"What'd you need to speak to the manager about?" Ava prodded. "Did they mess up your order?" She lifted one hand to play with her diamond A necklace, showing off her immaculate, black and white zebra-striped manicure.

"Actually, I was just here for my dad," Carina said. "He's

hosting a tea for some media people at our house and I just came in to see if they'd cater it for us." She couldn't believe she'd just thought of that off the top of her head.

Ava narrowed her eyes. "Really?"

"Uh-huh, but now that I think about it, this isn't really our speed," Carina said grandly, looking around. "I should probably go to Serendipity. Or Sant Ambroeus. Someplace a little more high-end."

"So you help your dad plan parties?" Ava asked, sounding genuinely interested.

"Oh yeah, all the time," she said. "I mean, I've been watching his people do it for years so I've really picked it up by now." She snuck a quick peek over her shoulder. The manager was still standing at the counter. She turned back around.

"You must have a lot of connections, then," Ava said, turning the A on her necklace backwards and forwards. "Like, with the best chefs, the best florists, the best DJs, right?"

"Pretty much. My dad and I only like to work with the best. You know how it is."

Ava folded her arms and leaned back on her heels. Carina half expected her to burst out laughing, but her expression was deadly serious. "How'd you like to plan my event?" she asked.

"What?" Carina wasn't sure whether she'd heard Ava correctly over the din of crying babies. "You mean the Silver Snowflake dance? Aren't you doing that?"

"Oh God no, I'm just dealing with the guest list." She sighed, pulling out a leather-covered notebook from her black

Hervé Chapelier bag. "This is everyone who goes to school in the city *and* at boarding school and of course I have to figure out who's actually cool enough to invite, you know what I mean?" She opened it to reveal a single-spaced list of names on the first page and then clapped it shut. "So I've got my hands full with that. All that other stuff – the DJ, the food, the decor – someone needs to handle that. And maybe it could be you."

Carina quickly mulled this over. This could be a job. If she could get Ava to pay her. "Well, I'm sort of busy with stuff for my dad right now," Carina said. "But if I were going to be *paid* for it, then that would be a different story." She held her breath and waited.

Ava didn't blink. "How much?"

"Food, DJ, decor, basically overseeing the entire thing…" Carina gazed into the middle distance, pretending to think. "A thousand dollars."

Ava's left eyebrow shot up. "A *thousand* dollars?" she asked.

Carina swallowed. "Uh-huh."

Ava's pearly white front teeth chewed her bottom lip. "Well, the charity people said they had a little money in the budget. And if we hired you for a party planner, it would totally be worth it. With your connections and everything." She paused. "OK. I think we could do that."

"Then what about the retainer fee?" Carina asked before she could chicken out.

"What's that?" Ava asked, suspicious now.

"That's how it works. You give the party planner a chunk of the money up-front to secure their services. I think the going rate is twenty per cent of the total charge. In this case, two hundred dollars." She had no idea whether any of this was true, but it was worth a shot. She needed some quick cash for that lift ticket.

Ava shrugged. "Fine, I'll have it for you on Monday."

"OK, great," Carina said, trying not to look shocked.

"Cool," Ava said breezily, pushing past her towards the counter. "I think together you and I could make this party totally *Times*-worthy. See you Monday."

Ava stepped on to the coffee line, and Carina did a discreet victory jig as she walked out of the door. She'd done it! She'd got a job! And not only was this going to be the easiest money she'd ever made in her life – well, the *first* money she'd ever made in her life – she'd get to go on the Carter trip after all! Of course, she didn't have any experience, but she'd learn. All she needed to do was sit down with a professional and get some pointers. And she already knew the perfect person to call: Roberta Baron was her dad's go-to woman for all his events, and the most sought-after party planner in New York. Roberta had done so many of the Jurg's parties that she was practically family. She'd be only too happy to answer her questions. And from what she'd seen of Roberta in action, party planning seemed pretty simple: telling the flower people where to put the arrangements, screaming at the caterers, making sure the band didn't play any Earth, Wind & Fire. How hard could that be?

She took out her mobile phone and tried to ignore the crawling panda as she dialled information. She would have just Googled her, but the Jurg wanted her to live in the Stone Age. "Roberta Baron, please," she said. "Of Roberta's Rare Events." As she walked back on to the street she didn't even notice the cold wind that blew through her hair and burned her cheeks.

I'm back, she thought as she headed towards the subway. *I am so very, very back.*

Chapter 9

She bounded up the red-carpeted steps, past the grey-suited doorman, and breezed through the shiny brass revolving doors of the Plaza. Her plan was going even better than she'd expected. After leaving Roberta a semi-rambling message saying that she had business to discuss, Roberta had texted her minutes later and given her a meeting on the spot: *Palm Court, Plaza Hotel, four o'clock.* That was the power of the Jurgensen name, she'd thought, tucking her phone back into her Botkier bag and turning west on Fifty-seventh Street. People always got back to you, even on a Saturday.

She hurried through the hushed, marble-floored lobby and the memories floated back to her. This was where they'd come, she and her mom, the day they'd left her dad. They'd taken a one-bedroom suite with a king-size feather bed and a majestic view of Central Park. For five days her mom cried in the bathroom and her dad made threatening phone calls and her mom's therapist, Dr Carla, made a few emergency visits. It was weird to be in the middle of such high drama, but she'd loved being here. They ordered room service from a white-gloved butler named Godfrey, took long freezing walks in Central Park, crunching over frozen snow, and one night even slipped into a party taking place in one of the private event rooms. Best of all, her mom called her in sick to school every morning, just so Carina could stay in the hotel and keep her company.

When the Jurg finally showed up, he was with a police officer and a lawyer, both of whom threatened to arrest his wife if she didn't allow Carina to come home. Carina wasn't surprised, and neither was her mom. They'd said goodbye to each other in the hotel room. Now as she made her way through the lobby, past the softly lit boutiques and the slow-moving tourists, she remembered the smell of peppermint shampoo in her mom's blonde hair and the touch of her freckled hands, and felt that same tightness in her chest from the night before. She'd gone home with her dad that day four years ago, thinking that she hadn't had a choice. Now she wondered whether she'd actually had one. At least if she'd gone with her mom, she would have had one parent who cared about her. Right now she didn't have any.

Carina rounded the corner and walked out into the entrance to the Palm Court, a large open dining area lined with potted palms and crammed with pink linen-covered tables.

"Excuse me, can I help you?" asked the skeletal hostess behind the podium.

"I'm meeting someone here," Carina said, craning her head. "Roberta Baron."

"Oh, right this way," said the hostess, beckoning Carina to follow her. They made their way past ladies in dresses and pearls sipping tea from china cups and nibbling on tiny crustless sandwiches. Carina felt her spirits instantly lift. This place was stuffy, but a little luxury was *just* what she needed right now.

Roberta was at a table in the corner, bent over her BlackBerry as she sipped a glass of iced water. Her flame-coloured bob looked like it had just been blown out that morning, and her bony wrists were draped with jewel-encrusted gold bangles. A fat yellow diamond glinted on her finger. If there was anyone who could teach her how to pull off being a successful party planner, Carina thought, it was Roberta.

"Carina, my darling," she said, standing up and giving Carina a hug. She smelled faintly of lemons and her beige cashmere twinset felt super-soft and super-expensive. "What a nice surprise. How are you, my dear?"

"Great, great," she said. "Thanks for meeting me."

"Please, sit down," Roberta said, and then turned to the hostess. "Could you please tell our waiter, wherever he is, that we'll have the English tea service with no clotted cream? And absolutely *no* watercress *or* milk – just lemon. And a plate of those little candied gingers. And no dawdling, please."

The hostess just nodded, mildly frazzled, and walked away.

"So, my dear, I was just thinking about you and I'm so glad you called," Roberta said, focusing her ice-blue eyes on Carina. She had to be almost sixty, but her pale face was eerily smooth. "If you're planning a sweet sixteen, you really should start thinking about venues now. The best places are always taken a year in advance. What about the University Club?"

"Actually, I wanted to ask *you* some questions," Carina said, circling the bottom of her water glass with her finger. "About your job."

Roberta's face went completely slack, as if she were trying hard not to make any unnecessary expressions.

"I've just been asked to plan the Silver Snowflake Ball this year," she said, leaning forward on her elbows. "It's this fancy private-school dance—"

"I know what it is," Roberta said abruptly.

"And um ... since this is my first party-planning job, I thought I'd ask *you*, the party-planning queen of New York, to give me a few pointers."

"Pointers?" Roberta repeated, as if she'd suddenly forgotten how to understand English. Tiny frown lines appeared between her eyebrows.

"I mean, I get the basic idea," Carina continued, "you kind of oversee everything, and tell people where to put stuff, and yell at people when things go wrong, but I'm sure there's more to it. Tricks of the trade, that kind of thing."

"So this *isn't* about an actual event that you'd like me to do?" Roberta asked. Her eyebrows edged closer and closer to her hairline.

"Oh no," Carina said. "Just advice."

Roberta pursed her lips so hard that they turned into a narrow pink dash. "I rescheduled a meeting for this, Carina," she said icily. "I thought you wanted to discuss an event."

"Oh," Carina said. "I thought I said I had some business to discuss—"

"Which I thought meant something for you and your father, not a school dance."

There was a sound of rolling wheels and trembling cutlery, and Carina looked up to see a white-jacketed waiter roll their tea service up to their table. On his cart were the largest silver teapot she'd ever seen, gold-edged china cups and saucers, several plates of scones and a three-tiered tray that held various tiny sandwiches.

"Wow, that looks delicious," Carina said, as the waiter began to serve the tea.

But Roberta didn't even look at the food. Instead she pushed her chair back. "Do you mind if we do this another time? I have more important things to do with my day." She slung her cream-coloured Chanel satchel impatiently over her shoulder.

"Um … OK," Carina stammered. "But don't you want to eat?"

Roberta waved her hand dismissively at the cart. "Just

tell your father we need to discuss what he wants to do about his holiday party this year. Everyone else already has their invitations printed. Goodbye, Carina."

With that she wrapped her cashmere cape around herself, wheeled around on her spike-heeled Jimmy Choo boots and set off towards the exit.

Carina watched her totter away in shock. What had just happened? Why was Roberta so angry with her? Or at least, why had she blown her off like that?

"Is everything OK?"

She looked up to see the skeletal hostess hovering over the table, fake smile blazing.

"Oh, yes," Carina said. "My friend had to leave."

"So you're done?" the hostess asked brightly.

"I guess."

"Then I'll have the waiter bring you the bill," the hostess said, before walking away.

The bill. Carina eyed the untouched stacks of sandwiches and scones, the huge teapot, the pots of butter and jam. Then she remembered that Roberta had left. Which meant that she would have to pay for it.

Her heart started to thump inside her chest like she was about to jump out of a plane. She had no idea how she was going to pay for this. Especially because this was probably the most expensive tea service on the face of the planet.

The waiter glided by the table and dropped the bill off.

"Everything all right, miss?" he asked.

"Fine," she said, barely able to look him in the eye.

Carina waited for him to leave, and then, holding her breath, she opened up the little leather book that held the bill.

1 English tea service............$75.00

She gulped and slammed the leather book closed. She had no idea what to do. She knew kids who'd "dined and dashed" before, but they'd done it at some broken-down diner on First Avenue under the Roosevelt Island tram, just for the fun of it. This was high tea at the Plaza Hotel. They probably arrested people for running out on the bill. But right now, it was the only option. If she could get away with it.

Slowly, she turned around. The restaurant seemed to be emptying. The hostess was at another table, speaking to the mother of three squirmy kids taking turns throwing mini quiches at each other. Carina reached down and grabbed her bag. It was now or never.

She got up and calmly began to walk to the exit. If anyone asked where she was going, she would say that she needed to use the toilet. No big deal. As she threaded her way past the tables, she imagined that she could feel the hostess's eyes boring into her back like lasers. Any moment now, she was going to notice Carina and ask her to stop. Any moment now...

"Excuse me!" a woman yelled. "Are you leaving?"

Carina slipped past the empty podium.

"Excuse me? I'm talking to you!" It was the hostess.

That was it. Time to run.

She zipped past the fancy boutiques, past the check-in desk, past a cluster of Japanese tourists who watched her, puzzled and amused, like she was another New York attraction. Out of the corner of her eye, she could see one of the clerks behind the front desk reach for his phone as she ran by, but she didn't care. With a push, she was through the heavy revolving doors and down the carpeted steps. Outside she didn't stop, zigzagging across Fifty-ninth Street, until she reached the lineup of smelly hansom cabs waiting to take tourists through the park and hid behind a big white horse. She stopped and bent over, panting. She could see the headline splashed across the cover of the *New York Post*: MOGUL'S DAUGHTER SKIPS OUT ON TEA TAB.

Finally she stood up. Her throat burned and the skin under her turtleneck dripped with sweat. The sun had set and it was getting cold. So Roberta wasn't going to help her. Fine. She didn't need her help. She needed to get home and come up with a plan B for Ava's party. Which right now looked like it would be called Winging It.

She took a deep breath and made her way to the subway. It was only when she'd reached the stairs to the subway that she realized that she'd forgotten one crucial part about the dine and dash. She hadn't eaten a thing.

Chapter 10

"Well, congratulations, C," Lizzie said, leaning back in the ratty, burnt-orange-coloured chair in the corner of the student lounge and stirring her instant Swiss Miss with a pen. "By taking this job, you may have officially punished yourself worse than your dad ever could."

"Did you even *go* to the Gap?" Hudson asked, looking up from the sheet music in front of her. "Or what about Jamba Juice? Or babysitting? My cousin is always complaining about her nanny going on vacation..."

"You guys, *chill*," Carina said, taking out a love poem by e. e. cummings from her bag. Another Ed special. "I'm gonna make a *thousand dollars* doing this – enough to go on the trip. And it's planning a party! This is gonna be fun." At the bottom of the page she wrote in big block letters I WANT TO KISS YOUR BALD SPOT.

"*Fun?*" Lizzie asked, almost spilling her Swiss Miss. "Dealing with Ava every waking minute for the next six weeks? That's not fun. That's heading for the psych ward."

"And you don't have any experience, C," Hudson almost whispered, twisting her rings.

"It's not like you have to be Martha Stewart to plan a party," Carina said, folding the letter to Ed back up and slipping it into her earth science notebook. "You just find people to do what you want and order them around. I've seen people do it before." She had decided not to mention her meeting with Roberta Baron. Not now, not ever.

"Carina, we're just—" Hudson started.

"Worried, I know," she cut in. "But don't be. Everything's fine. I can do this."

She pulled out her Spanish book as Lizzie and Hudson, she knew, traded dramatic, concerned looks over her head.

It wasn't fair. She was always the first one to get behind one of her friends' crazy schemes. Like Lizzie's secret modelling career, for one. If it hadn't been for Carina, they never would have visited Andrea's studio. She'd even signed Lizzie's modelling release for her. (Well, forged Katia's signature, but still…)

But whenever it was *her* crazy scheme, all Lizzie and Hudson ever did was ask her a bunch of nitpicky questions or make her feel like it was never going to work. Why couldn't they be the least bit supportive? She looked down at her book, trying to concentrate, until an overpowering scent of Issey Miyake perfume made her look up.

"Hey, C, can we have a quick meeting?" Ava stood over her with her leather-covered notebook tucked under her arm and a silver Tiffany fountain pen poised in her hand. She looked more like a businesswoman than Carina ever would. "There are just a few things I'd like to go over," she said, with a quick glance at her chunky silver Cartier watch. "Just to get you started."

"Sure," Carina said. She was about to get up, but Ava just sat right down next to her on the carpet.

"When I told the charity people that you'd be planning this party, they fuh-*lipped* out," Ava said, tucking an auburn curl behind one ear. "You know, because of all your connections and everything."

"Great!" Carina said proudly, making sure to glance at Lizzie and Hudson. But both of them were too busy staring at the back of Ava's head to notice her.

"So let's start with a quick overview of all the things you'll be taking care of," Ava said briskly, opening the cover of her notebook. "I've separated them into three categories. Food, music and decor. I figured the best thing to do would be to let you know what *I'd* like to have, just to give you something to work with."

"Sounds good," Carina said.

As Ava flipped the pages of her legal pad, Carina noticed that her nails had already been repainted a purplish black. "OK, the ballroom at the Pierre Hotel is our venue, and it has *amaaazing* acoustics. Which brings me to the most important thing we need to discuss. Music." She fixed Carina with a deadly serious look. "Music makes or breaks a party, so I think for this, we go for the best there is. We go for Matty Banks."

Matty Banks wasn't just a DJ. He was also a Grammy-winning music producer, trendsetter, model and generally one of the coolest twenty-two-year-old guys currently walking the earth. Who also charged thousands of dollars.

"Matty Banks? Really?" Carina asked.

"You've used him before, right?" Ava prompted.

"Yeah, sure, he played my dad's birthday last summer," Carina said, "but I don't know if he's gonna be available. He's, like, the busiest guy on earth."

"Even for *you*?" Ava asked.

"What do you mean, for me?"

"Well, *you'd* be the one asking him," Ava said. "You said you only like to work with the best."

Carina suddenly understood what Ava was talking about. She wanted Carina to use her "connections". After all, that's what Carina had pretended she could do. And even though Matty Banks was probably booked months, if not years, in advance, Ava would be expecting her to get him lickety-split.

"I'm sure it won't be a problem," Carina said, trying to sound confident.

"OK, then let's move on," Ava said, checking it off her list. "Now, appetizers. I'm thinking we go for comfort food. That new place in the Meatpacking District, Café Luz? It's supposed to do this incredible mac and cheese with shaved truffles. Your dad probably knows the chef, right?"

"Filippo?" Carina asked worriedly. "Since he's just opened that place, I'm sure he's going to have his hands full—"

"Let me know what he says," Ava interrupted, crossing the item off her list. "And then for dessert, I'm thinking vegan cupcakes from Sugarbabies."

"Wait. Isn't that the place that charges six bucks a cupcake?" Carina asked.

Ava wrinkled her nose. "They just won best red velvet in the city and they're totally in right now. And for the flowers, I think we should try to get Mercer Vaise. You've worked with him, right? He's supposed to be incredible with orchids."

"Mercer Vaise does weddings for sheiks and royal families," Carina pointed out. "Can the Make New York Beautiful people afford him?"

Ava scrunched up her face as if Carina had just spoken Swahili. "We're not *paying* these people. Is that what you thought? This is all for charity."

"Then how are we getting them?" Carina asked.

Ava rolled her eyes. "Because you *know* them. You've worked with them before. They should be happy to do this for you and your dad. Why else do you think we're paying you a thousand dollars?"

Carina glanced up at her friends. Hudson was aiming a furious stare into the back of Ava's head. Lizzie was shaking her head *no*.

"Wait," Ava said, giving Carina a steady, unblinking stare. "This isn't going to be a *problem*, is it?"

The seconds ticked by in slow, slow motion. Carina thought frantically. This was her chance. Her chance to say that, well, maybe . . . it might be a problem.

But that wasn't an option. She needed that money.

"Of course not," she said, shaking her head. "My dad's BFF with all these guys."

"*Wunderbar!*" Ava exclaimed, getting to her feet and brushing the dust off her burgundy tights. "Oh, and I almost forgot. We said two hundred, right?" She reached into her bag, took out a heavy Louis Vuitton wallet, and pulled out two crisp hundred-dollar bills. "For your retainer," she said, with the slightest touch of sarcasm.

As soon as Carina closed her fist over the money, she felt all of her doubts melt away.

"Let me know what happens with Matty," Ava reminded her. "By Friday?"

"No problem," Carina said.

"Perfect. I have a feeling that this is going to be the best Silver Snowflake in history." Ava tossed her hair and sauntered away as her rolled-up kilt swung back and forth like a wagging finger.

"Oh my God, this is worse than I thought," Lizzie said, almost leaping out of her chair. "You have to get people to do stuff for *free*?"

"And she's already given you money?" Hudson asked warily.

105

"It's just for the lift ticket," Carina said, trying to sound optimistic. "So I can save my place on the trip."

"But you *hate* using your dad's name," Lizzie said, playing with an elastic band around her wrist. "It, like, makes you nauseous. So why'd you tell her yes?"

"It's not like I have to throw his name around. Almost all of these people have worked with him already. It's asking friends for a favour. And it's for a really good cause."

"Free cosmetic surgery to the underprivileged?" Lizzie asked, arching a furry brow. "You're above this, C. Running around town, doing Ava Elting's bidding ... it's beneath you. Don't you think?"

Carina felt a flash of anger as she got to her feet. "I need to find Carter before the bell," she muttered and then grabbed her bag and ducked out of the lounge.

She sped down the hall to the stairs, trying to stay calm. As much as she loved Lizzie and Hudson, neither of them knew what she was going through. They'd never had to bail on plans with a guy they liked because they couldn't afford to get a pizza with him. They'd never had to live on twenty dollars a week. How could they judge her? She was just doing what she had to do. Of course, Ava had definitely thrown her a curveball with the favour thing, but she'd figure out a way to make it work. And she was already halfway to her romantic trip with Carter. As soon as she found him and gave him the money, it would be a fait accompli, as Hudson would say.

When she saw Carter walking out of the computer room

a few minutes later, her stomach did such a crazy free fall that she was afraid she might throw up.

"Hey, what are you in such a hurry for?" he asked, coming to stand a thrilling two feet away from her. He smiled in such a lazy, sexy way that the hairs on her arm stood on end.

"Just wanted to give you this," she said slyly, handing him the two bills. "For the lift ticket."

He looked down at the crumpled money in his hand. "I thought you'd just write me a cheque or something," he said.

"Nah, cold hard cash is how I roll," she flirted. "And you didn't think I was gonna forget about kicking your butt, right?"

"No way," he said, beaming, as he slipped the money into the pocket of his fleece.

"And … maybe we could even hang out before then," she said. For a second she was scared he wouldn't respond. But his grin only spread wider.

"Sounds good," he said. Just then, a deafening chime came from her bag. It was her vintage mobile phone. "What the hell was that?" Carter asked, looking around.

"I gotta go," Carina said, stepping backwards. "I'll Facebook you."

She raced down the hall and ducked into the girls' toilets. Once she was safely locked in a stall, she took out her phone. It was a text from her dad.

Party for Princess magazine tonight. 6:00 sharp. SoHo Grand Hotel.

She still hadn't seen the Jurg since the other night in the den. And the last thing she wanted to do right now was go to one of his events.

But maybe this was the perfect chance to let him see that she was just fine. She'd found herself a job and (possibly) a new boyfriend, all in the last few days. She was more than fine. She was kicking butt.

She tossed her phone into her bag and pulled her hair back into a ponytail. She'd go to his stupid party, smile her guts out and show him that his punishment had barely touched her. Now she almost couldn't wait.

Chapter 11

The party for *Princess* was well under way when Carina stepped off the elevator and into the penthouse suite of the SoHo Grand. She walked past a poster board mock-up of the December cover, featuring a brunette starlet who'd just played the lead in a popular horror movie, and checked herself in the mirrored wall of the foyer. She'd changed from her uniform into a parent-appropriate ruffled grey silk top from Anthropologie, dark blue skinny jeans, black ballet flats and her most expensive Martin Meloy bag. She wasn't crazy about Martin Meloy, especially after what had happened with Lizzie, but this seemed like the kind of crowd that'd be into him. OK, she thought, staring at her reflection. All she needed to do was show her face to the Jurg and then get out of here. Afterwards, she had a meeting with Matty Banks. And that was much more important than being here.

She moved into the main room of the suite. A few C-list celebrities lounged on the couches while the twenty-something *Princess* editors gawked at them from the open bar. Gorgeous waiters passed platters of tuna rolls and bacon-wrapped scallops, and paparazzi stalked the room, taking pictures. It was the usual scene, less a "party" and more just a reason to get *Princess,* and its cover girl, mentioned on Page Six and the gossip blogs the next day. And *Princess* needed all the press it could get. No matter how many times it changed art directors, or how many "cool" actresses it got for its covers, *Princess* got outsold by the other teen magazines every month. Her dad couldn't figure out why, but Carina had, a long time ago. It was because *Princess* was hopelessly lame. She'd always got the feeling that the editors had taken a seminar called "Getting to Know the Teen Girl!" in 1989 and been referring to their notes ever since. They were always too late with their trends and totally off with their fashion stories, and did articles on stuff that had been a big deal ten years ago, like "Teens and Technology." But she'd never shared her opinion with the Jurg. She doubted he'd appreciate it.

She moved through the room, on the lookout for her dad, when she almost tripped over Creepy Manservant perched on a suede ottoman. In his greasy comb-over and boring brown suit, he looked utterly out of place. "Hello, Carina," he said in his nasal voice. "Nice to see you."

"Hi, Ed," she said, unable to look him in the eye. She wondered if he'd been getting her anonymous love notes.

"Do you know Barb Willis?" he asked, gesturing stiffly to a plain-looking woman next to him who looked as out of place as he did. "She's the editor-in-chief of *Princess*. Barb, this is Carina. Karl's daughter."

"Hello, Carina," Barb said eagerly, extending her hand. Barb seemed to be in her mid-forties, and she had thin, staticky brown hair and wire-rimmed glasses. She didn't wear any jewellery or make-up, and her shapeless black suit hung on her angular frame. Unlike most of the female editors who worked for her dad, Barb seemed to be trying hard *not* to be glamorous.

"Hi," Carina said. "Nice to meet you."

"Carina was working for us in the office for a while," Ed said with one of his patented smirks. "So she knows all about the magazine."

And how much trouble it's in, Carina thought.

"Here's your father now," said Ed, and Carina turned to see her father striding towards her. People stepped aside to let him pass, the way they usually did whenever he moved through a crowded room. Even Carina had to admit that he looked like a movie star in his charcoal grey Armani suit.

"Hello, honey," he said, leaning down to kiss her on the cheek. He was always more affectionate with her in public. "Good to see you."

"Hi," she said, barely meeting his eye.

"I see you've met Barb," he said.

Carina noticed Barb staring at her dad intently. *Oh great,* she thought. *Barb's in love with him.* "Yes, we just met," she said.

"Carina loves the magazine," the Jurg told Barb. "She's had a subscription since ... well, for years now, haven't you?"

"Yes," Carina said, smiling right through the lie.

"Actually, Barb has a wonderful idea," the Jurg said. "I'll let her tell you about it."

Barb blushed a little and pushed her glasses up on her beaky nose. Carina couldn't help but think that Hudson could have done a seriously awesome makeover on her.

"We've decided to start doing a feature on a real-life 'Princess'," Barb began, putting quotes around the word with her fingers. "A real girl who lives a fabulous, glamorous life that all of our readers would love to have. And we figured, who better for that story than Carina Jurgensen?"

"What?" Carina asked. "Me?"

"Well, you do live a fabulous, glamorous life," Barb replied. "You go to Chadwick, you live in a penthouse, you spend your summers in Montauk, your father is one of the most successful men in the world..." Barb flashed Karl a grin. "That's a princess in our book."

"You'd just tell them about your life, the places you go, the stores you shop in, the kind of make-up you love to wear, all of that," her dad volunteered. "Sounds like fun, huh?" he asked, smiling his Public Appearance smile.

Stores she shopped in? she thought. Could her dad possibly be serious?

112

"I'm … uh … flattered, but honestly, I don't think I'm right for it. At least not these days," she added, shooting her dad a look he didn't catch.

"Oh come on," her father said. "They do a Q and A, they take pictures of you in some beautiful clothes. It'll be great." He gave her a brief, succinct tap on the middle of her back, which she knew meant End of Discussion. "We'll figure out a time for Carina to come by the office," he said to Barb.

"Thanks, Karl," said Barb. "Now if you'll excuse me, I think I see my beauty editor getting tipsy."

"I'll go with you," Ed said and the two of them melted into the crowd.

Carina turned to face her father. "Are you *kidding* me?" she said, fighting to be heard over the latest Zero 7 song.

"What, Carina?" he sighed. He grabbed a glass of iced water from one of the passing trays. "What's wrong now?"

"I thought you didn't *want* me to be a princess. I thought that was the whole point of what you did."

"It's a story," he explained, sipping his water. "Let's not dramatize it too much."

"But it's a lie. I know kids like the ones she's talking about and I'm not one of them. At least not any more. But I don't think I ever was, either."

"Carina, this magazine is in trouble," he said under his breath. "And if they want to do a sidebar on my daughter, then that's the least I can do for it."

"But why do you want people to think I'm something that *you* don't even want me to be?" she asked.

He slammed his glass down on a passing tray. "Everyone knows you live a good life. You're my daughter, for Christ's sake. You're not exactly suffering."

"Well, maybe I don't want to be your daughter any more. Maybe I'd just like to be Carina."

The Jurg's jaw muscle pulsed in and out as he looked at her. "What did you say?"

"I have to go," she muttered, almost backing right into a snapping photographer.

"Carina—" he said, but she didn't wait. She turned and hustled through the crowd, brushing past bulky handbags and pointy shoulders. She knew leaving like this was rude and immature, but right now, she didn't care. She was too angry. Her dad was a complete hypocrite and she just needed to get out of there. As she rounded the corner into the foyer, she bumped up against the mock-up of *Princess* on its stand. It tumbled to the ground.

People looked up from their champagne flutes. One of the photographers snapped a picture. Carina looked down at the mock-up, wondering whether to pick it up. In the suite, she could see her father watching her, his narrowed dark eyes glittering like black stars as he shook his head.

Then the elevator opened.

Oh, who cares, she thought, and ran inside.

Chapter 12

"I should be on the list," Carina said, knotting her scarf closer around her throat as a chilly wind blew down Spring Street. "Jurgensen with a J. Matty Banks put me on."

The bouncer glanced at his clipboard and then rubbed his stubbly chin as he sized her up. He was as big as a football player, and so thick around the shoulders that his leather jacket seemed liable to snap off at any moment. Standing in front of him Carina felt about eight years old. "You got ID?" he asked, tapping the list with his pen.

"I forgot it," she said confidently. Her dad had once told her that people will believe anything as long as you sound confident.

He looked her up and down. "Ten minutes," he said brusquely, unfastening the velvet rope in front of the door. "And no drinking."

"No prob'm," she said.

She had absolutely no interest in drinking, ever since she'd swigged a vodka and tonic thinking it was 7UP when she was ten years old and almost barfed. "Thanks," she said out of the side of her mouth, and walked into the Luxelle Lounge.

The Luxelle Lounge was so exclusive that it didn't have a phone number or a name on the door. Inside, it was as cool as Carina had pictured. Red velvet booths lined the walls, covered by gauzy curtains. Tea lights flickered along the massive cherrywood bar. Groovy French hip-hop played on the PA system. And on the stage at the back of the room, waiting like props for a play, were Matty's turntables and speakers, bathed in red lights.

Carina looked around self-consciously. She'd never been in a bar by herself and figured someone was about to call the police or Child Services. But nobody seemed to notice her. Not the silky-haired female bartenders shaking their martini shakers, or the beautiful waitress who glided past her without a word. The few people at the bar didn't turn around. But someone had noticed her. A guy who looked to be her age stood in the corner, sipping a glass of water as he quietly studied her.

He was thin and wiry like a skater, with dark hair that was cut a little too short on top to be stylish. He wore dark green trousers, scruffy Stan Smiths and an Arctic Monkeys T-shirt over a long-sleeved grey thermal. He was kind of cute with his sculpted cheekbones and big brown eyes, but he was a little on the small side, and he looked like an artsy guy. Artsy guys weren't really her thing. They were always way too into their music to be bothered with girls, or sports, or hanging out with the guys. But from the way this artsy guy was staring at her, he seemed much more interested in her than in, say, downloading another Arcade Fire album.

Suddenly a guy's howling voice made her jump.

From out of the shadows came "*CaREEEna! CaREENa JAY!*"

Matty Banks was half strutting, half shambling towards her, as if he were too cool to take actual steps. He looked even taller and skinnier than the last time she'd seen him and he'd grown a scruff of beard to go along with his permanent bedhead. Lots of girls thought Matty Banks was hot, but Carina was always a little turned off by guys who were thinner than she was. As he approached, he leaned backwards and sang her name out again to the ceiling.

"CaREEEna! What's *up*, Karl Junior?" he said, arching his back and giving her a big high five.

"Hey, Matty!" she said, returning the high five as best she could. "Good to see you."

Matty threw his arm around her and brought her face-to-face with his deliberately stained T-shirt. "Babe! So good to hear from you! Your dad like that iPod I set up for him?"

"He loves it. I think he's already lost ten pounds from running so much," she said.

"Yo, Amber!" Matty yelled towards the bar, cupping his hand. "Slide me a Rockstar when you have a sec!"

One of the silky-haired bartenders nodded at him.

"And one for my friend, OK?" he yelled again, taking her by the arm and steering her towards one of the red leather booths.

"So what's up?" he asked as Carina finally wriggled out of his grip and sat down. "You said you're doing a party?" His hands beat out a frantic staccato rhythm on the table as his eyes swept the room. She remembered that Matty had a classic case of attention deficit disorder.

"It's the Silver Snowflake Ball," she said. "It's for all the private-school kids in the city. It's black-tie, invitation-only. They do it every year. It's kind of a big deal."

"Sounds awesome, little J," he said, checking out the beautiful waitress as she came over with their drinks and placed them on the table.

"Anyway, all the money for tickets goes to charity," she went on, trying to regain his attention. "And nothing would make this event cooler than having *you* there to DJ. So what do you think?" She took a sip of the energy drink and almost gagged.

Matty gulped his drink, staring at something past her head. "So it's not for your dad?" he asked.

"Uh, *no*," she repeated. "But it's a really great cause. Cosmetic surgery for people who can't afford it, which is really important. And I'm pretty sure I could get you Rockstar drinks all night for free. But because it's a charity and everything, we wouldn't be able to pay you."

His eyes suddenly stopped roaming the room and landed on her.

"But I'm sure you're OK with that," she prompted.

Matty set down his bottle and studied the table for a moment. "Right, well ... I'd love to help you out, dude, but I don't think I can do it. I'm just too booked up."

"But I haven't even told you when it is yet."

Matty shook his head. "Doesn't matter. I'm just slammed. Like, all through Christmas, all through New Year's. Gotta make a living, right?" Before she could respond, he downed the rest of his drink and got to his feet. "Wish I could help you out. Seriously. But say hi to your dad for me. He knows how to reach me, right?"

"Sure," she said tonelessly.

He clutched her hand and gave her a bro-style handshake. "Awesome. Hope you're hanging around for the show. I'm taking requests," he joked, winking at her, and then he ambled off towards the bar.

She kicked at the table leg in frustration. That had been a total waste of time. Yes, Matty was still obsessed with her dad, and yes, he still liked her. But not enough to forget about getting paid. That was why he thought her dad was a rock star. That was why he'd taken a meeting with her. For the same reason Roberta had: because he thought it meant another fat cheque.

Out of the corner of her eye she saw the gargantuan bouncer approach the table. "Time's up," he said as he grabbed her arm. "You want us to lose our liquor licence?"

"I'm leaving, I promise!" she yelled as he yanked her to her feet. She twisted her arm to get free but the bouncer's hand was too strong. "Hey, hands off! What's your problem?"

Just as Carina was about to send a swift kick into the guy's massive leg, the skater guy with the big brown eyes stepped neatly in front of them.

"Ruben, man, chill," he said calmly, holding up the palms of his hands. "No need for theatrics."

"You know this girl?" the bouncer demanded.

"'Course I do and she's about to leave," the guy said calmly. He stepped closer, so close that she could see that he had nice white teeth and long dark eyelashes. "No offence, dude," he said, "but dragging her out of here kind of makes you look like a jackass."

Ruben released his blood-stopping grip on her arm. Whoever this guy was, it was clear that Ruben did not want to look like a jackass in front of him.

"If anything happens, it's your fault," Ruben muttered before stomping out of the door.

"Sorry about that," Artsy Guy said, coming closer. "They can get a little paranoid around here."

"But not about you?" she asked, rubbing her burning arm.

"I come here a lot," he said casually. "But you're obviously new." He cocked his head and stared at her. "I'm gonna say Park Avenue, tennis camp, East Hampton and only goes below Fourteenth Street to shop at Marc Jacobs," he said with a nod at her purse.

"Martin Meloy," she corrected, hiding her bag behind her legs. "And what are you? The Hipster Police?"

The guy smiled. "No, I'm Alex," he said, sticking out his hand. "Alex Suarez."

"Carina." They shook hands.

"And I'm *not* a hipster," he shot back.

"And *I* don't live on Park Avenue," she said.

"Got it," he conceded. "How do you know Matty Banks? Please tell me you're not dating him," he added, running a hand through his short black hair.

"I was just trying to hire him. For the Silver Snowflake Ball. It's this dance every Christmas—"

"I know what it is," he interrupted. "I go to Stuyvesant." He grinned. "Which means I've never been invited."

Stuyvesant was one of the city's public high schools, which meant that its students would never, ever turn up on Ava's list of potential invitees.

"Well, it's not life-changing or anything," she said quickly. "I wouldn't even be going if I weren't planning it."

"Uh-huh," Alex said, grinning even harder now. She felt her face get warm. Usually she was the one who called people out on their ridiculousness and now he was doing it to her. "So's Matty gonna do it?" he asked.

"No, he can't. He's all booked up."

"You just lucked out," Alex said. "He's terrible."

"*Terrible?*" Carina repeated. "He's the most famous DJ in the world."

"Doesn't mean he's good," Alex replied, hitching his hands under his armpits. "I've seen him spin three times in the past six months and he's played the same set every time. Just because he's got a Grammy and he sleeps with models, he thinks he doesn't have to try." Alex snorted. "He's a total disgrace to the DJ profession."

Carina folded her arms. "*You're* a DJ?" she countered.

"Yup," he said, scratching his neck. "And I can guarantee you I'm better than he is."

"*You* are?"

"Uh-huh," he said coolly, smiling at her.

"*What* grade are you in?" she asked.

"Eleventh." He looked up at the ceiling. "And my mom knows all about it, and I have an A-minus average. OK?"

"Fine," she said. "But you're seriously better than him?"

Just then the groovy French hip-hop was replaced with a remix of a Bee Gees song. They looked over and saw Matty standing behind the turntables, wearing his headphones.

"Now *that's* original," Alex muttered under his breath. "Look. If you really want someone good, you should have me do it. And if you're still not sure, then here. I'm spinning tomorrow. Come see me and decide for yourself." He pulled a flyer out of the pocket of his jeans and gave it to her. The headline said TUESDAYS WITH DJ ALEXX AT CLUB NESHKA.

"You have two x's in your name?" she asked sceptically.

"It's my stage name." He shrugged. "You gotta do something."

"Club Neshka?"

"It's one of the coolest places in the city. Trust me."

"I thought *this* was the coolest place in the city," she said.

Alex shook his head. "Then all the more reason you need to come to Club Neshka."

Carina dropped the flyer in her bag. "OK, I'll see you there. Tomorrow. Eight o'clock. And you better be good, Alex with the two x's."

"Don't worry, I will be," Alex said simply, and walked away.

As she headed to the velvet-curtained exit, she couldn't quite put her finger on Alex Suarez. Sure, he was a little bit of a know-it-all, and cocky as hell, but he seemed smart and to have a good heart. And talking to him was weirdly comfortable. Almost as if she'd known him her whole life.

She looked down again at the flyer. It seemed a little sketchy, hiring a guy her age for a party that Ava wanted to have mentioned in the *Times*'s style section. But maybe this guy was better than Matty Banks. And at least he wasn't wearing a deliberately stained T-shirt and singing out her name to the ceiling, she thought as she stepped through the front door.

Chapter 13

"So you just walked into this place and nobody even *carded* you?" Hudson asked incredulously, her chopsticks poised over a cucumber roll.

"Matty had me on the list. I told you guys he'd give me a meeting right away." Carina looked down at her soggy turkey and Swiss sandwich. She'd been so proud when she'd made it herself last night in the empty kitchen – spreading Dijon on the bread, folding in the lettuce, deseeding the slice of tomato. Now it looked and felt like a wet sponge.

"So is Million Dollar Matty gonna do this dance for free?" Lizzie asked.

"Well…" Carina hedged. "He turned out to be all booked up."

Just as she expected, Lizzie and Hudson gave her a We Told You So look.

"You guys, please," Carina groaned. "Stop."

"OK, fine," Lizzie said, biting off a piece of her delicious-looking spinach and turkey wrap. "But we're just worried. Especially since Ava's already paid you."

"OK, first?" Carina said. "Everyone's taken a meeting with me right away. The chef from Café Luz? Filippo? He's meeting me tonight. And as for the DJ, I've already found a replacement." She closed her eyes and bit into her sandwich. It didn't taste nearly as bad as it looked.

"Well, that's good," Hudson said. "Who is he?"

"This really cool guy I met at the Luxelle. He's our age. And he's DJing tonight at some place on East Broadway, if anyone wants to come with me."

"East Broadway?" Lizzie waggled her eyebrows. "Where is that?"

"Somewhere downtown," Carina said knowingly, even though she wasn't sure where it was either.

"Well, you know I would, but I'm still grounded," Lizzie said.

"And I have some last-minute studio stuff to do," Hudson explained. "And *then* I have dance practice."

"Wow," Carina said. "Your mom's really turning up the pressure on you."

"I know." Hudson put down her chopsticks. "I don't know if I can do this, you guys."

"Do what?" Lizzie asked. "Finish the album?"

"No," Hudson said carefully, picking the sesame seeds off

her roll with the pointy edge of a chopstick. "The performing. The singing and dancing. The stuff in front of people," she said, her voice so low it was practically a whisper.

"H, if there were ever anyone who was cut out to do this, it's you," Carina said, finishing her sandwich.

"It's normal to have jitters," added Lizzie. "You'd be weird if you didn't. But you can totally do this. And it's not like you're going to be doing your first show at Madison Square Garden. You'll have time to work up to it."

Hudson nodded, looking down at her half-eaten sushi. "Yeah, you guys are probably right," she agreed. "My mom says I just know too much. I'm not as naive about it all as she was. She says that I just have to turn off my mind."

Carina and Lizzie looked at each other. They both knew Hudson couldn't do that.

After lunch, Carina was rushing to get to her locker before English when someone tapped her on the shoulder.

"Hey, you."

She turned to see Carter McLean right next to her, so close that his right arm was almost grazing her left. His eyes were even more green and piercing than usual. "What's up?" he asked, flashing his sexy smile. "You never Facebooked me."

Her stomach did a somersault. "Oh. I wasn't home last night."

"Well, you still have a phone, right?"

Carina paused. There was no good way to tell him that her phone was older than he was. "Yeah, but my email isn't really working on it right now. But hey, are you around tonight? Like, later on? Around eight thirty?" That would give her plenty of time to go see Alex downtown.

"Sure," he said, looking pleased and a little impressed. "We can hang out at my place and watch a movie or something."

Score one for Carina Jurgensen, she thought. "Awesome."

"Here." He leaned over and shoved a piece of paper in her hand. "So now you don't have any excuses." His warm fingers lingered on hers, making her heartbeat triple. Then he smiled at her and loped off down the hall.

Carina staggered into class, holding the piece of paper. She could still smell his boy scent of soap and sweat, and it was making her heart knock against her chest.

They had a date. *Tonight.* At least five weeks before the trip.

When she was safely sitting down and sure that nobody was looking at her, she opened the piece of paper. There, written in adorably messy boy handwriting, was

CARTER
555-2322

She folded the paper back up before anyone could see. He liked her. He *definitely* liked her.

Chapter 14

Once upon a time in the far distant past – or, more specifically, before last week – the Meatpacking District had been one of Carina's favourite neighbourhoods. With Lizzie and Hudson at her side on a Saturday afternoon, she'd hit Martin Meloy, Diane von Furstenberg and Stella McCartney, and then pop into Pastis for a café au lait and *pain au chocolat*. Now as she walked through the rain into the triangle of cobblestoned streets, her plastic umbrella threatening to blow apart in the wind at any moment, she felt like those days had been part of someone else's life. Someone else's extremely fun, extremely lucky life.

She tried to ignore the store windows as she walked towards Café Luz, but the pull was too great. At Catherine Malandrino, she marched right up to the glass and looked inside. A blonde girl about her age was trying on a beautiful, fluttery, purple baby doll dress. Standing in front of the mirror, she turned around and around as the hem of her dress twirled up around her knees and the white price tag swung innocently from its safety pin.

Carina stepped closer, almost pressing her nose to the glass. She could practically feel the silk on her skin and smell that new-clothes scent. She wanted that dress. She needed that dress. It would have looked even prettier on her. Then her eyes drifted over to the display in the window. On one of the silver mannequins was the yellow halter top. *Her* yellow halter top. It was still beautiful, still in style, still perfect for her in every way...

Get a grip on yourself, she thought as she turned around and stomped back out into the rain. It was just clothes, for God's sake. Nothing important and nothing she couldn't live without. But they *were* important. Inside her stomach she felt a strange, gnawing void, as if she were denying herself a piece of cake. Maybe she really had liked to buy stuff. Maybe the Jurg had been right about her.

But no, he hadn't been right about her at all because here she was, on her way to meet with Filippo Mucci, chef extraordinaire, for the Snowflake Ball. When Filippo had heard that she was trying to reach him through the manager at Café Luz, he called her right back and told her that she absolutely had to come down to the restaurant, where he'd meet with her in person. She had a good feeling about this. And with any luck she'd get to eat.

She crossed the street and walked towards Café Luz, a tiny white carriage house from the nineteenth century that had been converted into a den of fabulousnesss. Even in the rain a small crowd of people waited outside for a table. Only Filippo's latest restaurant would have a line at five thirty in the afternoon.

"Good evening, can I help you?" asked the maître d' when Carina walked into the restaurant. He wore a dark suit and tie, and his shaved head shone in the candlelight. Behind him, Carina could make out a tiny, candlelit space with only about a dozen tables, all of which were filled. No wonder those people were waiting outside, she thought. This place was the size of her closet.

"Yes, I'm here to see Filippo. I'm Carina Jurgensen."

"Please, this way," he said, beckoning her towards a tiny vacant table for two that she hadn't noticed. "Filippo will be right out. But while you're waiting he'd like you to try some sample appetizers first."

"Wonderful!" she said a little too loudly.

After the maître d' had shown her to her seat, she took a look around. The gold-painted walls and wooden tables and chairs gave Café Luz a rustic feel, like being in a Tuscan farmhouse, but the small saucers of greenish olive oil and woven silk place mats screamed high-end New York. And the smell of butter and garlic wafting from the kitchen definitely wasn't cheap, either.

Suddenly a tall waiter in a black T-shirt and jeans arrived

with a plate of tiny bacon-wrapped goodies. "The pancetta-wrapped dates," he said, placing them in front of her.

Quickly she speared one with a fork and popped it in her mouth. The taste was rich and sweet, with an irresistible gooeyness. They *had* to get these for the party. Before she knew it, she'd eaten all of them.

Like magic, the waiter appeared again. "Tuna tartare on crispy tortilla chips with avocado," he announced.

Carina looked down at the mounds of raw tuna topped with a dollop of avocado and said a small prayer to the gods of luxury. She cleared the plate in a matter of seconds. Another definite, she thought. People were going to *love* those.

The waiter returned. "And now," he said dramatically, "our famous macaroni and cheese." He put the plate down in front of her with an extra flourish. "White cheddar, Gorgonzola, Gouda and Parmesan. Topped with shaved black truffles." He took out a small bowl of what looked like large raisins and sprinkled some on top. "*Buon appetito,*" he said with dead seriousness and disappeared.

Carina dug right into the bubbling casserole. As she took her first bite, there was an explosion of cheese and buttery goodness on her tongue. This was possibly the best macaroni and cheese she'd ever had in her life. Ever.

She opened the menu that she'd put aside and scanned it for the macaroni and cheese. It was fifty-five dollars. She almost stopped chewing in shock.

"*Buona sera*, Carina." The round, Santa-bellied Filippo Mucci stood next to her table and held out his arms for a hug. He was the size of a small bear, but his thin brown hair tied back in a punk-ish ponytail and his constantly twinkling brown eyes put her at ease.

"So you like?" he asked, pointing a meaty hand at her quickly disappearing plate of mac and cheese.

"This is incredible," she gushed. "We're going to definitely want this."

"*Bene,*" he said, clapping his hands. "So. How many people are we talking about?"

"About two hundred," she said.

Filippo squinted his eyes and cocked his head for a moment. "OK!" he cried. "Let's do it!"

She grabbed his hand with relief. "Oh, you've saved my life, you have no idea."

"Don't worry about anything, my Carina, we do this and make it *benissimo*," he said grandly, spreading his arms wide.

"Except you know this is a benefit," she said carefully, "and the food would have to be, um, donated—"

Filippo shook his head. "Please, please, I know. That is no problem. But my Carina," he said, holding on to her hand, "do you think you can do me a favour?"

"Sure," she said. "What?"

Filippo's gentle brown eyes began to look pained. "The last time I cook for your father ... last spring ... for his birthday, *ricordi*?"

"Yes, I remember," she said, uncertain what this was all about.

"There was a problem with the bill," he said in a lower voice. "My business partner, he overcharged your father – by mistake! – and now…" Filippo hung his head. "I invited him to the opening here but he didn't respond. I'm afraid he'll no longer use me. Ever again."

She hadn't heard about this, but she believed it. The Jurg did not like to be overcharged. "I'm sorry, Filippo, but I really don't know anything about it—"

"If I do this party for you, do you think your father will use me again?" he asked, grabbing her hand. His eyes were as large and imploring as a baby deer's.

Carina looked back at him, unsure what to say. If she said yes, he would do the food, Ava would be happy and Carina could at least check one thing off her interminable to-do list. But she couldn't do that. Her father wasn't the type to change his mind about someone, especially if he thought they'd tried to cheat him.

"I'm so sorry, Filippo," she said, pulling her hand away. "But I can't say for sure that he will."

Filippo's eyes filled with disappointment. "I will do it anyway," he said with a stoic nod. "It is my pleasure!"

"No, Filippo, that's OK," she said, pushing her chair back and standing up. "And I'd say that I'd put in a good word for you, but my opinion doesn't mean a whole lot right now with my dad."

She could barely look at his crestfallen face. It was killing her to turn him down, but she knew that she was doing the right thing.

Filippo looked up at her with astonishment. "But you're leaving?" he asked. "No, please, you must stay! Do you like zabaglione?"

"I can't. But thank you. The food was amazing. I enjoyed it more than you know."

With both hands on the table, Filippo helped himself to his feet with some difficulty. "Please tell your father he's always welcome here," he said sadly. "I'll even close the restaurant for him."

"I will," she said, even though she knew that her father didn't deserve such an extravagant favour. Then she picked up her umbrella and headed for the door.

So Lizzie had been right, she thought as she slipped past the maître d's podium. She should never have tried to score favours using her dad's name. No wonder Filippo had given her a meeting right away: he just wanted to rectify things with her dad. And Matty had just wanted another six-figure gig. These people didn't care about her. They didn't really even care about her dad. They cared about his money. For some reason, she'd never figured that out until now. From now on, she was going to have to plan this party on her own.

She stepped outside. The pattering rain had become a storm. As she tried to open her flimsy umbrella, a gust of wind turned it inside out and cold rain splattered her face.

"Ugh!" she said out loud. This whole trip downtown had been for nothing, and all she wanted to do right now was go home, take a nice hot shower and then meet up with Carter.

But she still needed a DJ. She dug into her bag and pulled out Alex's wrinkled flyer. She still had no clue where East Broadway was, but right now, DJ Alexx was her only chance.

The wind suddenly snapped her umbrella back into place. Hudson would have said that was a sign. Maybe this time, she thought as she made her way back down to the cobblestones, it was.

Chapter 15

By the time she walked up from the subway station, the rain had stopped, and there was only a damp, briny-smelling wind blowing down East Broadway. She ditched her wind-mangled umbrella in a metal garbage can and then turned to the left and right, searching the block for Club Neshka. From what she could see, East Broadway was definitely *not* the Meatpacking District. Instead of fancy boutiques and crowded bistros, this street was lined with a shabby-looking liquor store, a dry cleaner, and a tiny Chinese restaurant with a blinking neon sign that read JOLLY CHAN's. Above her, the roar of cars on the blue-lit Manhattan Bridge was almost deafening. There didn't seem to be a club in sight. No wonder she'd never heard of East Broadway, she thought. There was nothing here.

The creaky whine of an opening door made her spin around. Down the block, a young bearded guy and a girl in a white peacoat emerged from a building on to the street. Something told her that they'd just come from Club Neshka.

"Wait!" she yelled.

The couple held the door open for her until she reached it. Luckily, there was no bouncer in sight. She slipped past them and ducked inside, or almost ducked inside.

Club Neshka was so packed that she could barely get through the door. Rail-thin, scruffy guys in skinny jeans and waifish girls in vintage flea market dresses blocked the entrance, chatting and dancing and drinking their bottles of beer. It looked like every twentyish hipster in a five-mile radius had come to this desolate part of town just to hang out at this club.

She edged her way further inside. If the Luxelle had been trying hard to be chic, this place was trying hard to be cheesy. Strands of blue and white Christmas lights and bunches of silver tinsel were draped along the fake-wood panelled walls. A disco ball spun from the centre of the ceiling, and framed pictures from a Russian clothing catalogue hung on the walls. It looked like a demented Russian grandmother's living room. And even the music sounded weirdly retro. The song on the PA sounded like an old Motown number. It had a thumping bass line and blaring trumpets and a woman singing, "One hundred days, one hundred nights..." A handful of people danced and swayed to it in the centre of the room, mouthing the words.

Finally, she found Alex. He stood behind his turntables in the far corner of the room, looking like someone's kid brother who was sitting in for fun. He held a pair of headphones up to one ear and nodded to the beat, his brown eyes unblinking and totally focused. He almost seemed to be in another world. On the turntables were several milk crates stuffed with albums. Maybe it was all the DJ equipment and how lost he was in the music, but Alex seemed cuter tonight than he had at Luxelle. Except for his T-shirt silk screened with the cover of *The Queen Is Dead*. *Of course,* she thought. It was practically a law that artsy guys be into the Smiths.

"Hey," she said, walking up to him.

"You made it," he said, genuinely surprised as he put down the headphones. "I didn't think you'd come."

"Well, it turns out I do come downtown for other reasons than to shop," she said, dropping her bag to the floor and walking behind the turntables. "By the way, you were right," she said, looking around. "Cool place."

"No cover, six-dollar drinks and the best sound system on the Lower East Side," Alex said. "Always a crowd."

"So what are we listening to?" she asked, glancing down at the turning record.

"Sharon Jones and the Dap-Kings," he said.

"Cool, I love Motown."

"This isn't Motown. They played Radio City last week."

"Oh," she said, turning back to the albums, pretending not to be embarrassed.

"I'm gonna have to teach you that there's more out there than Lady Gaga," he said dryly.

138

"And I'm gonna have to teach you that being into the Smiths is soooo over. Don't you use an iPod?"

"First lesson of DJing," he said, selecting another record from the crate. "*Only* use vinyl."

"Why? Because it's so retro?" she asked sarcastically.

"No, because it's easier. DJing is really just about mixing."

"What's mixing?" she asked.

"Here," he said, dropping the record on to the empty deck next to the one playing. Then he pressed a button. The turntable began to move. "This is mixing," he said.

He held the headphones up to her ear. She could hear another song under the Sharon Jones and Dap-Whatevers, but the bass line of this new song was faster.

"Watch this," he said. He moved his hand to the console between the two turntables and slowly moved a dial to the left. Now both records were playing through the speakers. The new song's bass line had slowed down to match the one from the first song but was just a tiny bit different. She recognized it now: "I Feel Good" by James Brown. The crowd heard the James Brown, too, and a small cheer went up in the room.

"Isn't that cool?" he asked, watching the room. "That's what DJing is all about. Making sure one song blends into the other and timing the tracks."

"How do you know which songs will blend with each other?" she asked.

Alex shrugged. "You try stuff. Here, check this out." He put her hand on another dial on the mixing board. "You can either turn up the bass or the treble, see?" he said, putting his hand on hers.

She shivered at the warm touch of his hand. *But I'm not even into this guy*, she thought.

"This is taking away all the bass," he said as he moved her hand to the right. Now she couldn't hear the bass, only the high-pitched cymbals crashing in the music. "That's the treble," he said in her ear. "Now, here's the bass without the treble." He moved her hand in the other direction and all she could hear was the thump of the bass line. "See how many parts there are in a song?" he said. "It's like a whole landscape. And you're in control of it. That's DJing."

He kept his hand on hers, which gave her a funny, lurching feeling in her stomach. "Wow," she said. She'd never thought of a song as a landscape before.

They spent the next hour mixing together. She'd line up each record on the turntable, and then watch as Alex dropped the needle and turned the dials, coaxing beats out and into the song that was already playing, so that the two songs were actually playing at once, supporting each other, complementing each other. Alex seemed to know exactly what the crowd wanted. When he mixed in the *wamp-a-wamp-a* bass funk of "Brick House" over the disco beat of "Rich Girls," the crowd screamed and began to jump up and down. And when he went from "Brick House" to "Don't Stop 'til You Get Enough," people cheered. Carina wasn't a dancer, but she almost wanted to get out there on the dance floor and join the crowd. She'd never had this much fun when Matty Banks was spinning at one of her dad's parties.

"OK, you were right!" she finally yelled over the music. "You *are* good at this. Are you free December twentieth?"

"So you want me?" he said, grinning.

"You're hired. But there's one thing we should talk about," she said, pausing. "It's a benefit. Which means you'd have to do it for free."

"No problem," Alex said, dropping another album on to the spinning turntable. "As long as you introduce me to some cute girls."

"Sure." This was surprising. Especially because of all the hand-touching. "If you're into those snobby Upper East Side chicks," she added.

"I don't get it, though," he said, holding up one headphone to an ear. "You were gonna ask Matty Banks to work for *free*?"

"My dad's kind of a friend of his," she said. "It wasn't a big deal."

"Who's your dad?" Alex asked. Carina riffled through the albums in the milk crate. It was always the same dilemma: lie and say she was someone else, which she could never bring herself to do, or tell the truth, and know that the person she told would never see her the same way again. Usually when people found out who her father was, they either liked her a lot less or a lot more. She wasn't sure which one was worse.

141

"Karl Jurgensen," she said casually, looking straight at him.

"*What?*" Alex exclaimed. His brown eyes almost popped out of his head. "And you can't *pay* people?"

"This isn't a party for *me*," she said. "It's for a charity."

"Didn't he make, like, two billion dollars last year?" Alex asked.

"What does *that* have to do with anything?" she snapped.

"Just that I'd think he'd be helping you out, that's all."

"Well, he's *not*," she said. "So don't assume stuff like that, OK?"

"Fine," Alex said moodily. "But you are going after your dad's friends to work this thing."

"Because the girl who's in charge wants me to," she said quickly. "She wants the best DJ, the best food, the best flowers. And she thinks I can do that for her because of my dad." *Even though I let her think that*, Carina thought.

"Just tell her that the party doesn't have to be fancy to be fun," Alex said, picking out another album. "I mean, look at *this* place. It's a hundred times more fun than Luxelle. Because nobody's trying to be something they're not. There's no attitude. People are just free to be themselves and have a good time."

Carina surveyed the happy, dancing crowd. She knew exactly what Alex meant. But she also knew that Ava would think this place was frowzy, not fun. Still, she was beginning to come around to Alex's way of thinking.

"Would you be into helping me with this?" she asked

cautiously. "Just … suggesting some different ways to do stuff?"

Alex shook his head. "Do I look like a party planner?"

"You wouldn't be planning it. You'd just be giving me some inspiration. What's your number? I'll give you a—" She stopped. Carter. She'd completely forgotten about him. She checked her watch. It was almost nine thirty. "Oh my God!" she started, bumping her hip into the turntable and skipping a record. "I gotta go! I'm supposed to meet someone." She reached down and grabbed her bag. "Sorry!"

"Well, before you rush off, take this," Alex said, pulling a business card out of a little black box on the turntable. "That's my number," he said. "Most of the time I pick up."

She looked down at the card. Above his number the card read DJ ALEXX in block letters.

"You know, just between you and me, I'm really not into the second x," she said.

Alex cocked his head. "What are you, my manager?"

She grinned and stepped into the crowd. "I'll call you," she said.

She pushed her way through the dancing hipsters, still grinning. She'd finally found her DJ and she had no doubt that she'd picked the right one. Alex was blunt and kind of a smartass, but he was also talented and kind, and something told her that he might even turn out to be a friend.

As soon as she'd fought her way through the club and out of the door on to the empty street, she dialled Carter's number.

It rang as she walked to the subway, the damp wind whipping her hair.

"Hey, this is Carter," went his voicemail. "Do your thing."

Beeeeep.

"Hey, Carter, it's Carina," she said. "I'm soooo sorry I lost track of time, I'm just leaving my friend's thing and I'm still waaaay downtown, and I guess it's a little late—"

There was another loud beep, a click and then a strange staticky hum.

"Dumb phone," she muttered, flipping it closed. She could call him back, but that felt too desperate. She could text him, but that might be overkill. Maybe she'd just do nothing. Tomorrow she could explain everything.

As she put the phone back in her bag and crossed the street, she realized that she wasn't even that disappointed. DJing with Alex had been the most fun she'd had in weeks, maybe even more fun than watching a movie with Carter.

Just before she walked down into the subway, she looked back at the unmarked door to Club Neshka, hidden in the middle of the dreary street. She felt like she'd discovered a whole new New York tonight. All because of Alex. She hoped she'd see it again.

Chapter 16

For the rest of the week, Carina avoided Ava. It was a full-time job. Whenever she'd see Ava coming down the hall – curls bouncing, kilt swinging, gabbing with her friends, Ilona and Kate and Cici, who surrounded her like adoring bridesmaids – Carina would turn into the nearest empty space, which was sometimes a classroom, sometimes the girls' toilets, and, once, the janitor's closet. Hudson and Lizzie thought she was crazy, but Carina knew that she needed to buy some time. Before she made up a story for Ava about why Filippo couldn't help her out, she needed to find the perfect alternative to his pricey mac and cheese. And hopefully an alternative that she came up with herself. Alex's card was still in the pocket of her bag, but she couldn't bring herself to call him. Maybe it was pride, maybe it was stubbornness. Or maybe, she thought, it was actually some kind of work ethic.

On Saturday morning, Carina had Hudson and Lizzie over for brunch. A yummy brunch at Sarabeth's was out of her price range now, so Carina had decided to make it herself. And hopefully get their advice on the appetizer dilemma.

"I could take cooking classes," she said, deep in thought as she cracked an egg against the rim of a mixing bowl. "Or just follow a recipe. I mean, seriously, how hard can that be? Making some food by myself?"

"Really hard," Lizzie said next to her. Her hands and fingers and red curls were already dusted with spilled pancake mix. "Brunch for three people is one thing. Finger food for two hundred is another. And I think you just got some shell in there."

"Don't do it, C," Hudson warned, pouring a bag of frozen blueberries into a glass dish. "Just be honest with Ava. And why can't she just do Ruffles and Diet Coke like everyone else?"

"Because it needs to be 'Times-*worthy*'," Carina said in her best snooty accent as she started to whisk the batter. "Maybe I should just quit. Except I really want to go on that trip. I think Carter's forgotten about me. All I got this week were a few quick waves in the hall."

"Maybe he was just really busy," Lizzie said, pouring orange juice into tiny glasses.

"Or maybe he thinks *you* don't like *him*," Hudson said, pulling a strand of black hair behind her ear as she put the dish of frozen blueberries in the microwave. "Especially because you kind of blew off your date the other night."

"I didn't blow it off, I just lost track of time," Carina argued.

"Well, it's probably for the best," Lizzie said. "You've got enough on your mind with Ava. And I don't think Carter McLean's that much of a catch. I just don't."

Carina felt a flicker of annoyance as she went back to whisking. What kind of a comment was that? "How's Todd, Lizbutt?" she asked, deciding to ignore it. "What's up with his dad?"

"They let him come home after he made bail, thank God, but now he's under house arrest. And his mom flew in from London, so it's all been a little stressful for Todd."

"That's too bad," Carina said, unable to sound too upset about it.

Lizzie jumped up and sat on the edge of the marble countertop. "Hey, I've been meaning to ask you … Does it bother you that he hangs out with us a lot?"

"What?" Carina stopped whisking and glanced up at her. "No. Why?"

Lizzie shrugged. "Sometimes when he's around, you get a little quiet."

"I do?" she asked, even though she knew exactly what Lizzie was talking about.

"Yeah, you do."

"Well, that's weird, 'cause I love Todd," Carina said earnestly. "I totally do." Carina could feel Hudson looking at her.

"You sure?" Lizzie gave her a searching look with her

147

hazel eyes. "Because if he's annoying you or something, then let me know. I don't want to be one of those girls who falls in love and then drags her boyfriend around with her everywhere."

"Wait. Did you say in *love*?" Hudson asked, her perfect bow-like mouth hanging open.

Lizzie nodded excitedly. "Yeah. I think I am, you guys."

"*Already?*" Carina blurted out.

Lizzie's face crumpled. "Is that a problem?" she asked, sounding more hurt than angry.

"No," Carina said quickly, turning back to her bowl. "I just didn't know that you guys were so ... hard core."

Hudson shot Carina a warning look.

"We're not *hard core*," Lizzie said testily, jumping off the marble counter. "We're just really into each other."

"That's great, then," Carina said quickly, opening the microwave and taking out the berries. "I think he's a great guy." He and Lizzie had *just* started going out. And now they were in love? She dumped the warm berries into the batter.

"C, I think those need to be rinsed," Hudson said.

Carina looked down. The pancake batter had turned a bright blue. "Oops. Do you guys mind eating blue pancakes?"

Just then there was an ear-splitting chime from Carina's antique phone on the counter.

"Oh my God, C!" Lizzie said, holding her ear. "Get rid of that thing!"

"I wish I could," Carina said, flipping her phone open.

*Meant to check in yesterday. Where are we with Café
Luz? Are they doing the food??? Want an update ASAP. A*

"Who is it?" asked Hudson, ladling some batter on the piping-hot griddle. "Carter?"

"Ava. Asking where 'we' are with the food."

"Just be honest," Hudson repeated. "Tell her you don't have anything yet."

"Right," Carina said. "Because she totally won't freak out." She hit Reply and started typing.

*Found AMAZING new place! Undr-the-rdr. Will tell you
Monday.*

"At least this gives me the weekend," she said, pressing Send.

"But she's gonna want to know where the place is!" Lizzie said.

The phone chimed again a few seconds later.

Let's do a tasting tonight. Your place. Six o'clock.

"What's a tasting?" Carina asked.

"It's when you sit down and try out a bunch of sample appetizers from a caterer," Hudson explained.

Carina snapped her phone shut. "Then I need food for her to taste by six o'clock."

149

Lizzie pulled at a curl. "What are you gonna do?"

Carina paced the kitchen, listening to the pancakes sizzle. She was officially out of ideas. And maybe Alex was as creative with food as he was with music.

"I'll be right back," she said, walking out of the kitchen and taking the steps to her room two at a time. She just hoped he'd pick up.

In her room she turned her bag upside down. The DJ Alexx business card fell to the ground along with her well-used Metrocard and some peppermint candies. She crouched down, picked it up and, using her landline, dialled the 718 number.

"Hullooo?" It was Alex, and it sounded like he'd just woken up.

"Alex?" she said. "It's Carina. The party planner."

"Hey," he said in a groggy voice. "What's up?"

"Remember how you said to be less fancy with this party?

"Yeah."

She sat down. "Well ... I need some yummy party food. By tonight. For, like, no money. Can you help me? Like, now?"

Carina crossed Sixteenth Street and hurried into Union Square, trying not to trip over dog leashes and pushchairs. The unusually mild weather had driven most of New York outside, and the Saturday Greenmarket was packed with people buying fresh bread and bags of just-picked apples. Alex had told her to meet him on the Fourteenth Street side of the Square, and she zigzagged past idling shoppers, determined not to be late. She wasn't sure what he had in mind, but she'd felt better as soon as she'd hung up the phone. Alex seemed like the sort of person who could get you through any kind of emergency, even one involving food and Ava Elting.

After rushing past an African dance troupe performing under the Gandhi statue, she reached the steps that looked down over the plaza in front of Fourteenth Street. This area became a skate park on the weekends, and sure enough, some guys were gliding up and down over the concrete, practising their ollies. Her eyes swept the crowd sitting on the steps, looking for Alex's spiky dark hair, when she heard someone yell her name.

"Hey, Park Avenue!"

She looked up to see one of the skateboarders waving just before he leaped up on his board, gripping the sides, and did a perfect turn. So Alex wasn't just a music nerd, she thought. He was a skater guy. So much for her theory about artsy guys not liking sports.

"Not bad," she said as she walked down a few steps to meet him.

Alex pressed on his board with his toe and flipped the board upright. "Thanks," he said. "I'm sorta out of practice."

"So, is this what you do every Saturday?" She looked over her shoulder at the largely female audience on the steps. "Try to impress the ladies?"

"No, just you," he said, grinning. Then he rolled his eyes. "Kidding. So, tell me why this is such an emergency."

She couldn't help but feel a little offended. Why wasn't he into her? At least a little bit?

"The girl – Ava – wants to do a 'tasting' tonight," Carina explained. "Naturally, she's expecting food from a five-star restaurant. Which I don't have."

"No problem," he said, walking towards the corner. "Let's go to Trader Joe's. The cheapest food you can buy."

"Trader Joe's?" she asked. "Are you sure?"

He gave her a look that said *please*. "You sure you're not a snob?" he asked her. "Trust me."

They waited at the corner, watching the taxis race past. "So, besides being a skateboarder and a DJ, what else are you into? Do you have a girlfriend?" It hadn't been the subtlest question, but she was curious.

One of Alex's inky brows shot up. "Not at the moment," he said. "But to answer your other question, I guess you could say that I'm really into New York."

"New York?" she asked.

"Living here. Appreciating it. Taking advantage of all that it has to offer." He stepped on to his skateboard as they crossed Fourth Avenue. "I mean, look at that guy," he said as they passed a dog walker walking a Great Dane, a wheaten terrier, a Yorkie and a sour-faced pug all at once. "Where else would you see something like that?"

"Yeah, I know what you mean."

"Every weekend, I try to do one thing I've never done here before," he said. "Just one thing."

"It must get pretty expensive," she said.

"Not really," he said, hopping up on to the kerb. "There's *tonnes* of stuff to do here for free. You just have to know where to look. I mean, skateboarding for one," he said. "And biking up the West Side Highway. And Rollerblading through Central Park."

"You've just named three things that you can't do in winter," she pointed out.

"And getting free food," he said, turning towards the automatic doors that led into Trader Joe's.

"Free food?" she asked, suddenly interested. "Where do they serve food?"

"Now I can tell you've never been to Trader Joe's before," he said, grabbing her arm. "Come with me."

They walked inside, and he pulled her down an aisle. At the end was a small kiosk where a balding man in an apron made some kind of stir-fry on a stove.

"You mean, people just cook here in the store?" she asked in awe.

"Yep," Alex said, leading her over to the collection of paper cups lined up on a tray and stuffed with yummy-smelling noodles.

"Lo mein," Alex said, picking up one of the cups and sniffing. "We scored." He grabbed a fork from a nearby pile and took a bite. "Awesome."

Carina grabbed a cup and scooped out the lo mein with her fork. "Hmmm, you're right." she said, chewing. It happened to be delicious. "Do they always have this?"

"They always have *something*," he said. "If I'm low on cash and need a quick snack, this place always does the trick."

"Good to know," Carina said, making a mental note. She didn't want to tell Alex just how important free food was to her these days.

"So I think we want to go frozen, right?" he asked after demolishing three more cupfuls.

"Huh?" asked Carina, still eating.

"For the party," Alex added.

"Oh yeah," she said.

"Come with me," he said.

She tossed out her empty cup and followed him down another aisle. This one was lined with open freezers full of frozen goods.

"OK, first we have the chicken taquitos. Ten for three sixty-nine, and they're incredible." He held up the box. "And then we have the feta cheese and caramelized onion pastry bites," he said, holding up another box. "Twelve for five bucks."

"These are the appetizers?" she asked with uncertainty.

"Oh, and *these* are awesome," he said, reaching down and pulling out another box. "These are the three-cheese, two-bite soufflés. Also the same price. You can't go wrong." He added them to the other two boxes and handed the stack to Carina.

Carina looked down at the cold boxes. She wasn't sure if

heated-up appetizers were what Ava had in mind, but at these prices, she wasn't going to argue. "So how much do you think it would cost to do these for two hundred people?" she asked.

"About two hundred and fifty bucks." Alex reached back down into the tub and started grabbing every box in sight. "We might be able to get half right now—"

"That's OK," she said quickly. "I'll just get these. I'll get the rest later." Three boxes were all she could afford right now. As for the rest, she'd have to figure out a plan. They turned and walked towards the tills.

"So you think Miss Birkin Bag will be cool with doing stuff on the cheap?" Alex asked.

"I'll talk her into it," she fibbed. "I'm sure she'll love them." She knew that the only way Ava would love them was if she didn't know they came from Trader Joe's. She'd have to come up with a fake place. A fake, *fabulous* place.

"So she wants you to get all this expensive stuff for free, right?" he asked, scratching the side of his head.

"Yup."

"I don't get it," he said as they joined the line for the tills. "I thought these fancy charities had a pretty big budget for those parties. And now it sounds like they can't afford to pay anyone."

Carina fiddled with a bar of chocolate on display at the tills, trying not to think about her thousand-dollar payment. "I guess everyone's kind of cutting back," she said vaguely.

"And if you're so annoyed with this girl, why did you say yes to planning it?" Alex peered at her closely. "What are *you* getting out of this?"

A trip to the Alps, she thought. "She cornered me," she said uncomfortably. "And sometimes it's hard for me to say no to people." It wasn't the truth, but it was the best she could do.

Alex gave a small, bewildered shake of his head.

"What?" she asked warily.

"I'm not usually wrong about people," he said. "But I was about you. You're the opposite of everything I thought."

"Which was what?" she asked as they moved up in line.

"Come on. You're Karl Jurgensen's daughter. The guy could buy and sell my whole family. And that purse probably costs more than what my mom pays in rent," he said, pointing at her oversized Hayden-Harnett bag.

"So therefore I'm supposed to be mean?" she asked.

"Maybe not mean," Alex conceded. "But at least stuck-up. And you're not. You're ... cool."

Before Carina could smile at this, she heard a familiar *ka-CHUNG!* from inside her bag. It was so loud that the man ahead of them in line turned around and stared at her purse.

"Wait. Is that your phone?" Alex asked. "Didn't they stop making that ring in the third grade?"

"Whatever," she said, scrambling to find the phone inside her bag and turn it off.

"Take it out," he said. "Let me see it. I have to see it."

"No."

"Come on," he insisted.

Reluctantly, she pulled the ancient silver phone out of her purse and handed it to him. "There, you happy?"

Alex stared at it in his palm as if it were a fossil. "Oh my God. This is from nineteen ninety-*eight*," he said, awestruck.

"So what?" she asked, swiping it out of his hands.

"So what are you *doing* with that?" he asked. "Don't you have an iPhone? I'd be happy to take you to the Apple store," he said. "It's just down on Prince Street in case you haven't heard of it—"

"I already have an iPhone," she muttered. She felt her cheeks start to burn as she dropped the phone back into her bag.

"Then why are you walking around with *that*?" Alex demanded.

"Because my dad cut me off," she finally said, not looking at him.

There was an uncomfortable pause as the Trader Joe's clerk began to scan her items. "That'll be thirteen dollars and twenty-seven cents," he said when he was done. "Cash or credit?"

"Cash." Luckily she'd got her allowance two days earlier from the Jurg, but she'd already spent five bucks on eggs and pancake mix. She pulled out fifteen dollars from her wallet – the last of her money. The clerk gave Carina her change and she grabbed the paper bag of groceries. They walked to the doors in silence. She could tell from Alex's silence that he was either slightly off ended or really confused. Outside, a light rain was starting to fall.

"Cut off?" Alex asked. "What does that mean?"

"That means no iPhone, no credit cards. No money." She pawed at a gum wrapper on the ground with the toe of her Puma.

"Why? What'd you do?" he asked.

She pulled a damp strand of hair out of her eyes and thought about how to answer this. "You know when you're so mad at someone, and you have been for so long, that when something happens it just sets you off?"

Alex didn't blink. "Yeah," he said.

"Well, he did something that set me off."

"What?" The way he asked this question, it sounded like he really wanted to know. That he might even be on her side. She looked up the street. A falafel vendor was handing a pita stuffed with hummus to a heavyset guy. A homeless woman pushed a cart down the street, muttering to herself. She realized that she wanted to tell Alex the truth about everything – about the divorce, about her dad's cheating. About how the Jurg had ruined her family. But she barely knew him.

"Nothing," she said quickly. "It's not important."

"Does Miss Birkin Bag know?" Alex asked, a smile starting to form at the edges of his lips. "That you're ... broke?"

Carina shook her head. "It's not something I'm publicizing, if you get what I'm saying."

He stared at her and then nodded OK. "Well, just tell me how she likes those taquitos," he said finally, hopping on his board. "And if you need anything else, lemme know."

158

"I will," she said. "Thanks, Alex."

Alex stuck his earbuds into his ears. "No prob'm," he said as he pushed off with one foot. Then he glided away from her down the street into the falling rain.

As she watched him skate down the block, she felt exposed, as if he'd just wandered into the locker room and seen her changing out of her gym clothes. How had she ended up telling him so much? Was it him being nosy – or had she needed to tell him about it? And was there any chance she *was* into him?

No, she decided, watching him skate across Third Avenue and up to the subway. He didn't give her that squiggly, butterflies-in-her-throat feeling that Carter did. But she'd told him her secret, and now she didn't know what they were. Definitely more than acquaintances, but not quite friends. Not yet. They were something else.

And that something else made her feel unsettled but also comforted, in a strange way.

Then she remembered she'd got a text in the store. When she took out her phone, there was the name she'd just been thinking about. CARTER.

What r u doing l8r?

A jolt rocked her chest. So he *wasn't* over her, apparently.

Smthg with u ☺, she boldly wrote back and hit Send.

159

He wrote her back in under a minute.

Dinner 2nite. Serendipity. 8.

Her stomach did another free fall. She wrote back.

Can't wait.

Chapter 17

Carina was standing over the two outfits on her bed, trying to decide which one to wear on her date with Carter, when the intercom buzzed on the wall of her bedroom.

"Ava Elting on her way up!" came Otto's voice through the speaker. He didn't talk very often, but when he did it was always more of a scream.

"OK!" she yelled at the intercom, and turned back to the bed to scrutinize the clothes. She'd narrowed her choices down to the sexy black dress that she'd worn to the last Chadwick dance and the more casual, less high-stakes option of yellow cashmere V-neck and jeans.

She held the black dress up to her and checked herself out in front of the full-length mirror on her closet door. Since being cut off, she hadn't worn anything dressier than a nice top and jeans, and now the dress looked weirdly formal to her. Was it too formal? And had Carter been at the dance and possibly seen her in this? She went to her MacBook Air on the bed and was just about to iChat with Hudson about it when she saw that she had a new email. From Laetitia Dunn.

She clicked on the message.

To: Chamonix Peeps
From: TishD
Hey!!! Just wanted to let everyone know I've booked us all into the Ritz-Carlton for the night of December 26th since Carter's place won't be ready for us yet ... We'll each have a junior suite, unless you're Anton and need more room for your clothes (LOL!) ... It's all on my Amex so people PLEEEASE pony up the cash ASAP ... Thanks! LD

Carina reached for her stress ball. The Ritz-Carlton? That hadn't been part of the plan. There was no way she was going to be able to afford that.

The intercom buzzed again. "Your friend is here!" Otto called out.

"Coming!" she yelled. The last thing on earth she felt like dealing with now was Ava. But she just needed to get this dumb tasting over with. She pulled on the yellow cashmere top and jeans and ran down the stairs.

Ava stood in the hall, staring intently at the Andy Warhol soup can. Her burgundy J Brand cords were so tight that they looked painted on, and her hair was swept back in a series of knots behind a jewelled headband.

"Um, is that real?" she asked, pointing at the painting.

"I think so," Carina said.

"Huh, that's cool," she said, downplaying her disbelief with a haughty toss of her curls. "So, I don't have a lot of time. I guess we should get started?"

"Fine with me," Carina said. "Everything's in here." She led her into the dining room.

Ava glanced quickly at the Michelangelo-inspired painted ceiling, the gigantic crystal chandelier and the twenty-seat table, but didn't say anything. "OK," she said, taking a seat and pulling out a tall bottle of smartwater from her enormous bag. "Where's the food?"

"Coming right up," she said with an irony that Ava didn't catch, and walked through the swinging door into the kitchen. She grabbed the platter that she'd prepared a few minutes before and on her way back inside, she remembered her spiel.

"May I present feta cheese and sweet onion pastry bites, organic chicken and stone-ground corn taquitos, and four-cheese mini soufflés!" she announced, placing the platter in front of Ava with a little waiter-like flourish.

Ava squinted at the tiny appetizers. "Is this from Café Luz?" she asked doubtfully.

"It's from an even cooler place in the West Village that's not even open yet," Carina gushed. "But this place has *much* better buzz. And Jessica Biel's one of the owners."

Ava picked up a pastry bite, sniffed it and took a tiny bite. "Ummm," she said, looking at it with surprise. "That's yummy. What's this place called?"

"Oh, it doesn't have a name yet," Carina said. "Or a phone number. It's so hot that they're really trying to stay under the radar."

Ava nodded knowingly and then picked up one of the taquitos. "Stone-ground corn is the best," she said and then popped it in her mouth.

"Yeah," Carina said, still trying to keep a straight face.

"Yummm," she said with her mouth full. "Who's the chef? Mario Batali? Daniel Boulud?"

Carina pretended to think about it. "His name is Joe … something. Something French."

"Well, I can tell he uses really high-end ingredients," she said. "And I like the contrast between high-end and casual. That was just what I was going for, actually," she said, munching.

"So should we do them?" Carina asked, already knowing Ava's answer.

Ava popped a mini soufflé into her mouth and then pushed her chair back. "I'm cool with it. As long as he's not going to charge us."

"There might be a small fee, like … two hundred bucks," Carina said, pretending to pull the number out of thin air. She was still going to have to buy all this food.

Ava nodded moodily. "OK. Let's do a hundred of each."

She stood up. "And when this place is open, we're totally going, right?"

"Oh, totally," Carina fibbed, leading Ava to the door.

"Oh, by the way," Ava said, turning around. "I googled Alex Suarez and the only DJ I found was some guy who placed third in the Stuyvesant maths team and spins at some weird place downtown. That's not the same guy, right?"

Carina hesitated. She could tell Ava the truth. But she'd got away with the food so far. Another little fib wouldn't kill her.

"Oh no," she said, before she'd even thought about it. "This guy spends a lot of time in LA. I think he just did Mary-Kate and Ashley's birthday party at Chateau Marmont."

Ava fingered her diamond A as they walked to the front door. "Well, I'm impressed, Carina. At first I thought you might be full of crap, but your dad's right. You should do this for real."

Otto turned around at his desk and gave Carina a puzzled look.

"Thanks," Carina said, ignoring Otto's look.

"See you on Monday," Ava said. She glanced nervously at Otto. "You don't have to look in my bag again, do you?"

Otto shook his head.

"Oh, OK," Ava said, and walked out of the front door.

Carina ran up the stairs to her bedroom. Everything was going perfectly! Ava had completely fallen for her little ruse and now she was off to have an amazing time with an extremely cute guy. Things couldn't be going better. Thank God for Alex.

After a quick shower, an even quicker blow-dry, and a hurried sweep of her closet, she was dressed and finally ready for Carter McLean. Her V-neck sweater wasn't exactly the Catherine Malandrino halter top, but it would do. She took one last look in the mirror, checking her teeth for spare taquito bits, and gave herself a little pep talk. Just before she left, she took out her phone and texted Alex.

It WORKED!!!

She almost felt like giving him a hug.

When she walked out on to the street, she remembered that she hadn't even given her friends the update. She took out her phone and texted her friends:

Going on date with Carter! And Ava loved the food!

Hudson wrote back:

NO WAY – THAT IS FATE

And then Lizzie:

Call me as soon as it's done!

Serendipity had been one of their favourite places when they were kids. The food was incredible and so

166

was the house speciality: the Frozen Hot Chocolate. It was only fitting that she'd have her first date with Carter at a restaurant she'd always loved. *Another good sign,* she thought.

When she got to the restaurant, she saw Carter sitting alone at one of the white tables in the corner. He wore a pale blue shirt and a charcoal fleece jacket left casually unzipped, and his dark curls were brushed off his forehead with a little product. He waved to her and her mouth went instantly dry.

"You're late," he teased as she sat down.

"Well, I was just at Paragon, picking out my new snowboard," she teased back. "Have I told you that I'm going to crush you?"

"My uncle got you your lift ticket," he said. "So you better be serious."

"Me? Never," she flirted as she picked up the oversized menu. "OK, what do I want?" She opened the menu and her eye went straight to the prices. "*Fourteen bucks* for a chicken salad sandwich?" she blurted.

Carter looked at her strangely. "Are you OK?" he asked.

"Oh, yeah, that just seems a little pricey," she said, feeling a hot flush spread across her cheeks.

"Uh, dinner's on me," Carter said. "So don't worry about it."

"Oh, I know," she said, trying to smile, and then buried her head in the menu. She wanted to die.

Thankfully a moustachioed waiter appeared at their table a second later. "All set?" he asked, readying his pen.

"I'm gonna have the Young Chicken Sandwich," said Carter. "And a Frozen Hot Chocolate. And the banana split for dessert."

Her eyes went straight to the Outrageous Banana Split. *Twenty-two dollars? For a banana?* she wanted to say, but stifled herself. "I think I'll just have an iced tea and the Ultimate BLT," she said with a pleasant smile.

The waiter scribbled their order and walked away.

"Do you have some issue with money?" Carter asked. He was pretending to smile, like his question was almost a joke, but she could see in his eyes that he was serious.

"No. Of course not," she bluffed, smoothing her hair. "I just haven't been here in a while. They raised their prices."

Carter was still looking at her oddly. "Uh-huh," he said. She could practically hear him thinking *FREAK. FREAK. FREAK.*

"So we're gonna be in Florida for Thanksgiving," he said, mercifully changing the subject. "My family's got this place on Fisher Island."

The only thing she'd heard about Fisher Island was that it was one of the wealthiest neighbourhoods in Miami. People who had condos there usually paid millions for them.

"That's nice," she said. "I've never been there."

"It's amazing. Killer waterskiing. And right off the coast from South Beach. I think we're gonna go deep sea fishing. Last

168

time I almost caught this marlin that was huuuge." He held his hands as far apart as he could. "Sucker was, like, fourteen feet long."

She searched for something interesting to say but could only come up with "Oh yeah?"

"Yeah," he said.

There was a long silence. *Yikes*, Carina thought. They'd only been together ten minutes and already this date was tanking.

"That's a nice watch," she said, noticing the gigantic silver Rolex on his wrist.

"It was a birthday present," he said proudly, absently twisting the band. "It wasn't the one I really wanted, but it does the trick."

"What was the one you *really* wanted?" she asked.

"The one with the chronograph, for when I dive," he said. "I used to have one but it fell off in the Caymans."

"So you lost a Rolex in the ocean and then you got another one?" she asked.

He grinned. "Yep."

"*Ugh*," she said.

Carter's grin vanished. She realized with a shock that she'd said that out loud.

"I mean ... um ... *ugh* that you lost it," she stammered.

It didn't work. Carter was still looking at her like she had an infectious disease when a busboy walked up with their plates.

"Young Chicken Sandwich?" he asked.

"Over here," Carter muttered.

"That looks really good," she said, hoping to make peace.

Carter smiled thinly. "Thanks."

"And this looks amazing," she said to her sandwich.

Carter didn't say anything.

As Carina bit into her twelve-dollar BLT, she realized that her dream date had suddenly gone AWOL.

"So I saw Laetitia's email," she said. "I guess we're all gonna stay at the Ritz-Carlton for the first night?"

"Yeah, my uncle's still gonna be at the chalet," he said offhandedly. "He doesn't leave for Greece until the next day."

"So your uncle's not gonna be there?" she asked. This entire time, she'd assumed that he would at least be in the house.

"Oh, no way," Carter said. "I wouldn't have wanted to go if he were. It's gonna be just us."

"And your parents are cool with that?" she asked.

"Yeah, why wouldn't they be?" he asked, his voice curdling with irritation. "Do you need to be chaperoned or something?"

"No," she said carefully. "I just … I didn't realize that was the plan." She picked at her sandwich, feeling like a shamed child. But it had been an honest question. Why had he been so obnoxious? Lizzie was right. Carter McLean was kind of a jerk.

When the bill finally came, Carter slapped his Visa card down on the tray without even looking at it.

"Thanks," she said awkwardly. "That was really good."

Carter just shifted around in his chair. "Glad you enjoyed it," he muttered, reaching for his coat.

When they walked out on to the street, a bitter wind was blowing down Sixtieth Street. Carina looked at her watch. It wasn't even nine fifteen yet, but this night definitely felt over.

"Well, thanks for hanging out," he said tonelessly as he zipped up his fleece.

"Yeah, that was really fun." She smiled at him, waiting. Maybe if she tried really hard, maybe if she could get him to kiss her, she could somehow salvage this date and turn him back to the Carter she'd had a crush on.

But he just looked up and down the street, distracted, his green eyes searching for something – or someone – that wasn't her.

"Did you want to go somewhere else?" she asked.

"Nah, I'm really tired," he said. "And I'm getting up early to run the reservoir tomorrow. But can I get you a cab?"

"That's OK, I can walk," she said. "See you Monday."

He leaned down and gave her a quick, barely there kiss on the cheek.

"See you," he said, backing away from her like she had the plague.

It was crazy, she thought, turning around and setting off down the block. From the moment she'd sat down at the table, the night had been a complete, unmitigated disaster. But had that been her fault, for opening her big mouth and saying *Ugh*? Or had it been Carter's for being a spoiled jerk? And if he was a spoiled jerk, then why had she been so disappointed with how the night had ended – with a lame kiss on the cheek?

She needed to call Lizzie and Hudson and figure this out with them. But when she pulled out her phone, she saw that she had a voicemail from her mom. She listened to the message, turning up the volume.

"Hi, honey, it's me, and I'm so, so, SO sorry that it's taken me this long to get back to you. Things have been just *insane* here … One of my instructors quit without giving me any notice, and I've just been *inundated* with new students … Anyway, I wanted you to know that I'll be in town on the thirtieth – before I leave for India – I'm going to another ashram – and I'm looking forward to a nice long catch-up session then. I miss you, honey!"

She hung up the phone. She was happy to hear that her mom would be in town but she was also relieved that she'd missed the call. Having to recap all the strange and difficult events of the past couple of weeks wasn't something that she felt like doing right now. It was hard enough just living through each moment. And for now she couldn't wait to get home, curl up on the couch and eat the rest of those cheapo taquitos.

Chapter 18

"C, you know I would totally come out to Montauk for the day or something, but my mom's freaking out that we're still in the studio," Hudson said the day before Thanksgiving as they walked to their last class. "She wants to do a couple of tracks over. And you should hear them – it already doesn't even sound like my voice. She's put it through the compressor so many times I sound like Gwen Stefani on helium."

"Is your cute producer still kissing her butt?" Lizzie asked. The day before Thanksgiving break at Chadwick was always Free Dress Day and Lizzie had on a very cool electric purple top with a deep V-neck and a silk cardigan with a huge flower appliqué. Carina had glimpsed both pieces in the Anthropologie catalogue before she'd tossed it sadly in the trash.

"Of course he's kissing her butt," Hudson said, untangling her silver necklaces. "The good thing is my mom seems to love him. And you know how she hates *everybody*." Hudson looked amazing, as usual, in a metallic silver empire-waist dress and black opaque tights. "At least it makes my life easier."

Carina pulled at the zip of her favourite Vince hoodie. She'd paired it with a cute striped top from Barneys that she'd bought last year, but standing next to her stylish-looking friends right now, she wished that she had something newer to show off.

"So, C, I would go too but I'm going down to North Carolina with Todd and his mom," Lizzie said. "I guess all of his mom's family is down there."

"That's OK, you guys," Carina said, trying not to sound as pathetic as she felt. "I can figure something out."

"Aren't you and your dad sort of getting along?" Lizzie asked.

Carina thought about the handful of times she'd seen him since their fight two weeks ago at the *Princess* cocktail party. She definitely wouldn't say that they were getting along. They'd barely spoken at dinner, except for his routine questions about school and her one-syllable answers.

"Not really. But today I'm being summoned back to the Death Star for that dumb interview on being a 'real-life princess'," she answered. "Maybe that means I didn't totally piss him off at that cocktail party."

"I thought you were getting out of that," Lizzie said, scanning the hallway for Todd.

"Yeah, I thought you told your dad that it was a bad idea," Hudson said.

"And you think he listened to me?" Carina said. "No way. He thinks it's amazing. Just what I want to do as soon as I'm off for Thanksgiving break."

There'd been a time – back when her mom was still around – when Thanksgiving had been Carina's favourite holiday. They'd all gone down to Jamaica to their house on a cliff overlooking Montego Bay. They'd spend their days walking the beach, swimming in the infinity pool and reading in the hammocks on the gigantic flagstone-paved veranda. And then there'd been the yummy Jamaican-style feast of jerk chicken and conch fritters instead of traditional turkey and stuffing.

But those days were over. Now Turkey Day meant staying with her friends to avoid spending four days with the Jurg in his cold, glass-walled Montauk mansion. But this year, staying with her friends wouldn't be possible. Which meant that Carina would be on her own in Montauk, tiptoeing around her dad's house, and her dad.

"Wait – doesn't Carter have a place in East Hampton?" Hudson asked. "Invite him over!"

"He's going to Florida. And I think we're kind of over each other."

"C, just because he didn't kiss you—" Lizzie started.

"No, it's not that. I just feel like something's changed." She hitched her bag on to her other shoulder as they stopped in front of the lockers. "I was sitting there in Serendipity and all of a sudden it was like he morphed into a completely different guy. Right in front of me."

"Maybe *you're* the one who's morphed," Hudson said.

"Huh?" Carina asked.

"You've changed, C," Hudson said, putting books in her locker. "You can't see it, but we can. You're calmer. More mature. Not so impulsive any more."

"Maybe he just doesn't look that good to you any more," Lizzie said, tying her red hair into a knot.

Carina thought about this. She did feel different. But why did it have to make other people different, too? "Well, maybe we were just having an off night," she said.

"Are you still going to go on the trip?" Lizzie asked.

The trip. She'd received another one of Laetitia's group emails, this one about getting a reservation at Rue de Soleil, which, according to the Fodor's website, was one of the most expensive restaurants in Chamonix. Like the other email about the Ritz-Carlton, she'd just ignored it.

"I guess so," she said listlessly.

"Well, I guess that's good," Lizzie said, slamming her locker closed. "Otherwise you'd be crazy to want to keep dealing with Ava."

"Speaking of," Hudson whispered. "Time to enter Crazytown again."

"Carina?" Ava called out behind her. "Can I talk to you?"

Carina turned around to see Ava striding towards her in fringed Uggs, leather jeans and a fur-trimmed poncho. Trailing behind her were the Icks, looking more subdued in skinny jeans, ankle boots and long cashmere sweater coats, but still a tad overdressed for a four-hour school day.

"Hi, Ava," Carina said, trying not to sound apprehensive. She hadn't done more work on the party lately, but she figured that after her Trader Joe's triumph a week and a half ago, she could relax a little.

"So, now that the dance is less than a month away," Ava said, training her glittering eyes on Carina, "I've been thinking. I know we already have a DJ, but wouldn't it be cool if we could get someone to sing?"

"*Sing?*" Carina repeated, dumbstruck.

"Well, we have this great stage," Ava explained. "And how awesome would it be if someone could come out and do one or two really great songs?"

What is this? Ava-palooza? Carina thought. "Who were you thinking of?" she asked, trying to ignore Ilona's piercing blue-eyed stare.

"I dunno," Ava said, annoyed at being pinned down. "Didn't your dad get Justin Timberlake once for one of his things?"

"Justin *Timberlake*?"

"Or what about the Jonas Brothers? Your dad's used them, right?" Ava asked, batting her long lashes. "I mean, if he has, then it's not *that* big a deal to ask."

That was it, she thought. This was getting ridiculous. She had to finally tell Ava once and for all that her dad had nothing to do with this party.

But then she got a brilliant idea.

"You know, there's someone we could get who's even *better* and *newer* than JT or the Jonas Brothers," she said. "Someone who's about to break out any minute."

"Who?" Ava asked sceptically.

"How about Hudson Jones?"

Carina looked over at her friend. Hudson had gone almost as pale as Lizzie, and her Chanel berry-stained mouth was popped open in shock. *Oops,* Carina thought.

"*Hudson?*" Ava asked, as if Carina had just said that she would sing herself.

"Well, she's just about to finish recording her first album and she's totally on the verge of becoming a star," Carina said proudly as she put her arm around her friend. "We'd be the first ones to get her live. It'd be like seeing Robert Pattinson in his school play."

Hudson winced a little under her arm.

Carina glanced over at Lizzie. She had two furious-looking pools of red in her cheeks as she stared at the floor.

"Actually, I really don't think I'm ready to do anything live yet," Hudson said in a wavery voice. "But I totally appreciate the invitation—"

"Oh, but it's just one night," Carina persisted. "And you'd be going to the dance anyway, right?"

She knew that she was putting Hudson on the spot, but with Ava and the Icks all staring at her, she couldn't stop herself.

Hudson bit her bottom lip and nodded her head.

"Well, I *think* that could work," Ava said with a sigh. "I mean, I've heard you have a great voice and everything."

"Great!" Carina jumped in. "We'll chat later about it over the break, OK?"

"OK," Ava said, oblivious to Hudson's ashen face. "We'll talk about songs later. I have very specific taste."

Ava and the Icks moved off into the stream of people in the hall, leaving the three of them in an awkward silence.

"Hudson," Carina whispered as they walked into class. "I'm so sorry. I hope you don't hate me."

Hudson was quiet as they found three empty seats in the back and sat down.

"Don't worry, I can get you out of it," Carina said.

"Then why'd you get her *into* it?" Lizzie whispered.

"It's fine," Hudson said, putting a hand on Carina's arm. She would do anything to prevent a fight. "Really. It's not a big deal."

Carina felt like the worst friend in the world as she leaned down and pulled out her *Survey of World History* textbook. But objectively speaking, Hudson really *was* the perfect choice for the dance. She was a better singer than anyone else they could get and it would be the perfect way for her to get used to being onstage.

"Hey," she said, putting her hand on Hudson's arm. "At least your first show will be in front of people you know."

"That's what I was trying to avoid," Hudson said, trying to smile. "But that's OK. I'll do it."

"Thanks, H," she said, giving Hudson a quick hug. As she pulled away, Carina could feel the heat of Lizzie's critical glare. She clearly didn't approve. The rift that had been growing for weeks between her and Lizzie had just got a little bigger. And Carina was starting to wonder when it was going to explode.

Chapter 19

"Barb'll be right in," said the baby-faced assistant as she showed Carina into Barb's plush corner office at *Princess*. "But can I get you something to drink? Iced tea? Cappuccino? Vitaminwater?"

"Nothing, I'm fine," Carina said.

"You sure? We have Pellegrino," she offered, tipping her head so that her blonde highlights glowed under the halogen light.

"No, really, I'm cool."

The assistant gave Carina a quick, all-business nod, and then hightailed it out of the office.

Carina dropped her bag on the thick white carpet and sighed. Seeing how eager people were to be nice to her always made her uneasy. The same thing had happened when she'd interned at her dad's corporate headquarters, fifteen stories above the *Princess* offices. Everyone – assistants, vice presidents, even the cleaning staff – seemed harried or just plain scared around her. Maybe that's why she'd felt so uncomfortable being there. There was no way she'd ever be *just* an intern.

She walked over to Barb's floor-to-ceiling window and looked out at the grey, wet canyons of Midtown below. Things had still been a little weird between her and Lizzie and Hudson after class. When they said goodbye on the street in front of school, Hudson had just shrugged when Carina told her to hang in there with the recording stuff. And Lizzie had called out "Have fun!" when they went their separate ways on the street. Lizzie never said stuff like "Have fun!" Clearly they were still upset with her for how she'd got Hudson involved in the party. But she knew that if she called Hudson and asked her whether she was OK, Hudson would just say she was.

Sometimes girls were so frustrating, Carina thought. At least with boys you knew where you stood. Like with Carter. She'd seen him for only a second through the window of the pizza place, sitting with Anton and Laetitia as soon as school got out. But he had looked right at her, and then through her. No smile, nothing. Which could only mean that he'd come out of their date just as disappointed as she'd been. At least he didn't try to still be her friend, she thought. It was almost a relief.

"So sorry to keep you waiting," a woman called out from the hall, and Carina watched Barb Willis speed walk into the office, looking more dishevelled – and frazzled – than she had the other night. Her thin, shoulder-length brown hair was so staticky that some of the ends stood up, and her dark brown blazer seemed to be covered in white dog hair.

"Did Jamie offer you something to drink?" she asked, blinking at Carina behind her glasses as if she couldn't see her. "Or how about some of those cookies?" she asked, pointing to an opened plastic sleeve of oversized chocolate chip cookies on her desk. "Please. Have some. I've already blown my diet three times over."

"I don't think you need to be on a diet," Carina said.

Barb gave her an odd look and then smiled. "Please, sit down, Carina. Make yourself comfortable." She gestured with a piece of paper in her hand to the plain white sofa against the wall. Barb Willis was a far cry from the icy Glamazons who ran her dad's other women's magazines, but so far, all of her imperfections had started to win Carina over.

"We're all a little out of sync today because of Thanksgiving," she said. "And since almost everyone is gone, I think I'm going to be the one to interview you – oops!"

The piece of paper in Barb's hand floated to the floor. It was a test cover of *Princess* magazine, printed on regular-size computer paper.

"That's a cover try for the March issue," Barb explained as Carina bent down and picked it up. "The design director just finished it."

Carina took in the familiar, hot-pink-coloured PRINCESS logo in flowery script, and the cover lines crammed with numbers ("353 Ways to Do Your Hair!"). And there was the cover girl, a television actress who'd already graced several other magazine covers in the past six months, and had looked cooler and prettier on all of them.

"What do you think?" Barb asked.

Carina tried to think of something positive to say. "I like her hair," she said.

Frowning, Barb took the page back from her. "What *don't* you like about it? It's OK. Just tell me what you think. As a reader."

"Well, to be perfectly honest, I'm *not* a reader," Carina said.

Barb smiled. "Oh. May I ask why?"

"It all just seems a little forced," Carina said. "See this?" she said, pointing to the *Princess* logo on the cover page. "See how it's in hot pink and in script and it has a heart to dot the i? It's *way* too frou-frou. I'd say get rid of the heart, do the logo in a chunky boldface, and *then* you can get away with the hot pink. Funk it up a little bit. Make it a little edgy. Don't be afraid to be bold. Bold can be girly, too."

Barb looked uncertain, but nodded with her chin cupped in her hand. "Go on," she said.

"Is this the rest of the issue?" Carina walked over to a bulletin board covered with more miniature pages of the magazine.

Barb nodded. "Yes, that's the layout right now."

"OK, this section on trends," Carina started, pointing to

where the Trend Report page was tacked to the wall. "This needs to be edgier. *Much* edgier. Most of these things are in other magazines before this even comes out." She pointed at one of the boxed photos. "And I really don't think ponchos count as a trend. I mean, they kind of do to this one girl in my class, but she just looks ridiculous in one."

"O-kay," Barb said slowly, sounding a little overwhelmed.

"You guys should find a couple of cool kids who hang out downtown and go to the flea markets and all those vintage stores," Carina said. "Just have them talk about cool stuff they want to wear, or are wearing, and you could re-create the looks. This page needs to *start* trends, not find them. And these fashion stories," she said, jumping over to the fashion pages on the board. "I mean, look at this." She pointed to a layout featuring a girl in a silver tutu and tiara under a headline that read "Bring Him Under Your Spell". "What is *this* all about?"

"That's our prom dress story," Barb said proudly. "The photographer is very, *very* well-known, and it was his idea to do something magical—"

"Nobody's gonna wear a tutu to prom," Carina said bluntly. "Especially if it's a lot of money. What if all your clothes were under a hundred and fifty bucks? If you show stuff like that, kids at least won't feel so bad about themselves for not being able to afford them."

Barb straightened her glasses. "Is this something you and your father have discussed?" she asked nervously.

Carina shook her head. "No. It's just my own idea."

"I see," Barb said, sounding relieved. "Well, we should probably start that interview," she said, gesturing for her to sit on the couch.

Carina sat down. She knew that she'd probably offended Barb, and that there was a ninety-eight per cent chance this would get back to her dad. But she almost didn't care. It had felt good to be honest for a change.

Barb perched herself on the edge of an upholstered chair and placed an old-fashioned tape recorder on the glass coffee table in front of the couch. "OK, first question. You know that this is a story about your fabulous everyday life. So let's start with what you did last weekend." Barb leaned over and gave her a meaningful smile behind her glasses. "What did you do? How'd you spend your afternoon last Saturday?"

Carina thought about this. "Do you really want to know?"

"Sure," Barb said gamely.

"I made blue pancakes and I went to Trader Joe's."

Barb frowned again. "Did you say Trader Joe's?"

"Uh-huh. And the blue pancakes were kind of an accident. But they were still really good."

Barb nodded slowly, trying to regroup. "Was there anything else you did?"

Just then there was the sound of footsteps out in the hall, and before Barb's assistant could announce him, the Jurg entered the room.

"Hello, ladies," he said, flashing the hundred-watt smile he saved for work events. "Hope I haven't missed too much."

Of course he was here, Carina thought with a sinking feeling in her chest. She took a deep breath and tried not to look irritated.

"Karl," Barb said, running a hand over her electrified hair as she leaped to her feet. "What a nice surprise."

"Don't get up," he said, sitting down next to Carina on the couch. "I thought I'd just pop downstairs and sit in for fun. Hello, C," he said, kissing her on the top of her head. "So, where are we?" He sat down next to her and clapped his hands over his knees. "Don't let me get in the way. I'm just observing."

"I was just about to ask Carina about shopping," Barb said, still beaming at him. "Of course that's of big interest to our readers. So, Carina. What are your favourite stores?"

Carina glanced at her dad. Maybe having him here for this wasn't such a bad thing, after all. "You mean right now?" she asked. "I don't have any."

"None at all?" Barb repeated.

"I guess you could say I'm not shopping much these days," she said evenly.

"Now, that's not exactly true, C," said the Jurg good-naturedly. "You like that place, what's it called . . . Intersection?"

"Inter*mix*."

"And she loves the Meatpacking District," he added. "All of those stores. She can't get enough of them."

"Yeah, right," she muttered just a little too loudly.

"And she's been known to clean out the shops on Newtown Lane in East Hampton," he said, grinning.

187

Now she understood why her dad was here. He wanted her to stay on message. He wanted her to pretend that she was still living a "fabulous" life. She couldn't believe it.

"Right," she said as sarcastically as she could. "I clean 'em out."

Barb darted her eyes from father to daughter. She'd caught the sarcasm in Carina's voice. "OK, what about travel? Where's the last place you went?"

"That would be California," Carina said archly. "But it wasn't a pleasure trip."

Barb looked down at her sheet once more. "Any extra-curriculars?"

Carina snorted. "No."

"Actually, Carina's favourite thing to do is come into the office and learn about Metronome," her dad cut in as he put his arm around her shoulder. "She's already got quite an interest in business."

"Really?" Barb asked.

"Yes, she used to love to come to the office when she was a little girl and sit at the head of the table in the boardroom," he went on. "And then just recently she expressed some interest in interning for me—"

Carina leaned over, found the stop button on the tape recorder, and pressed it. "I'm sorry, but could my dad and I have a minute alone?" she asked, her eyes on the coffee table. Her face felt hot.

Barb stood up suddenly as if she'd just remembered she had a flight to catch. "Take your time," she said.

She walked out and shut the door behind her. As soon as they were alone, the Jurg put his head in his hands and clutched at his hair. "Carina, what am I going to do with you?" he asked.

"Why did you come down here? Are you just afraid I'm not going to be able to do this right?"

"I had a feeling you couldn't be trusted to do this in an appropriate way," he said. "And clearly, I was right."

"You're just afraid I'll disappoint her," she said, forcing herself to stay calm. "That Karl Jurgensen's kid won't turn out to be a real-life princess after all. Or anything else you approve of."

"Carina, please," he said, rubbing his eyelids with the tips of his fingers. "You're still privileged no matter how much money I give you."

"Because I'm your daughter?" she asked.

He took a deep breath and looked at her. "Yes," he said firmly.

"Right. Because all you can see is that I'm your kid. That's it. You don't know anything about me. You don't even *look* at me. It's like I'm invisible or something. Why did you even want me to live with you?"

"What?" The Jurg shook his head. "What are you talking about?"

"*Mom* wanted me. Mom loved me. Mom knew who I was.

And she wanted me with her. But you wouldn't let her have me." She let out a choked laugh. "It's pretty ironic when you think about it. Since *you're* the one who cheated on her."

There it was. She'd finally said it. The thing no one had ever dared to mention.

Her father's entire body seemed to freeze. For a moment, he seemed too shocked to speak. "Go home," he finally said. "Just go."

Grasping her bag with one hand, she got to her feet. Her words still ricocheted between them, filling the air, making her dizzy. She couldn't look him in the face any more. He was right. She needed to leave.

She turned the knob and walked out. In her peripheral vision, she could see Barb and her assistant huddled in the corner like a couple of teenage girls. They'd probably heard everything. But it didn't matter. She hurried past them, her eyes on the carpet, and headed to the elevators.

She wished she could have taken it back, but it was too late. She hated herself for saying such an ugly thing, but she hated him more because it was true.

Chapter 20

Carina lay on her bed, staring out of the window at a blinking helicopter as the afternoon dwindled into night. Her insides felt scooped out and emptied, like she'd just thrown up. That's what crying did to her. It made her feel weak. And she hated to feel weak.

She scrolled down to Lizzie's number on her panda phone. Normally, the three of them would have been huddled at Pinkberry by now, cheering Carina up over plain yoghurt topped with Cap'n Crunch and Oreo pieces. But this was no ordinary fight with the Jurg. She wasn't even sure this was something she could talk about with her friends. She'd never mentioned her dad's cheating to them. And the memory of Hudson's face that morning in class – quiet and scared – kept her from calling them. Even if they weren't full-on mad, Lizzie and Hudson were probably a little annoyed at her. Leaning on her friends right now probably wasn't the best idea.

So she called her mom. She was stunned when someone actually picked up.

"Hello?" It was a man. Behind him she could hear the dim racket of a party.

"Hi, is Mimi there?" she asked.

"No, I'm sorry," he said. "She's with a private client. Who's this?"

"This is her daughter, Carina."

"Who?" the man asked.

"Her *daughter*," she said. "Can you tell her I called?"

"Sure thing," the man said. "Aloha."

"Aloha yourself," she muttered as she hung up.

Why was some random guy answering her mom's mobile phone? And why did he sound like he'd never heard of her before? Didn't people know that she had a child named Carina?

Her mother had always been too classy to say anything to her about her dad's affairs, even during those four days at the Plaza. But she hadn't needed to. Carina had figured it out herself. For the last few months before her mom had left, the Jurg had done everything he could to avoid his wife. If she walked into a room, he left it. If she wandered into his den while he was watching CNBC, he'd pick up his BlackBerry and make a phone call. During dinners, he'd wolf down his food as he read a pile of magazines, and her mother would stare at her plate, as if a movie were playing somewhere between her pounded chicken breast and steamed broccoli. Carina would sit between them, furiously texting her friends under the table to distract herself.

It got worse as the school year went on. By the winter her mom had started crying in the mornings and walking through the house like a zombie on Xanax. When she'd finally asked her mom if she was all right, Mimi had just given Carina a weak, red-eyed shrug. "Oh, honey," she'd said, and there had been novels of despair in those two words.

Finally, there'd been the night when she passed her parents' closed bedroom door and heard shouting.

"Do you have to treat me like this in front of our daughter? She notices, Karl!" her mother yelled. "She notices everything! For her sake, can't you be a little decent?"

"I can do whatever I damn well want," her dad yelled back. "And you *deserve* it if you're going to be so selfish—"

And then someone's hand was on the doorknob, twisting it to open the door, and Carina fled down the stairs, all the way down to the first floor, where she hid in the powder room and sat on the toilet lid, holding her breath.

For a few minutes she could only hear their voices on a loop inside her head, like a recording she couldn't stop. And then finally, it came to her.

He'd cheated. Of course he had. There'd always been women around her father. Even as a little girl she'd sensed his power over them. And now something had gone too far and he'd broken her mother's heart. It made her sick to her stomach. But it also made perfect sense. He always got what he wanted. As upsetting as it was to think about him with other women, down deep inside she knew that it wasn't too much of a stretch.

Ka-CHUNG!

The chime of her mobile brought her back to the real world. Carina sat up on her bed and eyed her battered phone, which was sitting on her dresser. It was probably a text from her dad, telling her in no uncertain terms how disappointed he was in her. She lay back on her bed, waiting to get up the necessary courage to look at the message. But when she finally got up and walked over to it, she saw that it was a text from Alex.

U free tonite?

She hadn't seen or spoken to him since their shopping trip at Trader Joe's. But right now he was the only person on the planet she felt like talking to.

Yep, she wrote back.

Lincoln Centre. Fountain. Half an hour.

She would have thought that New York's opera, ballet and classical music centre would be far too stuffy for someone as hipstery as Alex, but then again, he was an unpredictable guy.

C u there, she wrote back. Then she said a small prayer that whatever he had in mind cost less than five dollars.

She took the Fifty-seventh Street cross-town bus and got off at Broadway. It was fully dark out by now and a damp wind blew against her face as she walked uptown. Lincoln Centre was another place that reminded her of her mom. Every December when she was little, Carina and her mom would come up here to see a matinee of *The Nutcracker*, and then get hot chocolate and apple torte at Cafe Lalo. Her mom called these trips their "girl dates", and Carina had loved them. But in fifth grade, they'd come to a screeching halt, thanks to her dad's antics. Her dad had ruined everything, she thought as she dodged a woman running for a cab in front of the Mandarin Oriental Hotel. There was no reason to feel bad about their fight today. He'd deserved everything she'd said to him and more.

She bounded up the white limestone steps to Lincoln Centre Plaza, and when she reached the top, a smile came to her face. She'd forgotten how beautiful the fountain was at night. Steam drifted off the golden-white jets of water as they bubbled up into the sky, while the sound of rushing water blotted out the horns and sirens. People criss-crossed the plaza, hurrying to get home and out of town for the holiday weekend. But one person stood still in front of the fountain, waiting for someone. It was Alex. He wore a long, military-style coat and knotted red scarf. His normally spiky dark hair seemed to have been smoothed over with some gel. If she didn't know better, she would have thought that he'd dressed up just for her. But she already knew that this wasn't a date. How could it be, after how much he knew about her?

"Hey," she said as she walked over. She felt suddenly embarrassed that she'd only worn jeans and a black Gap turtleneck under her coat. "You look nice."

"Thanks," Alex said. She thought she saw a slight reddening in his cheeks. "I know it was kind of last minute."

"So are we seeing something here?"

"Maybe. Just think of this as Music Ed, pre-Lady Gaga." He grinned.

"We're seeing classical music?" she asked.

"Don't worry, you'll survive," he deadpanned.

As they walked down the block to the gleaming glass cube of Alice Tully Hall, she said, "I wouldn't think that a guy who's into German electronica would also be into Beethoven." They stepped inside the sleek, glass-walled lobby. It was nearly empty. An usher standing by the escalator ripped their tickets.

"I kind of grew up with classical music," Alex said as he stepped on to the escalator. "My mom used to be a concert pianist, until she married my dad. And my sister plays the flute. And I used to play violin."

"Really? The violin? Why'd you stop?"

Alex looked at her as they travelled upward on the escalator. "When you're a guy and you're kind of small for your age *and* you're getting beaten up on a regular basis, you stop playing the violin as soon as possible."

"Oh, right," she agreed.

On the second floor, another usher directed them through

a set of doors.

"So, do you have season tickets or something?" she asked as they walked into a large, wood-panelled auditorium that glowed with soft amber lighting.

"Nah, this is free," Alex said, making his way into an aisle. "Every Wednesday some of the Juilliard students perform for school credit. Anyone can come to see them. Except no one really knows about it."

"But you do," Carina said as they sat down.

Alex unbuttoned his coat. "And now you do, too."

As Alex took off his coat, she snuck a quick glance at his clothes. Instead of his usual T-shirt and thermal combo, he wore a collared, grey-striped shirt. And she definitely smelled hair gel.

"What?" Alex asked, catching her stare.

"Nothing," she said, red-faced, turning back to face the stage.

What is going on? she thought. Did he like her or not? The old Carina would have made a joke to find out. Something like *Where's the Smiths T-shirt? Or is this a date?* But she was a different person now. The sort of person who didn't know how to crack jokes and flirt with guys any more. Or maybe she was just that person around Alex. There was something about him that made her feel like she had some growing up to do.

"This is a string quartet," Alex whispered into her ear. "Two violinists, one cellist and a violist. I think they're playing

Beethoven."

The lights dimmed and two girls and a guy, wearing dark blazers and jeans, walked onstage carrying what looked like violins. A fourth guy walked out, carrying a cello.

"What's a violist?" she asked.

"It's someone who plays the viola," he said.

"Oh." She'd never heard of a viola. As far as she could tell, it looked just like a violin.

The audience's applause died down and the lights dimmed all the way. And then they began to play.

Carina sat there in the dark, ready to listen politely for the first five minutes and then discreetly take a nap. But from the sound of the first note she was completely transfixed. Instead of lulling her to sleep, the music actually woke her up. It was invigorating and relaxing at the same time.

"Close your eyes," Alex whispered into her ear.

She did. The music filled the space around her. She remembered what Alex had said to her about music having a landscape. She could hear it now – the different parts separating and coming together. Like waves, it washed over her, calming her. All of the things she'd said to her dad, all of the questions that had been racing through her mind, quietened down. There was nothing in her mind right now but the music. Until she felt Alex's arm press up against hers.

She opened her eyes. There it was: his arm, nestled right up next to hers, the skin of their wrists just barely touching. The contact sent a current of prickly heat right up to her shoulder.

But Alex seemed oblivious to it. He sat watching the musicians onstage, totally absorbed in the music.

Carina tried to refocus on the music, but she couldn't. Was this an accident? Or did he mean to be touching her arm? The old her would have done something to find out, like reach down to grab his hand or tickle his palm. But now she just sat there motionless, feeling the warmth from his skin seep right through the sleeve of her turtleneck.

The old her wouldn't have been surprised that he liked her. But the new her was. Alex *knew* the new her. And he liked her anyway. And now, as she sat perfectly still amid the swelling music, her heart pounding like crazy, she realized that she liked him, too.

Chapter 21

When the concert was over and they stood up to pull on their coats, Carina wondered if things were going to be a little awkward after more than an hour of semi-accidental arm touching. But Alex didn't seem the least bit weirded out.

"Pretty cool, huh?" he asked on the escalator as he buttoned up his coat. "I can't believe those guys are still in school."

"Amazing," she agreed. "Do you think you'd like to go to Juilliard, too?"

"Sure, but I missed my chance," he said. "I stopped playing a couple of years ago."

"So start now. I'm sure you can catch up. I mean, if that's really where you want to go."

Alex gave her a playful nudge as they walked off the escalator and into the now-crowded lobby. "Thanks for the life coaching. Where do you want to go?"

"I don't know," she said. "I think somewhere in Colorado so I can go hiking. That's what I really love to do."

"What does your dad think about that?" he asked as they walked out on to the street.

"My dad?"

"I just figure he'd probably want you to go into business, right? Go work for him or something?"

"Well, I don't want to work for him. How would you feel if someone told you what to do?"

"I'd love for my dad to tell me what to do," Alex said.

Carina walked beside him in silence. It sounded like Alex's dad wasn't in the picture any more. Suddenly she felt embarrassed for complaining so much.

"So just tell me what he did that made you so angry," he said. "You know, that made you do the thing you did to piss him off."

"It's a long story," she said, fumbling for her gloves in her coat pocket.

"Just so you know, I don't have Page Six on speed dial or anything."

"I know you don't. But I actually know a girl who might."

"I'm serious," he said, giving her a probing look. "Tell me."

"OK. My dad cheated on my mom," she said bluntly. "He was seeing some other woman and my mom left him. She wanted me to live with her but my dad threatened to sue her for custody. And she didn't have any choice but to do what he said. Like always."

Alex walked quietly beside her. "That's what you're still mad about?" he asked.

"He's so obsessed with his company he doesn't even know I exist. And I just have to wonder why he wanted me so bad. If it had anything to do with me, or just, you know, winning."

Alex was still quiet as they passed a row of dark brownstones.

"You can't tell anyone that, by the way," she added. "I mean the cheating part. *Any*body."

"I won't," Alex finally said. "And that sucks. Really. But at some point, you're just gonna have to get over it. You can't spend the rest of your life hating your dad for something he did."

"So I'm just supposed to forget about it?"

"No. I'm just saying there's nothing you can *do* about it. It's over. Now you have to figure out how to live with the guy. And it's not all up to him to make sure it's easy."

"What do you mean, it's not all up to *him*?" she asked, starting to get angry. They turned the corner on to Central Park West. A bus was lumbering towards them down the street, and for a moment, Carina thought about jumping on it.

"I'm just saying that you need to meet him halfway," Alex said. "*You* have to try to get along with him, too."

"Look, you don't know the situation."

"And what about the other woman?" Alex asked. "Is he with her now?"

"No," Carina said.

"Well, who was she?" he asked. "Did you meet her?"

"No, but who cares?" she asked, truly annoyed now. "It still happened. What does *that* have to do with anything?"

"Well, at least she's not in your face the whole time," he said, shrugging.

Carina stopped walking and turned to him. "What's your problem?" she asked.

"My problem?" he repeated.

"Why are you trying to make me feel like I don't have a right to be upset?" she asked.

"Carina." Alex sighed. In the glow of the orange streetlight above them his gaze was intense and direct. "I'm just saying that you have to move on. This is your life, too. You can't give it all over to something that happened in the past."

Carina stared at him, biting her lip in frustration. "Thanks for being so understanding," she grumbled. "I think I'm gonna go." She turned back in the opposite direction down the street.

"Hey, wait!" Alex grabbed her arm. Despite her anger, her knees went weak at his touch. "I'm sorry," he said, smiling as he turned her around to face him. "I'm on your side. I am. I just have kind of a big mouth sometimes. Just ask my mom and sister."

"I will," she said, trying to resist a smile.

"In fact," he said, pulling out his phone, "you can ask them right now." He started typing out a text. "You want to meet them?"

"*Now?*"

"I'm on my way to meet up with them," he said, pointing up the street.

Carina squinted as she looked uptown. In the distance, she saw crowds, lights and what looked like giant buildings hanging suspended in midair. "What is that?" she asked, staring. "Oh my God," she said, as it dawned on her. "It's *that*!" They were blowing up the balloons for the Macy's Thanksgiving Day parade on Eighty-first Street, just across from the Museum of Natural History. It was a New York tradition, but one that she'd never seen in person. "I've never gone to this!" she squealed.

"You've never come here with your parents?" Alex asked.

"Nope, but I've wanted to," she said. She didn't want to explain that her two best friends were the daughters of Katia Summers and Holla Jones, who could probably start a stampede in crowded public places like this. "Come on! Let's go!"

They half ran, half walked up Central Park West towards the surreal sight of a gigantic Kermit the Frog bobbing up and down in the sky, tied down with ropes. They turned on to Eighty-first Street. "My mom should be right over here," he said, taking Carina by the arm and pulling her into the crowd massed behind police horses. "We sort of always have the same spot."

"Alex!" a girl yelled, just as they were halfway down the block.

A girl Carina's age elbowed her way out of the crowd and skipped towards them. She had a brilliant stripe of purple in her hair, a mess of earrings all up and down one ear and a charcoal wool dress with big red buttons and black-and white-striped tights.

"Thank *God* you showed up," she said desperately, taking Alex's arm. "Mom's hijacked about twenty people so far, *and* she's invited half of them over for Thanksgiving tomorrow. Help." She nodded towards a short, dark-haired woman a few feet away, busily chatting to a young couple.

"Carina, this is my sister, Marisol," he said. "Who also thinks I have a big mouth."

"God, does he ever." Marisol laughed pleasantly as she shook Carina's hand. Alex's sister shared his large, wide-set brown eyes and graceful cheekbones, but she was even artsier-looking than her brother. "So nice to meet you. My brother's told us a lot about you."

"He has? Like what?" Carina asked, shaking her hand.

Alex gave his sister a hard nudge, and she gave him one right back. "Um, only that you're really cool," she said brightly. "So what happened? Did he say something stupid to you?"

"No, not at all," Carina said, feeling herself blush a little. He'd told his sister about her? She'd never expected that. "Cool dress. Where'd you get it?"

"The Williamsburg Goodwill. It cost five dollars, which was, like, super-expensive for that place. You ever been?"

"Uh, no," Carina said. "But I'd like to check it out."

"I can take you there sometime," Marisol said. "You're so tiny, you'd probably find more stuff there than me."

"Wait, before you get further into girl talk, Marisol, did you get us the tickets for Texas?" Alex said.

"Mom got them," Marisol said. "We leave the day before Christmas Eve. That OK with you? Or do you have another fancy DJ gig?"

"What are you guys doing in Texas?" Carina asked. "Do you have family there?"

"We're going down to build houses for Habitat for Humanity," Alex explained. "We started doing it a couple of years ago. It's actually really fun."

"Because my brother likes to hog all the good jobs," Marisol put in, nudging him again. "I just get stuck with carrying all the lumber around."

"Oh come on, you're in charge of the best part," he said. "My sister's an artist," he said to Carina. "So she gets to boss us all around when the time comes for painting the houses."

"Wow," Carina said, genuinely impressed.

"You know, I was thinking," Alex said, rubbing his hands together, "you still need to get flowers for the party, right?"

"I do." She'd almost completely forgotten about the party.

"Well, Marisol does these really cool flower sculptures she paints by hand," he said. "They might be a little more unique than real flowers."

"Could we use them?" Carina asked.

Marisol tugged at the purple stripe in her hair. "As long as they don't get torn apart by the end of the night, sure."

"And maybe she can go to the dance," Alex suggested. "Everyone'll be around her age, right?"

Marisol blushed as she swatted her brother. "Alex," she said.

"No, no, I'm sure that would be fine," Carina said, trying to picture someone as edgy as Marisol trying to fit in with Ava's crowd. "I can get her a ticket. And I'd love to use the flowers."

"Great," Marisol said, beaming. "And I can help you pick out something to wear."

"It's a deal," Carina replied just as the small, dark-haired woman Carina knew was Alex's mom stepped out of the crowd and threw her arms around Alex.

"Hello, honey!" Mrs Suarez was so petite that she had to stand on her tiptoes to plant a big kiss on Alex's cheek. She had a neat shoulder-length bob and doe-shaped eyes, and Carina could see that ten years ago she would have been astonishingly beautiful. "How was the concert?" she asked.

"Amazing," Alex said. "Mom, this is Carina."

"Hi, Mrs Suarez," Carina said, putting out her hand.

Alex's mom waved her hand away and threw her arms around her, too. "Oh, your face is freeeeezing," she said, patting Carina's cheek. Mrs Suarez reached down and put a cup of something dark into Carina's hand. "This'll warm you up."

Carina took a sip. It tasted like a latte but it was sweeter and stronger. "Thanks," Carina said. "What is this?"

"*Café con leche,*" Mrs Suarez replied. "But don't worry. It's decaf. When Alex's father was still alive, we used to go to the Macy's parade and I'd bring a whole vat of this I'd wheel around like a suitcase," she said. "But caffeine didn't agree with him. And he'd start telling terrible jokes," she laughed. "So now, decaf."

So Alex's father was dead, she thought, sipping her drink. No wonder he'd said that he'd love for his dad to tell him what to do, and no wonder he'd been so kind about the Jurg. She felt so bad for him that she wanted to hug him right there in front of his family.

"Mom, you can stop monopolizing my friend now," Alex said, touching Carina on the shoulder. "We've gotta go."

"Do you have plans for the holiday tomorrow?" she asked Carina. "Please! Come over."

"Oh, I would love to," Carina said genuinely. "But I'm going to be out of town." *Or imprisoned,* she wanted to say.

"Well, if you change your mind, we'll have enough food to choke a horse!" Mrs Suarez said as Alex steered Carina away.

"Sorry, my mom can be a little overbearing," he said.

"That's OK, I see where you get it now," she said, smiling. "But I should probably get going. My dad likes to leave for Montauk at night to avoid the rush-hour traffic. But thanks so much for the concert tonight."

"Sure thing," he said, leading her out of the crowd and into the park in front of the glowing pink ball of the Hayden Planetarium. "I think my family wants to adopt you."

"Well, they can," she laughed. "You're really lucky."

"Yeah, I guess," he said, running a hand through his

hair. "But you know how it is. Sometimes it doesn't feel that way."

They came to a stop under one of the large elms in front of the planetarium, and Carina hugged herself to stay warm. "I'm sorry about your dad," she said. "Why didn't you tell me?"

Alex nodded and looked down at the ground. "It's not my favourite topic," he said.

She reached out and touched his arm. "You know, *you* can tell *me* stuff, too," she whispered. "If you need to."

Alex looked up at her, and she could tell from the way his brown eyes took in her entire face that he was surprised by what she'd said.

"OK," he said under his breath.

They were only a few inches apart, and in the darkness, she felt that familiar, pre-kiss adrenaline begin to course through her body. She stepped closer to him and closed her eyes. This was it, she thought. They were going to kiss. She held her breath, waiting for him to make his move … when she felt his hands gently squeeze her arms.

"Have a great Thanksgiving," he said.

She opened her eyes. It was as if a splash of cold water had hit her in the face.

"Yeah. You, too," Carina said, stumbling over a rock in the dark. "Have a good time in Texas."

"That's not this weekend," Alex said. "That's Christmas."

"Oh, right." She stumbled again. "Well. Happy Thanksgiving. Bye."

"Bye."

She gave him a silly, half-hearted wave and walked to Columbus, thrilled that the dark was hiding her burning face. All of her instincts had been wrong. He didn't like her. Tonight had just been a friendly hangout. Maybe he talked about *all* his friends with his sister. She'd read him wrong this entire time, she thought, with a panic that gripped all of her internal organs and turned them inside out.

But it didn't surprise her. After all, Alex was nothing like the other guys she knew. He was thoughtful and kind, and he listened to Beethoven, and he got into any club he wanted *and* he did social service on his vacations. Maybe she wasn't deep enough for him. Maybe, she thought with a tiny gasp, he felt sorry for her.

Another bus was coming down the street and Carina ran down the block to the bus stop, waving her arms frantically so it would see her. If this had been just a few months ago, she would have had to push Alex away, hail a cab, and get in the back seat with a flirtatious blown kiss in his direction. Now she was running like a banshee towards a city bus, after getting royally blown off. What had happened to her?

The bus wheezed to a stop and Carina ran on, just as her phone went *Ka-CHUNG!* It was a text from the Jurg.

Where r u? Leaving in 30

She sat down and dropped the phone back into her bag. She was in for a long four days.

Chapter 22

"Carina? *Carina?*"

Her dad was calling her, but Carina didn't move from her spot on the couch except to pick up the remote and turn up the volume. So far she'd spent Thanksgiving weekend mostly immobile, lying under a mohair blanket and watching TV. The Jurg had invited her to join his annual Thanksgiving dinner party the night before, but their fight in Barb's office still hung in the air, making things even tenser than usual. Plus she wasn't in the mood to watch the Jurg's female guests contort themselves to show off their cleavage. So she'd eaten her turkey and sweet potatoes in front of the flat screen, watching *The Sound of Music* and feeling sorry for herself. Until she started thinking about Alex.

Actually, she'd been doing a lot of thinking about Alex. Ever since their near kiss at the balloon blow-up, she'd been imagining a whole slew of actual kiss scenarios. Like in the park in front of the Planetarium, where they'd said goodbye; or in the frozen food aisle of Trader Joe's; or at Club Neshka in front of all those dancing hipsters. She wanted to see him, talk to him, be with him, walk the streets of New York with him. And she *really* wanted to text him. But every time she typed out something, such as "Happy Turkey Day!", it felt like code for I'M TOTALLY INTO YOU, and she'd turn off her phone.

It was only four o'clock on Friday, which meant that she had at least four more days before she could get in touch with him without it looking ridiculously obvious. She sighed into the throw pillow. She was completely into him and it was making her miserable. Outside, past the swimming pool, the Atlantic lapped at the shore, frustratingly calm. She would have killed for some waves, just to take her mind off him.

"Carina?" Her dad walked into the den. "You're still in front of the TV. What a surprise." In his Montauk uniform of beige cashmere sweater and jeans, the Jurg looked a little dorky and bereft of his usual power, like a modern-day Clark Kent. "Don't you want to go into Amagansett? Or East Hampton?"

"And what am I supposed to do in town?" she asked.

Her dad sat down on one of the sleek black leather settees. "I don't know. Get some fresh air. Leave the house."

"It's freezing out. Is it bothering you that I'm in here?"

"No, it's not bothering me. Look, about the fight we had the other day—"

Carina heard the muffled ring of his BlackBerry.

"Hold on," he said, taking it out of his back pocket. "Yeah?" he said into it. "I thought Ed was taking care—" He let out a long, annoyed sigh. "Fine, I guess I'll just get ready then."

He clicked off. "I just found out that I have to go to London again for a few days," he said. "Are you going to be all right here by yourself? Or do you want to go back into the city?"

She sat bolt upright. Going back to the city meant seeing Alex again. "I'll go back in," she said brightly.

"I'm sorry I have to go," her father said.

She eyed her panda phone, sitting on the coffee table. Now she knew the perfect text to write Alex...

"Carina? Did you just hear what I said?" her father asked.

"Yeah, you're going to London," she said, reaching for her phone. "Got it loud and clear."

She flipped open her phone as she heard her dad get to his feet. "Carina..." he started.

"Yeah?" she asked, looking up from her phone.

Her dad looked past her, and suddenly he seemed lost. She wondered if he'd said something she hadn't caught. "Nothing," he finally said, shaking his head. "I'll see you when I get back."

He drifted out of the room as Carina started typing her text.

Hey. Coming back into the city. Wot u up to?

Alex wrote back two minutes later:

213

Leftovers. Come over. 45 Forsyth Street. #5W. 7 p.m.

Dinner at his house? she thought in shock. So maybe *he'd* been thinking about *her*, too.

Cool, bring anything?

Just u, he wrote back.

She dropped the phone. She didn't want to read too much into two words, but that had to be a sign. *Just u.* Her heart started to pound. She couldn't wait to see him. If she could only figure out where Forsyth Street was.

"Hey, Carina!" Marisol said when she opened their front door. "Come on in!"

Marisol wore a denim button-down dress with a ripped hem, rainbow tights and scuffed-up plimsolls, but the effect was so cool she looked like a stylist had dressed her.

"So psyched you're here! And you didn't have to bring those!" She pointed to the plastic-wrapped daisies that Carina was carrying and grabbed Carina's arm as she pulled her inside. "You look great," Marisol said admiringly.

"Really?" asked Carina. She'd been too excited to stop at the apartment to change out of her J. Crew sweater and jeans and had gone straight from Penn Station to Alex's apartment on the Lower East Side. "Thanks so much for having me—"

"Oh, come see my flower sculptures!" Marisol cried,

tugging her by the arm down the hall and into a room. "I got them all out for you. Here!" she said, flipping on the light. "Whaddya think?"

Carina hesitated for a moment in the doorway. Marisol's room was the size of Carina's closet and the walls were plastered with pictures. Pictures of modern art paintings. Pictures of sculpture. And most of all, pictures from fashion magazines. There were hundreds of them, going back almost two years. It was like an altar to high fashion. Carina was so distracted by them that she almost didn't see the row of brilliantly painted papier-mâché flower arrangements standing on her dresser. Each one was at least three colours, all swirled together and spinning outward all over the petals in a kind of kaleidoscopic explosion. Alex had been right. They were definitely unique.

"Oh my God, Marisol," Carina said, walking over to them. "These are beautiful. You made these?"

"Uh-huh. You still want to use them?"

Carina reached over and picked up one of the sculptures. "Of course I do. Did you paint all these yourself?"

"It didn't take too long."

"I can only do paint-by-numbers. You're really talented, you know that?"

"Well, thanks," Marisol said, touching the petals lightly with her fingers. "I was thinking, if it's not too much trouble, maybe at the dance you can put up a sign and say that they're mine?"

"Done." Carina wasn't sure how Ava was going to feel about

an eighth-grader doing the flowers, but she'd worry about it later.

"Great!" Marisol said, reaching for a binder near her bed. "Because I'm already trying to figure out my dress. I can't decide between something with bat sleeves or a strapless corset-style thing." She opened the binder and inside were plastic-covered pages from fashion magazines.

"What are these?" Carina asked.

"Inspiration," Marisol said, sitting cross-legged on her bed. "Stuff I like to keep in mind when I'm creating my final look."

"You make your own *clothes*?" Carina asked, dumbfounded.

"It's easy," Marisol said cheerfully. "I usually find something at one of the vintage shops and then add to it a little. Have you ever tried that?"

"Tried what?" Alex said.

Carina turned to see Alex standing in the doorway, watching Carina with a shy smile that made her hands start to sweat. He was back to his usual Artsy Boy self, wearing a brown thermal under a black T-shirt with a silk-screened illustration of Blondie. It was ridiculously cute. "Marisol, can we let Carina eat?" he asked.

"We were just talking about the dance," Carina said. "I'm totally using these sculptures, by the way."

"And I'm definitely going," Marisol said proudly. "I just need to figure out what I'm wearing."

"You guys can talk fashion later. I'm hungry," Alex said. His hand on her arm was warm and comforting as he led her into the hall. "Thanks for coming down. My mom almost had a coronary when I told her you were coming, she was so excited."

"Oh, these are for you," she said, giving him the daisies that she still held in her hands. "I mean, your mom."

Thankfully Alex didn't catch her slip. "Huh," he said, taking the flowers. "Now she's really going to be obsessed with you. Daisies are her favourite. Welcome to the family."

They turned into the narrow, cramped kitchen, where several adults stood drinking wine. Odours of cinnamon and pumpkin and sweet potatoes made Carina's stomach wake up. Mrs Suarez, looking even younger and prettier in a burgundy turtleneck and jeans, removed a bubbling casserole from the oven.

"Hi, Mrs Suarez," Carina said.

"Carina! I'm so glad you could make it," she cried. "Here, take a plate and help yourself. You better be hungry."

Mrs Suarez gestured to the kitchen table, which was laden with dishes of baked sweet potatoes, cranberry sauce, wild rice, cheese enchiladas and the remains of a roast turkey.

"Everything looks amazing," Carina said, grabbing a plate.

Mrs Suarez put the still bubbling dish on the table. "Green bean casserole," she said. "Even better the next day."

"This all looks better than anything I had last night," Carina said, dishing a healthy scoop of sweet potatoes on to her plate. "Thanks for having me."

"Didn't you spend yesterday with your family?" Mrs

Suarez asked, pulling cling film off a dish of warmed-up gravy.

"Just my dad," Carina said. "He had some people over but it was more of a work thing. Not really family."

"And what does he do?" Mrs Suarez asked.

Carina stared at her. Normally people already knew that. It was the headline when people talked about her: *She's Karl Jurgensen's daughter*. But Alex apparently hadn't mentioned it.

"Um … he's a businessman," she said simply, eyeing Alex from the other side of the table.

After she'd gone back into the kitchen for seconds and then thirds, and chatted more with Marisol, Alex turned to her across the table. "OK, time to go," he announced, putting down his napkin. "We're on a tight schedule."

"Where are we going?" she asked.

Alex shook his head. "It's a surprise."

"Oh God, is this more music education?" Carina said.

"Trust me," Alex said, grabbing his military coat.

Next to her, Marisol beamed and then quickly went back to her green bean casserole. "Have a good time, you guys," she said in a secretive way.

They threw on their coats and said their goodbyes to Mrs Suarez and Marisol. When they had walked out of the building into the cold and gone almost a block in silence, Alex said, "Thanks for getting my sister that ticket to the dance. This is going to be the high point of her year."

"No problem. Thanks for letting me know about her artwork. She's brilliant. And seriously, anything I can do."

"It'll be good for her to go," he said. "She's been having a tough time at school. Her friends turning on her, stuff like that. It'll be good for people to know she's going to that. As much as I think it's a total waste of time." He winked, pulling a green wool hat over his head.

"So you didn't tell your mom who I was," Carina prompted.

Alex looked at her closely. "Did you want me to tell her?"

"No, but that's just what I'm used to. Everyone does that."

"And is that why you think people like you?" he asked.

Carina knew that he wasn't trying to offend her, but his question still stung. "No, of course not," she said carefully. "It's just that it's always part of me. Wherever I go. Whatever I do. It's like my hair colour or my eye colour or my first name. Just part of me. I'm just surprised you didn't mention it."

"It wasn't important," he shrugged. "You're just Carina to me. Always have been."

Her heart was beating so rapidly that she thought it was going to rise up into her throat and get stuck there. For the first time, she wondered who else could say that, outside of Lizzie and Hudson. She doubted that anyone could. "Your mom's really wonderful, by the way," she said, changing the subject.

"Yeah, I know. Whenever I think about her being alone the rest of her life, it kills me."

219

"Were you close with your dad?" she asked.

Alex didn't say anything for a minute as they walked. "Not as close as I should have been," he finally said.

Carina snuck her hand around his arm. "I'm sorry."

Alex squeezed her hand. "I'm really glad you came down tonight," he said quietly. "I didn't think I could wait until next week to see you."

She let herself lean her head slightly on his shoulder as his words sunk in. "Me too," she whispered.

They turned on to Houston Street and Alex slowed his steps. *Oh my God, he's going to kiss me,* she thought. *It's finally gonna happen.*

But instead Alex removed his arm as he came to a stop. "OK, we're here," he said.

"Here? There's a surprise *here*?" she asked, looking up at the deserted warehouse in front of them. "Are you sure?"

"No judgements," Alex said, grinning. "Just trust me." He pressed a button on the grimy front door. At the buzz he pulled it open. Inside were a dirty vestibule and a freight elevator.

"OK, I'm scared," Carina said as they walked into the elevator.

"Don't be," he said as the doors closed. "What would you say if I said this actually was a concert? Another stop on the Carina Music Appreciation Tour?"

"I would say that you're probably delusional," Carina said, looking around the graffiti-scarred elevator.

"No imagination," Alex said mournfully as the elevator

shuddered to a stop and the door opened on to a large, almost empty loft.

Inside, several men in black T-shirts were busy setting up what looked like amps, microphone stands and a drum set in the back of the room. Several large black cases of equipment were stacked right in front of them, and there, right on a guitar case, she saw THE KILLERS stenciled in big white letters.

"Wait," she said. "Why does that say that? Are we picking up tickets to a Killers concert?"

"No, we're *seeing* a Killers concert. Here."

"But ... how?" she stammered as one of the roadies walked past them with a gleaming guitar.

"My friend rents this space out for rehearsals. A lot of really good bands use it the day before a big show. And he always lets me know when there's someone I like coming in."

"So we're basically the *only* outside people coming here to see them?" Carina asked in disbelief. Besides the guys setting up, there only seemed to be a handful of men and women, walking around the loft, talking on their phones or texting.

"Yup. Pretty cool, huh?" Alex turned to a tall, scraggly haired man in his twenties coming towards them. "What's up, man?"

The scraggly haired man gave Alex a bro shake. "Alex, man, what is *up*? Glad you could come by."

"Ted, this is my friend Carina," Alex said.

"Hey, Carina," Ted said. "You're probably gonna need these." He handed her a pair of foam earplugs.

221

As Carina watched Alex and Ted talk, she couldn't believe where she was. Not even her dad could have got her into something like this. Alex had been right that day at Trader Joe's. The best things about New York – and the best experiences – didn't cost a dime.

After Ted had hurried away to take care of some last-minute business, and just before the band was about to come on, Alex took her by the arm and brought her over to the window.

"There's the Manhattan Bridge," he said, pointing to the looming blue bridge dotted with lights. "Isn't it cool-looking?"

Carina put her hand on his arm. "This is the most amazing night of my life," she said to him.

Alex smiled at her, letting her get lost in his deep cocoa-coloured eyes. Then he leaned in towards her and she closed her eyes.

Before she knew it, his lips were on hers. She drew her arms up around his neck. There were the sounds of dissonant guitar chords and some drumming as the roadies prepared the band equipment, but she barely noticed. She'd waited for this moment for so long and now that it was finally here, she wasn't going to let anything interrupt it.

Finally their lips pulled apart.

"So, I've been wanting to do that a long, long time," he said.

"Me too," she said, keeping her arms around his neck. "But I thought it was better you go first."

Alex smiled and leaned into her again. As his lips found hers, and her arms tightened around his neck, Carina knew that for the first time in her life, she was exactly where she belonged.

Chapter 23

"I am *exhausted*, you guys," Hudson said. "Remind me *never* to do boot camp with my mom's new trainer. Five straight days of two-hour 'dance classes' and I have, like, swine flu." Hudson scrunched up her face and went *a-CHOO!* as people all over the diner turned their heads from her ear-splitting sneeze.

"Couldn't you have just stayed home today?" Carina asked, discreetly pulling out her packed lunch under the table.

"And risk being pulled into another torture session? No thanks," Hudson said, sniffling into her Kleenex. "C, let me order you something, OK? You can't bring food in here."

"No, it's fine," she said, darting her eyes at the waiter's turned back as she snuck a bite of her homemade sandwich, which she held under the table. "By the way, you sound really sick."

"Have an Airborne," Lizzie said, reaching into her backpack

and pulling out a tube of meds. "I was behind some guy on the plane back from North Carolina who was really sick and I think this saved me."

"Was it weird not being home for Thanksgiving?" Carina asked Lizzie.

"Sort of, but not really," Lizzie said, taking another bite of grilled cheese. "His mom's side of the family really made me feel welcome. And North Carolina was so beautiful. How was Montauk?"

Carina smiled and snuck another bite. "So you guys remember my friend Alex? The DJ?" In a rare bout of self-control, she'd decided to wait until Monday to tell Lizzie and Hudson the news in person.

"Yeahhhh," Hudson prompted, dipping a spoon into her chicken soup. "When's his birthday again?"

"I have no idea," Carina said. "But guess what? We hooked up."

Hudson dropped her spoon in the bowl. "You *did*?"

"Yep," Carina said, scooting closer to the table. "We went to this concert at Lincoln Centre, and saw these Juilliard students play Beethoven, and then we went to the balloon blow-up, and I thought he was going to kiss me, but he didn't," she said breathlessly. "And then the night after Thanksgiving, I went back in the city and we went to a rehearsal for the Killers. We had our own private concert. It was amazing."

"Holy crap," Hudson yelled. "The Killers? Are you kidding me?"

"And he's so sweet and funny and cute and wonderful," Carina went on. "You guys'll love him."

"What happened to Carter?" Lizzie asked abruptly, digging into her side of coleslaw. "I thought *he* was the one you were really into."

"Well, he was," Carina said, a little irritably. "But you know what happened with that. Now everything's kind of changed."

"So you're in love with the DJ guy?" Lizzie asked with a sour note in her voice.

Just then Todd walked over to their booth and for the first time ever Carina was happy to have him interrupt.

"May I sit with you guys? Or am I interrupting?" he asked, in his adorably Britishy way.

"Sure, siddown," Carina said, scooting over to make room for him in the booth.

"We're just talking about guys," Lizzie said. She reached out and gave Todd's hand a girlfriend-like squeeze. "Carina's into someone."

"Oh, right – Carter," Todd said distractedly as he picked up a menu from the table. "How's that going?"

Carina looked at Todd, frozen. She wasn't sure if she'd just heard him correctly. Had Lizzie told Todd about her crush on Carter?

She glanced at Lizzie, whose pale face was starting to redden.

"Did you tell him?" Carina asked.

"I didn't mean to," Lizzie said, giving Todd a stern you-blew-it look. "It just slipped out."

"Oh, sorry," Todd said quickly. "I don't know anything. Nothing."

Carina almost couldn't swallow. It was one of their oldest rules: crush gossip – and anything crush-related – stayed strictly between the three of them. And now Lizzie had broken their rule.

Carina put her food back in the brown bag. "I have to go," she muttered, feeling her cheeks start to blaze.

"Carina—" Lizzie said.

She almost pushed Todd out of her way but he gallantly stood up. "Carina – don't," he said.

"C," pleaded Lizzie. "Come on. I'm *sorry* , I—"

Carina didn't let her finish. She grabbed her bag and went right to the door. She could feel everyone watching her as she walked back on to the street, but she didn't care.

She marched down the street to school, barely noticing the tiny flakes of snow that drifted down from the sky. When had she *ever* breathed a word to Todd about Lizzie's crush on *him*? All those months when Lizzie was pining for him – had Carina ever told anyone? Would she *ever* betray her friend that way? Absolutely not. And now Lizzie felt it was OK to tell Todd about her friend's crushes on other guys? She was almost nauseous. And even if it had "slipped out", it still felt like a betrayal.

"C! Wait up!" a voice called out.

Carina turned around and saw Hudson running down the street with her coat unbuttoned, her pigtails flapping in the breeze.

"C, come back!" Hudson called out, brushing a strand of black hair out of her green eyes. "Todd's totally mortified. And Lizzie feels awful."

"Then why'd she tell him?" Carina asked. "It's our biggest rule."

"I don't know." Hudson shrugged. "He's her boyfriend now. People in relationships tell each other stuff. When you're in love, sometimes those rules go out of the window."

"Oh come on, they're not *in love*," Carina spat. "They're just going out like everyone else."

Hudson swallowed. A flake of snow hit the top of her tiny snub nose and melted. "Not any more. I think they said it to each other this weekend."

Carina felt something heavy shift inside of her. "They *said* it to each other?"

"That's what she told me," Hudson said.

And she didn't tell me, Carina thought. This felt like an even worse betrayal than what had happened with Todd.

Carina edged backwards down the street. "I think I gotta go up to the computer room and print something out. See you in Spanish?"

Hudson's face fell. "Come on, Carina," Hudson said. "Don't do this."

Carina wheeled around and hurried towards the school

228

entrance, feeling Hudson's eyes watching her go. She knew that she was being ultra-dramatic, but she was too mad and too confused right now to know how to act or what to say. Lizzie had betrayed her trust, plain and simple. And now she'd betrayed their friendship by keeping something from her.

It was just so crazy. Of the three of them, *Carina* had always been the one with the boyfriends. She was the one who routinely gave Lizzie and Hudson advice on how to talk to guys. She was the one who'd been kissed first, who'd been on a date first, who'd received more love letters – OK, *emails* – from guys than anyone else she knew. It had always been a given that *she* would be the one to be in love first. Now Lizzie, who'd never really gone out with anyone before, had beaten her to the Holy Grail of romance. And she hadn't even told Carina about it. Was it because she could sense Carina's feelings about Todd? Among the three of them, nobody ever kept information from one person but not from the other. They were all practically the same person. So why would Lizzie tell Hudson and not her?

She threw open the door to the school and came face-to-face with Ava and the Icks, headed outside. Ava's normally auburn hair was now almost blonde, and her skin glowed with what could only be a Caribbean tan. As usual, she didn't seem the slightest bit surprised to see Carina, even though they'd almost ploughed into each other.

"Oh, hey, I meant to text you while I was down in Mustique, but for some reason my phone wouldn't work on the beach," she said, popping almonds in her mouth from a small plastic bag. "Where are we with the flowers? Have you talked to Mercer yet? We're starting to run out of time."

"Who?" Carina asked. She knew that the name Mercer sounded familiar but she couldn't remember why.

"Mercer *Vaise*. The florist I said I wanted. Have you spoken to him?"

Carina thought fast. "Actually, I was just gonna tell you," she said. "I found someone even cooler than that to do the flowers."

"You did?" Ava asked, shooting a sceptical look at Ilona, who smirked back at her. "Who?"

"Marisol Suar—" She stopped herself. Ava would find out that Marisol was fourteen. But she didn't need to know that she was the DJ's sister. "*Willis*. She does these arrangements that are so perfect they almost don't look real. And would it be possible for her to come to the event?"

Ava scribbled something in her pad. "She wants to come?"

"I guess she just likes to see her pieces all set up."

"And what about Sugarbabies?" Ava pressed. "Have you called them yet about the cupcakes?"

"Yup," she fibbed. "But we're still working out the details."

Satisfied, Ava put her notebook away. "Just so you know, the Make New York Beautiful people are *très* psyched at everything you've done so far. You've got your invitation, right?"

Carina nodded. It was still sitting unopened in its gold-lined envelope on her desk. How she was ever going to scrape together the cash to actually go to this dance she had no idea. "Hey, I gotta get to Spanish," she said, hoping to make a graceful exit.

"Wait." Ava grabbed her arm. "A bunch of us are going to Intermix after school to pick out dresses. So we can be sure that we don't all wear the same thing but that we all look like we're in the same, you know, group."

"Um – I really don't –"

"We'll see you in the lobby. Three thirty," Ava said firmly, and then she and the Icks breezed out on to the street. Carina let the door swing closed behind her.

There was always the janitor's closet, she thought. But this time, she didn't think she could lie her way out of this one. And the lies she'd already told were starting to pile up into a confusing, treacherous mess. The dance was in less than three weeks now and for the first time she wondered if she was actually going to get away with any of the stuff she'd kept from Ava. And thinking about her thousand-dollar payment only made her feel guiltier. Especially because she knew now that she didn't even want to go on Carter's ski trip any more.

She pushed through the door on to the Upper School floor and as if to answer her question, there were Carter and Laetitia walking towards her down the hall. They'd both just come in from outside as well. The fine dusting of snow in Carter's curly hair clashed with the tan he'd got down on Fisher Island. Laetitia sipped a gigantic Starbucks takeaway coffee, and from the way she chatted in Carter's ear she looked as blasé and over it all as usual.

Carina's first instinct was to run. She still hadn't responded to any of Laetitia's emails about the Ritz-Carlton or the restaurant reservation. But it was too late. Both of them saw her. And then Carina realized that she needed to tell him that her plans had changed.

"Hey," Carter said, walking over, unwinding his scarf. "How was your break?"

"Great," she said, shifting her weight shyly from foot to foot. "How was Florida?"

"Amazing as usual," he said. "I caught another marlin. It was *hella* big, like this," he said, stretching out his arms. "Took me all day to reel it in. I was like that guy..." He shrugged. "You know ... from the book..."

"*The Old Man and the Sea*?" she prompted. They'd all had to read it in eighth grade. Apparently, the title had left little impression on Carter.

"Ex-*actly*," he said, pointing at her.

"Um, have you got any of my emails?" Laetitia asked in a withering voice as her bored blue eyes looked Carina up and down. "Because you're the only one who hasn't responded."

"Actually, I came over to tell you ... I don't think I can make the trip any more. My dad wants to spend the break down in Jamaica and he's forcing me to come with him." It was a lie, but this time she didn't feel guilty telling one.

"Your dad is forcing you?" Laetitia asked in disbelief.

Carina could feel Carter looking at her.

"I'm not really sure," she said. "But I can't go."

Laetitia smiled wryly, as if she'd known this was coming all along. "See?" she said to Carter. "I told you she was too young for this." She turned back to Carina. "So sorry you won't be joining us." She took Carter by the arm and in that moment, Carina finally understood why Laetitia never seemed to leave Carter alone. She was completely in love with him. "Let's go," she said to him.

They stalked off, leaving her standing in the hall. Carter didn't even give her one last look. Things were definitely over with him. But right now, it just felt like one less person that she had to play a part for.

Chapter 24

"So here's the question, you guys," Ava announced as they walked down Madison Avenue under a light snowfall. "I just had my colourist go a little lighter, and now I don't know if I can pull off purple. I mean, when I was sort of reddish brown, it worked. Now it might look gross."

Lagging a few feet behind her, Carina considered stepping quietly into a L'Occitane shop and hiding until the group was three blocks down the street. But she knew she couldn't.

"Oh my God, you guys, they have a killer Stella McCartney top in there I want to try on," said Ilona, ignoring Ava's statement. "It has sequins and it is to *die* for."

"You're going to do *separates*?" asked Kate in mock horror, twirling a strand of black hair around her finger.

"Uh, sequins are *so* last year," drawled Cici.

What a supportive, close-knit group of friends, Carina thought. She checked her watch. Five minutes was all she was giving them. Just enough time for a polite "Yeah, that looks great!" on Ava's dress, and then a speedy exit.

As they walked inside, the pounding music, bright halogen lighting and shimmering dresses and tops hanging on their racks almost made her dizzy. She felt like a diabetic walking into a candy store. She glanced around at the gorgeous clothes, feeling that old hunger come back. There were so many beautiful things and she immediately had to have all of them. No wonder she'd spent so much money here.

Then she saw the salesgirl behind the till. She had a familiar pile of copper hair and a super-scrawny chest. And then she remembered that this was the same Intermix where her cards had been declined that fateful night. Now she really had to get out of here.

"OK, what do you guys think?" Ava said, walking over to them with an electric purple side-slit dress held up to her chest. "Nice or slutty?"

Cici narrowed her eyes and cocked her head. "Slutty," she decided.

Ava ignored her and looked at Carina. "Carina? What do you think?"

Carina looked at the dress. The purple was definitely pretty with Ava's hair colour, and the long slit went with Ava's accidentally sexy look. But then Carina saw the three zeros on the price tag.

"It's … nice," she said haltingly. "But don't you think Forever 21 probably makes the same thing?"

Ava only looked at her. "What'd you just say?"

"I said try it on," Carina said quickly. "It looks great."

Ava shrugged as if she hadn't heard her. "OK. Be right back." She trotted off towards the fitting rooms, leaving Carina alone with Ilona, Cici and Kate, who were all looking at her like she'd just sprouted another head.

To get away from them, Carina ambled over to a display of python stilettos. She picked one up. The sticker on the sole said $985. She almost laughed out loud. Who spent nine hundred dollars on shoes?

"Hey! Carina, right?"

It was the salesgirl behind the till, waving at her. "We've been *wondering* when you were going to be back in! Actually, I think I still have that Catherine Malandrino halter. You were a two, right?" She stepped out from behind the till and headed towards the racks.

"That's OK," Carina said, looking anxiously at the Icks browsing a few feet away. "Don't worry about it."

"Oh, it's no problem," the girl said, waving her off. "And lemme grab you some stuff to try on. Have any special event coming up?"

"Um, uh, no," she lied, avoiding Ilona's stare.

"OK, you guys! Here it is!" Ava called out. She flung back

the curtain of her fitting room and emerged in the purple dress. Cici had been right – it was Slutty Central. The slit showed off almost her entire leg.

"What do you guys think?" Ava asked, turning to admire herself in the mirror. "Isn't it insane?"

"It looks great," Carina said in a cheery monotone. "Get it."

The salesgirl looked from Ava to Carina. "Are you guys together?" she asked.

Carina tried to shake her head, but Ava interrupted her.

"Yeah, we're shopping for the Silver Snowflake Ball," she said. "I'm the chairperson. *She's* the party planner," she added, gesturing to Carina.

"Great!" the salesgirl said to Carina. "Then I have the *perfect* thing for you. Don't move!"

Ava turned to Carina with a disapproving glare. "She *knows* you?" she asked as the salesgirl rummaged through the racks.

"Not really," Carina whispered.

"OK, here we go," the salesgirl said, returning with an armful of clothes. "I grabbed a bunch of things that we just got in. Hope you don't mind."

As Carina watched, powerless to stop her, the salesgirl whisked open the curtain to the fitting room beside Ava's and laid all the dresses down on the small chair inside. "Let me know if you need any sizes!" she burbled.

Carina racked her brain trying to think of an excuse not to try anything on. But she couldn't come up with anything. "Uh, thanks," she finally said as she fled into the fitting room.

She flung the curtain closed and stood in the stall. She felt just the way she did that day at the Plaza when Roberta had stuck her with the bill – the same sense of panic laced with shame.

"How's it going in there?" the salesgirl asked on the other side of the curtain. "Can we see something?"

Carina looked down at the pile of dresses. She had to try on something. The one on top was a delicate silk ombré dress, which went from a milky white to mauve to lavender to a deep rich burgundy. Carina fingered the price tag. It was $1,400.

"Can we see something?" the salesgirl asked again.

"Hold on!" Carina yelled.

She pulled off her turtleneck and her kilt and stepped into the dress. She zipped it up, barely noticing that it fitted perfectly. "Looks OK!" she yelled back. She slid the curtain aside just an inch.

The salesgirl yanked the curtain open all the way and gasped. "That *kills*," she muttered, pulling Carina out of the room.

Ava and the Icks turned around. They looked her up and down. Despite their stony expressions, she could tell that they were impressed.

Carina looked over at the full-length mirror. The dress was stunning. She looked like some beautiful blonde TV actress on her way to a premiere. But it only made her panic more.

"You should get that," Ava managed to say.

"Really? I don't think it's me," Carina said.

"Are you *kidding*?" the salesgirl exclaimed. "It fits you like a glove. And it makes your butt look phenomenal. It comes in a halter style too, if you want to get both."

"That's OK," she said, edging her way back to the fitting room. "I don't think it's right for the dance…"

"Then get it for something else," Ava said. "You'll always wear it."

"No, I don't really like it," Carina said.

"And it's *soooo* reasonable," the salesgirl said. "I'm gonna bring it up to the till while you try on the others. Because you really ought to have it—"

"No!" Carina yelled, so loudly that it surprised even her.

The salesgirl jumped. Ava and the Icks flinched.

"I don't need this," she said. "I have tons of dresses already. And do you really think that fourteen hundred bucks is *reasonable*?"

Nobody said a word. Ava wrinkled her nose. Ilona's patented deathstare reached another level of iciness. Cici and Kate covered their mouths, as if they were on the verge of cracking up.

"That's *Chloé*," the salesgirl said, disapproval coating her voice.

"Well, whatever it is, it's out of my price range," Carina said. "I can't spend that kind of money. Not even for the party of the year."

She turned on her bare toes, walked back into the fitting

room and pulled the curtain closed. Her trembling hands went to the zip and yanked it down. As she stepped out of the dress, it was as if someone had finally taken something heavy off her shoulders and she could breathe again. She'd always known that she didn't care what those girls thought of her, but she'd never had the courage to really stand up to them. Now she finally had. She couldn't believe it. She'd told the truth.

When she walked out with the pile of dresses in her arms, the Icks were still in an ominous-looking huddle, Ava was nowhere to be seen and the salesgirl was eyeing her from the till with pursed lips.

"Here," Carina said to the salesgirl, laying the dresses on the counter. "And the next time I tell you I'm not looking, I'm really *not* looking."

A giggle made her turn around. Cici whispered something into Kate's ear. Kate giggled again, covering her mouth and then gave Carina a smug so-what? look. *Whatever*, Carina thought, mentally rolling her eyes. Let them make fun of her.

But it was Ilona who scared her. She pawed a rack of silk Stella McCartney tunics, but she wasn't looking at the clothes. She was looking at Carina. A half smile curled across her pouty lips, while her eyes gave off the impression of a hundred wheels turning inside her head. She was thinking of something – something that, as soon as Carina walked out of the store, would undoubtedly be said to Ava.

Ava walked out of the fitting room again, this time in a pale pink baby doll shift. Even though Carina was standing right in front of her, Ava didn't seem to see her.

"That looks good," Carina said, suddenly feeling a little bad, as if she'd ruined someone's party. "You should get that."

Ava drew herself up, put her hands on her hips and finally gave Carina a half-withering, half-furious look.

"Just don't forget the cupcakes," she sneered before she stomped back into the fitting room.

Chapter 25

Frosting, it turned out, was tricky. Carina dug her spatula into the jar of Duncan Hines chocolate and smoothed another layer on top of the yellow cupcake, trying to get it even in the centre and swirly around the edges. But it wasn't easy. Maybe because she was still furious with Ava. After three applications, the frosting was patchy in places, and overly thick in others, and it rose in uneven waves all around the edges. The girls behind the counter at Magnolia Bakery would probably be horrified, she thought, but maybe, just maybe, she could get away with it for the party.

Of course, she'd have to come up with another white lie for Ava. And after today's incident in Intermix, it would have to be a good one. The bakery couldn't be Sugarbabies – it would have to be some new, not yet opened place in SoHo, or better yet, a tony LA chain that catered to movie stars. What would it be called? Morsels? Frosties? And then she'd have to actually bake a few hundred cupcakes herself. Luckily, Duncan Hines was on sale this week at the Food Emporium. As soon as she mastered frosting, she'd stock up on cake mix (and maybe some food dye for the "red velvet" ones) and then her planning would finally be over. And at the end of it all, she'd have her money.

Her money, she thought. She brushed a stray piece of blonde hair away with her spatula handle and felt the same sinking feeling that arose whenever she thought about her payment. Why was she even doing this any more? Especially now that she'd met Alex?

Their magical night at the Killers concert three days ago had been on constant replay in her mind. She'd sent him a text the next day to thank him, but he hadn't responded. Now it was Monday night and she still hadn't heard anything from him. But she wasn't going to obsess over it, she reminded herself as she filled in a bare spot on her cupcake. She had dinner with her mom tonight to think about. Maybe she'd bring the best cupcake with her. Her mom had texted her that morning saying that she had made reservations for them tonight at Nobu, and she couldn't wait to have their rock shrimp tempura.

The kitchen door suddenly swung open. Instead of Nikita coming in to check that Carina wasn't setting the apartment on fire, in walked her father. She'd almost forgotten this was the day he was coming home from London.

"Carina, can I talk to you?" he asked. He was dressed in

his workout clothes and perspiration still beaded his unlined forehead.

"Sure," she said, placing her badly frosted cupcake down on the counter. "What?" Normally her dad never asked if he could speak to her. He just went ahead and started talking. This was interesting.

Her dad took out a bottle of water from the Sub-Zero fridge and frowned at the cupcakes. "First . . . what are you doing?" he asked.

"Oh, I'm planning a party. The Silver Snowflake Ball," she said, sitting up tentatively on the marble counter. "These are for the dessert." This was another first, she thought. Usually the Jurg was so distracted that he didn't even notice his surroundings.

Her father stared forlornly at the badly frosted cupcakes. "You're going to make them all yourself?"

"Well, we wanted to go with Sugarbabies, that place on the Lower East Side with the awesome red velvets, but they're a little pricey," she said. "So I'm going with Duncan Hines instead. It's almost just as good."

"I can't imagine it is," he said disdainfully. "When is this party?"

"The last day of school before Christmas break," she said. "The twentieth. Don't worry. Exams will be over by then."

The Jurg didn't pick up on her semi-snarky tone. Instead he rubbed his chin and went quiet. "I spoke to Barb Willis today," he said.

Carina sat straight up on the counter, gripping the marble edges. She'd almost managed to forget that embarrassing fight with her dad at the *Princess* offices. "Oh, really?" she said.

"We decided to cancel the story on you," he said, unscrewing the cap on his water bottle. "It was a mutual decision. I figured you'd be happy to hear it."

"Oh," she murmured, strangely disappointed.

"It wasn't your fault," he said. "The more I think about it, the more I realize that you were right. It probably wasn't a good idea." He took a sip of water. "They're going to find someone else. Someone more appropriate."

Carina had never seen him look this regretful before. She'd also never heard him say that she could be right about something.

"Barb also told me about your critique of the magazine."

Carina gripped the edge of the counter harder. She'd almost forgotten that, too.

"She loved what you said," he went on. "In fact, she's going to revamp the trend section based on your suggestions. And possibly redesign the logo. I'm not crazy about that logo, either. I always thought it was too pink. But what do I know about a magazine for teen girls?" He shrugged and took another sip. "She wants you to go back in there and meet with the entire editorial team. And be her new trend spotter, if you want to be."

"Are you serious?" she asked.

"You know, I was thinking," he said, smiling faintly, "*this* is what I should have had you working on to begin with. The teen titles. All this time I've got an expert in my house and I never even thought of it." He shook his head. "Would you ever consider coming back to work for me? Being my consultant on my teen properties?"

"Dad..." she started.

He nodded and held up his hand. "OK, OK. I'm not going to force you. I'm done with doing that, God knows. But I'm very impressed with you, Carina. I really am."

Carina blinked. Her father had never been impressed with her. Ever.

"So can I think about it?" she asked, putting the cap back on the frosting. "Doing the stuff for *Princess*?"

"Absolutely. And there's something else I want to discuss with you. What you said the other day about your mother."

She slid off the counter. With the tip of her finger she started to scrape off cooked cupcake from the sides of the baking pan. "We don't have to talk about that," she said.

"No, I think we do," he said. "I think it's time I cleared up a few things with you. Some things you don't know. Some things I wanted to spare you until you were older—"

"Then spare me," she blurted out, putting the cupcake pan in the sink. "We really don't have to talk about it."

She ran water noisily over the pan.

"Fine," her father said, getting to his feet. "Suit yourself. But if you don't want to know what really happened, then I'd keep the accusations to yourself." He glanced once more at the unappealling collection of cupcakes lined up on the counter. "If you need to bake you should at least have Nikita help you."

"OK."

"Are you going to this dance or are you just planning it?"

She crouched down to the ground with a paper towel and cleaned up some drops of frosting. "I don't know," she said breezily. "I'm not sure I really want to go."

The Jurg tossed his empty water bottle into the stainless steel recycle bin. "You should call Roberta. If you want I can get her on the phone right now. I'm sure she'd be happy to help you—"

"Dad, I've got it under control," she said. "But thanks."

Her dad nodded and looked down at the ground. "OK. See you later then," he said, and he walked through the swinging door.

She watched the kitchen door swing back and forth and listened to him walk up the steps. That's when she realized that her dad had finally tried to have a real conversation with her. And she hadn't let him.

When she got back up to her room, there was a voicemail waiting on her phone. From her mom's mobile.

"Hey sweetie, it's me! I'm running around getting some last-minute things for my trip ... And honey, I'm so, so, *so* sorry, but it turns out I'm leaving for India tonight. It was just easier that way. But I promise we'll get together on my way back. I'll text you from the ashram, K? I love you!"

Carina let the phone drop on to her bed. Now she wondered what it was that her dad had wanted to tell her.

247

Chapter 26

"*Bonjour*, Mademoiselle Jurgensen," said Madame Dupuis, as one pencil-drawn eyebrow rose sky-high on her forehead. "How nice of you to join us."

Carina rushed through the doorway of homeroom, pulling off her hat and slamming herself into the nearest empty desk.

"Sorry, overslept," she muttered. Oversleeping was a serious problem now that she had to take the subway to school. Unbuttoning her coat, she said a silent hi to Lizzie, Todd and Hudson across the room. Lizzie returned the wave and pointed to the seat next to her, but it was too far away to reach. At least Lizzie didn't seem to be mad at her for storming out of the diner at lunch the day before. As soon as homeroom was over she'd go and try to smooth things over. But now she had at least three more geometry problems she had to solve before maths class.

As she opened her book, a vague sense of dread came over her, and suddenly she remembered her nightmare.

She'd been ten years old again and crouched in front of her parents' bedroom door, listening to them fight. Her mother was crying and pleading with her dad to be decent. Her father was yelling that she'd lost her mind. And then someone – or something – began to claw at the door.

Somehow Carina knew that it was her mom. She grabbed the doorknob and tried to turn it, but it wouldn't budge. She tried and tried to open it, but the doorknob was locked in place, and her sweaty hands kept slipping, kept losing their hold on it…

She'd woken up with tears streaming down her face and her hair stuck to her forehead. Just a nightmare, she'd thought, but her throat burned and she knew that she was getting sick. The clock said seven fifty-five and the radio was chattering. Somehow she'd slept through her alarm. She leaped out of bed, splashed cold water on her face, and threw on her uniform. Five minutes later she was out of the door and running to the subway in the cold. But the terror of the nightmare had stayed with her until she'd got on the train.

Now as Madame Dupuis finished calling roll and Carina began last night's homework, she tried to shake off the icky morning feeling once and for all. But then behind her, she heard a familiar giggle. The hairs on her arms stood up. She knew that giggle. She'd know it anywhere.

Slowly, she turned around. Cici and Kate were sitting right

behind her. Without taking their eyes off her, Kate whispered into Cici's ear, and Cici cracked up again. Beside them Ilona kept staring at Carina with the same mocking half smile from yesterday. And on her other side, next to the blackboard, was Ava, calmly writing in her leather-covered notebook with her Tiffany pen. For a second, her brown eyes flicked up from her notebook and gave Carina a scathing glare. Carina whipped back around in her seat. Without even noticing, she'd sat down right in the middle of their territory. And now she was going to have to answer for what she'd done at Intermix. Clearly Ava and the Icks hadn't forgiven her for her little outburst.

When the bell finally rang, she stood up and gave Ava a radiant smile. "So did you get the purple dress?" she asked.

Ava barely looked at her as she closed her notebook. "Yep," she said tonelessly. "Thanks for your feedback."

"It looked great on you," Carina said, hoping she didn't sound too obvious. "The colour was perfect."

Ava gave her a thin smile. "I think it was better than going to Forever 21, don't you think?"

Carina paused. "Yeah," she said, unsure what to say.

"So … what happened with the cupcakes?" Ava asked, tossing her purse over her shoulder. "Did you talk to Sugarbabies?"

Carina hadn't expected Ava to launch into party talk. "Ye-es," she fibbed, "but I decided to go with someone else. They didn't think they could do that number of people. I guess they're really booked up this time of year."

250

"Well, that's funny," Ava said, gesturing for the Icks to go on ahead. "I called Sugarbabies first thing this morning and they knew nothing about it. They said they never even heard from you."

Carina followed Ava to the door, starting to panic. She scrunched her wool hat in her hands. *Be confident,* she thought. "Well, I *called* them," she said. "But maybe they didn't remember because I never ended up placing an order."

Lizzie and Hudson gave her do-you-need-us? looks but Carina nodded for them to keep going.

"Hmmm," Ava said in an exaggerated way. "Are you sure? The manager said that *none* of the clerks there took a phone call about this. He said he'd remember a call about the Silver Snowflake Ball. Unless he's lying, of course."

Carina stepped into the hall. Ava's saucer-shaped eyes were locked on hers and burning their way past her skin. "Well, I don't really know what to say. I definitely spoke to them. But I decided to—"

"Go with someone else," Ava cut in. "And who was that?" She cocked her head and waited.

She knows I'm lying, Carina thought. *She totally knows.* "I have to look in my notes."

"You don't remember?" Ava asked, almost smiling. "That's weird. Where'd you hear about them?"

Carina bit her bottom lip. She felt like she was on the witness stand. "Just through word of mouth."

"Right. Like that restaurant in the West Village. The

one that's 'under-the-radar'," she said sarcastically, hooking her fingers around the phrase. "By the way, I really need the contact info for that place. Just to make sure we're all on track for the food. Or have you forgotten what that's called, too? Oh, wait!" Ava batted her eyes. "It doesn't have a name, does it? How convenient."

Ava's tone cut right through her. "Um, I'm gonna have to get back to you," Carina said, her heart beating faster. "I can't really remember right now."

"And you know this DJ you keep telling me about?" Ava said, starting to play with her diamond necklace. "Alex Suarez? I called the Chateau Marmont and they've never heard of him."

Carina's stomach dropped. She'd forgotten all about that little white lie. "Huh, that's weird. I mean, he told me that's where he was."

Ava's expression turned stony. "Right," she said thickly. "Are you just making all this stuff up?"

"Of course not," Carina said. "That's crazy."

"Then what exactly have you done for this party?" Ava demanded. "Anything?"

"Of course," she stammered. "I've done tonnes of stuff."

"Yeah, like what? I don't have names, I don't have phone numbers. All I've seen are a couple of mini quesadillas and God only knows where those came from," she said. "You want to know what I think? I think you've done *nothing*. I think you've been lying this entire time."

Carina felt a flicker of rage in her gut. Ava could accuse her of lying, but she couldn't accuse her of not doing anything for her stupid event.

"OK, I've had to deviate a little from the plan," she admitted. "Because – news flash: *nobody* likes to work for free. Not even for the Silver Snowflake Ball."

Ava narrowed her eyes. "You said they were all your friends."

"They weren't my friends. They're people my *dad* has *hired*. And they don't work for free."

"Not even when he asks them to?" Ava asked, folding her arms.

"He didn't ask them to."

"Why not?"

"Because I didn't tell him about it."

Ava shook her head. "Well, that was stupid," she sneered. "Why *didn't* you?"

"Because I wanted to do this myself," Carina answered.

Ava snorted. "That's the dumbest thing I've ever heard. You're Karl Jurgensen's daughter."

"So *what*? Does that mean that I'm rolling in money and that I have Matty Banks on speed dial? That I can just snap my fingers and get Filippo Mucci to cater my party for free? That I can ask for someone to donate five hundred orchids just because it's a good cause?" Carina almost shouted. "I don't have a gazillion dollars. I've got nothing, OK? *Nothing.*"

Ava took a step back from her in the hall.

"You want to see my phone?" Carina went on. "Here." She pulled out her mobile and flipped it open. "My dad cut me off and now I have zilch – no money, no pull, nothing. No help. Not even for your stupid dance."

Ava's shiny mouth opened a little in shock.

"And I *did* plan everything," she went on. "I have food, I have decorations, I have a DJ. It was still gonna be a great party. I just couldn't get the people you wanted me to. I thought I could, but I couldn't."

"Look, I don't need to know the gory details of your personal life," Ava said, holding up her hand. "I have a party to throw in two weeks. So where *did* you get that food?"

Carina looked past her at a row of lockers. "Trader Joe's," she said quietly.

Ava recoiled. "What? And the DJ?"

"He's this guy who goes to Stuyvesant," she answered.

Ava's nostrils flared. "And the florist?"

"That was his sister. But she's this amazing artist—"

"And the cupcakes?" Ava asked, her voice starting to get wavery.

Carina paused. "Those I was probably going to do myself," she confessed. "But this event was going to be incredible. Really, if you'd just trust me—"

"Trust you? I didn't hire Carina Jurgensen to slum it, OK? You're a total fake. And a liar."

"I didn't lie to you. You assumed stuff about me," Carina argued.

"Uh, no, you *wanted* me to think all those things," Ava said, pointing a finger at her. "That day in the coffee shop, you totally bragged about how good you were at this and how connected you were. So don't try to pin this on me. You've *always* worked your dad around here. To get guys, to get invitations to things... So please. You can't have it both ways. You can't let people think something and then be upset when they do."

Someone behind them slammed a locker. The hallway was empty now. They needed to get to class, but Carina couldn't move.

Ava gripped the strap of her Kooba bag. "You're fired. And I want that two hundred dollars back ASAP."

"What?" Carina sputtered. "But ... but I don't have it."

Ava glared at her. "That's *so* not my problem."

Before Carina could say anything, Ava pushed past her, around the corner and out of sight, as the heels of her ankle boots clip-clopped down the hall.

"Ava!" Carina yelled.

Just then the tall, bony frame of Mr Barlow appeared in the doorway of his office. "Don't you have class, Carina?" he asked in his Marine-style baritone. "Or are you just visiting today?"

"Sorry," she said, hitching her bag up her shoulder and taking off in a run towards world history.

Once she got to class, she found Lizzie and Hudson sitting close to the door. She claimed the empty seat next to them just as the bell rang.

"What was all that about?" Hudson whispered. "We wanted to go over to you guys but it looked a little intense."

Carina pulled out her textbook and her binder, trying to figure out the best way to spin this. She was still shaking. And she still hadn't spoken to Lizzie since their mini fight in the diner the day before.

"I had to tell her the truth," she said. "That I couldn't get the people she wanted."

"And she flipped out," Lizzie guessed.

"Well, yeah," Carina said. "She fired me."

Up at the front of the room, Mr Weatherly started writing on the board about ancient Sumer and the room got quieter.

Hudson put her hand on Carina's wrist. "Does this mean I still have to sing?" she asked.

Carina gave Hudson a look. "Yes. And I need to get back that two hundred dollars," she said. "You know, what I paid for Carter's lift ticket."

"How are you gonna do *that*?" asked Lizzie.

"I don't know." A headache pulsed behind her forehead and she remembered that she'd left the house without breakfast. "It's completely unfair, though. I worked really hard. I did stuff. And this party was gonna be incredible. And she says I *lied* to her. Can you believe that? That I lied?"

"You kind of did," Lizzie said, turning to the board.

"No, I didn't."

"You weren't honest with her," Lizzie pointed out. "Same thing."

256

"Don't talk to *me* about honesty," Carina muttered.

"If you're talking about the Todd thing, I apologized," said Lizzie. "It's not like I did it on purpose."

"So what?" Carina asked. "You still did it."

"You guys, *chill*," Hudson said, waving her hand in between them.

"What are you so mad about?" Lizzie asked. "I feel like you've had something against him since the start."

"And I feel like you've been totally unsupportive of me this whole time," Carina shot back. "It's like I'm always being judged or something. Do you even remember how I was about your modelling stuff with Andrea? I never judged you. Not ever."

"You guys, *stop it*," Hudson whispered.

Mr Weatherly looked over at them from the board. "Ladies? Would one of you like to come up here and explain the difference between the Ubaid and the Uruk period?"

They all looked down at their desks, mute.

Carina dug her pen into her notebook, furious. She hadn't had a fight with either Lizzie or Hudson since sixth grade, and that had been over which one of them she'd accompany to the Chadwick Mother-Daughter Tea. Now the disapproval in Lizzie's voice threatened to send her into a tailspin. There had to be someone out there who wouldn't judge her for this.

As soon as class was over, she pulled out her phone and typed out a text.

Need to c u. U free after school?

Alex wrote her right back.

Kim's Video. After 4. See you soon.

She flipped her phone closed. Alex would help her figure out what to do. True, she'd have to tell him that his DJ job was no longer happening, but he'd understand. She knew he would.

Carina searched the hallway for her friends. They'd walked up ahead, leaving her by herself. She couldn't remember a time they'd done that, or a time when she'd felt so alone.

She started up the hall by herself. All she had to do was make it to four o'clock.

Chapter 27

A thick snow was falling when Carina walked up from the Astor Place subway station into the East Village. The few other times she'd been here it had been late summer and early fall, when the rank smell of garbage mingled with the smell of incense from street vendors, and the pavements were jammed with shoppers and tourists. Now it seemed quiet and almost romantic, as people hurried past the tattoo parlours and coffee shops under the gently blowing snow.

Her stomach ached with hunger and her legs felt filled with sand as she trudged down St Marks Place. It had been one of the longest days of her life. After their whispered argument in history, she and Lizzie hadn't spoken for the rest of the day. Hudson had done her best to stay in the middle, trying to talk to both of them, but it was way too awkward. Finally, at lunch, Hudson and Lizzie had gone to get pizza, and Carina, terrified of running into Ava, had gone back to the janitor's closet, where she'd eaten her tuna sandwich standing straight up next to a collection of mops.

But now Alex was going to cheer her up. She knew that Kim's Video was supposed to be the coolest place to find underground art movies and bootleg albums, but she'd never set foot in the place. As she turned on to First Avenue, butterflies swam up from her stomach. She couldn't wait to see Alex again.

She pushed open the door and stepped into an overheated store crammed with shelves of videos and DVDs.

"I'm sorry," somebody said. "But I don't think we have anything with Matthew McConaughey here."

She turned to see Alex leaning against the graffiti-scarred counter. He had earbuds in his ears and an open comic book in his hand.

"Hey," she said, striding up to the counter. "Nice store. Don't you think you could spend some time organizing?" she said, looking around at the millions of movies.

"Nah, we have a secret system," he said. "You tell me what you're looking for and then I hunt around for it for hours," he said, smiling at her with his soft brown eyes. "Actually, I've already picked something out for you. One of my favourites." He walked out from behind the counter in his Stan Smiths and pulled a box off the shelf and gave it to her. "You're hereby ordered to love it."

"What is this?" she asked, looking at the Chinese writing on the box.

"*In the Mood for Love*," he said. "By Wong Kar-Wai. He's a genius."

"Is it in English?"

"Cantonese. With English subtitles," he said, pressing it on her. "It's beautiful. It reminds me of you."

The memory of his lips on hers flooded back to her as she looked at him. "Thanks," she said. "It's really good to see you."

"You, too," he said. He walked back to the counter and leaned towards her on his elbows. "Oh, hey, I found this incredible remix by Mastercraft the other day. I'm totally playing it at the dance. Here. Listen." He reached for the record turntable and CD player on the shelf above him.

She watched, slightly cringing as he placed a record on the turntable and dropped the needle. Driving technobeats filled the store. "Isn't that cool?" he yelled over the sound. "I think I'll put this on first."

"Alex?" She still didn't know how to tell him, but she knew she had to as soon as possible. "I need to tell you something."

He turned the volume down just a little. "Yeah, what?" he asked, his head bobbing. "Isn't that great?"

She swallowed past the lump in her throat as she stepped closer to the counter. "The DJ job isn't happening any more."

Alex turned to her. "What?" he asked. "Did they cancel the dance?"

"No. I had kind of a fight with that girl today. The one in

charge. The one who wanted me to get all those fancy people for her."

Alex reached up and turned the knob to lower the volume even more. "Fight about what?" he asked seriously.

"Well, I never really told her that I was going to do things differently. And then when I told her what I'd done she got a little mad."

Alex shook his head. "So she thought Matty Banks was still DJing?"

"No, she knew it was you, but…" She wondered if there was a space under the counter for her to hide. "I told her you were in your twenties and you played Mary-Kate Olsen's birthday party."

Alex blinked. "*What?*"

"I knew she wouldn't go for someone who was our age and went to Stuyvesant, so I had to fib a little," she said. "I didn't think it'd be that big a deal."

"What else didn't you tell her?" he asked, perfectly still.

"That the food was from Trader Joe's. And that your sister was gonna do the decorations. And that I was gonna bake three hundred Duncan Hines cupcakes." Her face burned as she looked down at her feet. "But she totally flipped out on me. She said that she wouldn't have hired me if she knew that we were going to have to 'slum it'. That I lied to her. And then she fired me."

Alex leaned against the wall. His eyes looked dark. "So I was included in her idea of 'slumming it'?"

"No, it wasn't like that," she said desperately. "She's just a snob anyway."

"Who you still wanted to impress," Alex said. "Why couldn't you just tell her the truth?"

Carina kicked at the counter with her toe. *Because I couldn't tell her that I wasn't the person she thought,* she wanted to say. "I told you what my situation was. How this girl just assumed stuff about me because of my dad. And then expected me to follow through. I *had* to lie."

"Right," he said. "Don't give me that, Carina."

"You don't know how my school operates, OK? Or what people are like there. What they *think*. What they think of *me*. Do you think I can tell them that I can barely take a cab right now?"

Alex shook his head. "Sounds like you were just afraid this girl wasn't gonna like you or something."

"No, there's a little more to it than that." She turned the DVD over and over in her hand. "She was paying me."

"You were getting *paid* for this?" he exclaimed. "And the rest of us had to do stuff for free?"

"Alex." Of course she shouldn't have told him that she was getting paid. Now she looked like a coward and a hypocrite.

"OK, I'm done feeling sorry for you," he said. "I assume my sister can't go to the dance, either, right? Were you ever gonna get her a ticket? Or did you just want to make sure she gave you her artwork to use?"

Carina realized that she'd completely forgotten about Marisol. "Alex, I'll make it up to you both, I promise—"

"Do you have any idea how excited she was to go to that stupid dance?" he asked. "She's made three outfits for it already. And now I have to tell her that she never had a ticket in the first place?"

"Alex, please," she pleaded. "Don't be so mad at me, OK?"

"Why shouldn't I be?" Alex said. "I really like you."

"You do?" she said. "I haven't heard from you since the Killers concert. That was practically five days ago. What's up with that?"

Now it was time for him to avoid her eyes as he fiddled with his iPod. "Every time I thought about that night, I'd remember who your dad is," he said softly. "And how I'll never, ever be the kind of guy he'd want you to be with." He looked away, curling and uncurling his fist. "But then I realized that *I'm* the one with the problem. That all of that stuff shouldn't matter to me. Because it doesn't matter to *you*." As he looked back at her, the hurt and disappointment beamed out from his eyes. "Except obviously it does."

"Alex." She moved towards him but he stepped back behind the counter. "Please. You're the coolest, most interesting person I've ever met. I can't handle it if you're mad at me."

He just looked at the door. Through the dirty glass the snow blew in thick white sheets down the street. "I think you should probably go," he said quietly.

He looked down at his comic book and paged through it. It

was obvious that he didn't even want to look at her any more. There had to be something she could say or do. But from the way he was studying his comic, she knew that she'd missed her chance.

She laid the DVD down on the counter. "You can keep this," she muttered, and then she blew through the door.

Chapter 28

Snow drifted into Carina's face as she walked uptown. It wet her eyelashes and the tips of her ears and melted instantly on her cheeks. It was the first serious snowstorm of the year, and already a thick layer of white covered the pavements and the tops of mailboxes and the pointy spires of Grace Church. Normally she loved the first snow in the city, when traffic slowed down and sirens got quieter, and the whole city seemed to go on mute. But tonight she didn't notice. As she trudged up a deserted Broadway, Alex's hurt, angry voice rang in her head like a car alarm.

In one day, she'd lost everything. The job. Alex. Her reputation. The money. And maybe even Lizzie.

Lizzie. She stopped at the corner, where snow was silently filling up a metal garbage can. Only Lizzie could bring her back to herself right now. Only Lizzie could assure her that her life wasn't completely over. She had to talk to her. Now.

She dialled Lizzie's number. The phone was freezing against her ear. *Pick up,* she thought. Please *pick up*.

It rang twice, three times, four times, and then went to voicemail. She hung up. If Lizzie couldn't get to her phone, she usually sent calls right to voicemail so that it didn't even ring. The fact that she'd let it ring four times meant that she didn't want to speak to her. That she wasn't picking up on purpose. Carina had never felt this alone. Not ever.

By the time she got off the subway at Fifty-ninth Street, she was damp and chilled. She pushed past some Christmas shoppers on the platform and sprinted up the steps. She couldn't wait to get into a hot bath, climb into bed and forget this day.

But as soon as she walked in her front door, she saw the coat-rack set up in the hallway and the waiters scurrying in and out of the kitchen with drinks on trays, and the extra security men standing with Otto at his desk, monitoring the tiny television screens with stony expressions. *Great,* she thought. It was her dad's holiday cocktail party.

Her dad's holiday parties weren't really her scene. It was always a mix of the same groups: the Money (usually men in dark blue three-piece suits), the Models (stick-thin, bobble-headed women with sharp, alien-like features and long, slick ponytails), and the Media (more average-looking men and women in fancy clothes and bad haircuts, staring with envy

267

at the Money and the Models). She'd walked around these things before, usually with a glass of eggnog and either Lizzie or Hudson in tow, but tonight it was the last thing she felt like doing. She was almost at the stairs when she heard a woman shriek with amped-up laughter. She looked over and there was her father in the middle of a crowd of people. He stopped talking when he saw her.

"Carina? Are you OK?" He walked towards her, stopped short, and took in her dishevelled appearance. "You're soaked."

"I got caught in the snow," she said.

"Come with me," he said sternly. "We need to get you dried off." He put his hands on her shoulders and steered her to the kitchen.

"Dad, this isn't *ER* or anything, I'm fine," she said.

"You look like something out of a Dickens novel," he muttered. "Come on."

The shrieking woman, who had small eyes and a blonde pageboy, pulled him aside. "Karl, about the *Vanity Fair* piece, I think the best thing to do is speak to Graydon directly—"

"Be right back, Elise," he said gruffly, and kept going. Carina made a mental note. She'd never seen him blow off one of his party guests like that before. Especially for her.

When they walked into the kitchen, white-suited cater waiters were moving gracefully around the room, refilling their trays.

"Marco?" her dad yelled out. "Can we get some towels here,

268

and some hot chicken soup?" He helped her off with her coat and her gloves, pulled off a bunch of paper towels and dried her hair. "Here, sit down," he said, leading her to the kitchen table. "And Marco? That soup? We're waiting!"

Marco ran over with a steaming bowl of chicken noodle soup and a stack of towels. Where he'd got it so quickly, she had no idea.

"Did something happen to you today?" he asked, taking a towel to her hair as she wiped her nose with a napkin.

"No, I'm fine," she said, picking up her spoon. She sneezed loudly.

"Did something happen at school?" he asked. "You get in a fight with someone?"

"No." She sneezed again. "Well ... yeah. Maybe."

"What happened?" He finished drying her hair and covered her hand with his own.

Suddenly she felt tears come to her eyes. It was the first nice thing anyone had done for her all day. And the fact that it was coming from him, the last person on earth she expected to be nice to her, was overwhelming.

"Carina?" he asked, even more gently. "What happened today?"

The inside of her throat burned and she felt that tingling in the tip of her nose. But she refused to cry in front of him. Just out of habit.

"I got fired," she said.

"Fired?" he repeated. "From what?"

269

"Remember how I said I was planning that party? The Silver Snowflake Ball?"

Her dad nodded.

"Well, I got in a fight with the girl in charge. Ava Elting. And she fired me."

"Why?" he asked. "On what grounds?"

"Misrepresentation of services, I guess."

Her father let her go and tilted his chair so that he faced her. "OK, tell me everything. Just start from the beginning."

Carina wiped her nose with the back of her hand. "Well, it all started with this guy," she said, cringing a little. She'd never talked about her love life with her dad. But there was no way around it now. "This guy, Carter McLean. He asked me to go on this snowboarding trip with him and some friends, to the Alps."

"The *Alps*?" her dad repeated.

"Yeah, his uncle has a place there. And I said I would go."

"You did, huh?" he said wryly.

"Anyway, it was free except for the airfare and the lift ticket and food," she went on. "Which I figured would cost about a thousand dollars." She put her hands in her lap and took a deep breath. "Which, obviously, I don't have."

"Yes," he said, more seriously.

"So I decided to get a job, but I couldn't find one, and then this girl, Ava, said she needed a party planner, someone to take care of all the details for this Christmas ball that's ultra-fancy and totally a big deal and all that. And I said I could do it. And she really wanted me to do it."

"Why did she want you to do it when you don't have any experience with party planning?" he asked.

"Because…" She sighed. "Because I'm your daughter. And she figured that I could get her Matty Banks and Filippo Mucci and the fanciest flowers. And I let her think that. But she wanted me to get them for free. As *favours*. But nobody wanted to do me a favour. Everybody wants to get paid."

Her father gave a rueful smile. "Yes, they do."

"So, I had to kind of…improvise." She gulped. "I found this guy who's an incredible DJ, but he's my age and just starting out. And this guy's sister was going to do the table decorations. And then I got these awesome appetizers from Trader Joe's – that she loved. And I was going to bake the cupcakes myself. I was going to do the whole thing for practically nothing."

"But you didn't tell this girl that," he prompted.

"No. I couldn't. She wouldn't have gone for it. Not at all. She wants this party to be in the Style section."

Her father frowned slightly. "So she found out?"

She nodded. "Yeah. And she fired me."

"But how could she fire you? This wasn't a real job."

She hung her head and picked at her napkin. "She was going to pay me a thousand dollars."

"A thousand dollars?" he said in disbelief.

"So I could go on this stupid trip. Dad, I did the work," she argued. "I planned the party. I did everything she asked me to. I just didn't want to tell her that I had to 'slum it'. To use her words."

"First of all, you didn't slum it. But why couldn't you just be honest with her?"

Carina shredded the napkin between her fingers. "Because if I told her that I couldn't get these people, she would have expected me to ask you to do it for me. And I wasn't going to do that. Not with, you know, what's been going on," she said delicately. "So it was easier to just pretend I could do it. People expect me to be a certain way. They think of me a certain way. You know that. That's why you wanted me to do that interview, remember?"

The Jurg rubbed his chin and looked away.

"I'm not gonna tell this girl that I'm walking around with a mobile from ten years ago. Well, I finally did, actually," she pointed out. "But I'm fine with it. I really am. I've changed. I'm a different person now. But I just couldn't be that different person in *front* of people yet."

She sniffled one last time and nudged at some noodles and carrots with her spoon. "Sometimes the way people see you is the way you see yourself," she said.

Her dad stayed quiet beside her. She thought she could feel his disappointment getting stronger every second.

"I'm proud of you," he said at last. "You *have* changed. You have." He squeezed her shoulder. "Now let's just fix some of this mess." He reached into his jacket and pulled out his BlackBerry Pearl. "Who did you say she wanted? Matty and who else?"

She put her hand on his arm. "Dad, don't. It's too late anyway."

He put the BlackBerry to his ear. "I'm sure Matty'd be happy to do it. What was the date again?"

Carina yanked his hand down. "Dad, *stop*."

Slowly, he put his hand down and hung up.

"It's done," she said. "*I* messed things up. And now *I* have to live with it."

"Carina, I'm just trying to help you," her father said.

"No, you can't," she said. "This is *my* problem. Not yours. And not even you can swoop in and save people every time."

She pushed her chair away and stood up. She was so tired. She really needed to lie down. And her head was starting to get woozy.

"Well, what happened with that guy?" he asked.

"Which guy?" she asked.

"That Carter fellow."

"Oh. *Nothing*," she said. "That's totally over. And for the future ... can we just pretend I never told you about him? Or any guy?"

Her dad nodded. "Fine with me. Now go get some rest." He stood up, and for a moment she thought they might actually hug, but instead they walked to the door.

When she got up to her room, she collapsed on her bed and pressed her face into the pillow. Her head was pounding and her forehead felt hot. She could feel herself starting to get sick. Really sick. But as she drifted off, something inside of her knew that from now on, she was going to be OK.

Chapter 29

B-rrring!

At the sound of the bell, Carina put down her pen and pushed her blue book away. The world history final had been easier than she'd expected, but it was still a relief for exams to be over. Now she just had to get through one more day of school until Christmas break began. She couldn't wait. Ever since the day of the snowstorm, she felt like she'd been trapped in a bad dream. Two weeks in total winter break seclusion was just what she needed.

Her pounding headache and fever the night of her dad's holiday party blossomed into a flu the next morning, and for five days she lay in bed, stuffed up and miserable and watching *Oprah*. In a rare display of parental concern, her dad came and sat by her bed and even took her temperature a couple of times. Hudson visited her almost every day, bringing

Carina's favourite s'mores-flavoured Luna Bars and even some vanilla cupcakes with chocolate icing from Magnolia Bakery. Thankfully, she seemed to have forgiven Carina for putting her on the spot with Ava.

But Lizzie stayed away. She just sent get-well texts and emails. Their fight that last day in class had left its mark and Carina knew that she'd have to smooth things over with her in person as soon as possible.

And, of course, there was no word from Alex. She'd finally broken down and called him – twice – but her voicemails had gone unanswered. It was clear that he hated her guts.

And he wasn't the only one. When she returned to school for the start of exams, the Icks were the first people she saw, standing in a vicious cluster near the bulletin board in the Upper School hall. The hate vibes that they beamed in her direction could have felled a large animal. Every morning in the lounge before exams, Ava iced her completely, keeping her back to her as she studied. Carina wondered how the party was coming along but didn't dare ask. She still had no idea how to pay Ava back and figured the better move was just to stay away. But something told her that the party was in trouble. Ava had been so incredibly clueless about how to do anything practical. She couldn't imagine that she'd got everything together on such short notice. But then again, Carina told herself, why did she care if Ava failed? She was a snob and a jerk. Maybe a completely screwed-up event was what Ava deserved.

She stood up, stretched, and dropped her blue book off on

Mr Weatherley's desk before following the stream of people into the hall. Carter McLean sailed right past her, not meeting her eyes, for the third time that week. She wasn't sure, but she could only assume that Ava had shared the "gory details" about her personal life with everyone in the school. She didn't even care. If people wanted to treat her like a pariah, then that was their problem.

Down the hall, she saw Lizzie and Hudson walking with Todd. She felt a stab of loneliness. How had things got this weird between all of them? All week she'd felt like it was two against one. She needed to finally get up the guts to go to Lizzie, pull her aside and somehow repair things. She was just about to talk to them when Hudson craned her head around, waved at her and fell out of step to come walk by her side.

"Hey, can I talk to you?" Hudson asked breathlessly. Even during this past week of finals, Hudson had managed to look polished and put together, but today she had dark circles under her eyes and she was dressed in hole-ridden jeans and a simple black sweater. She pulled Carina against the wall, out of the stream of people. "So I did my rehearsal last night for the dance and they are in *trouble*."

"What do you mean?"

"Ava had to dump everything on the charity people at the last minute and they have no clue what they're doing," Hudson said, rolling her sea green eyes and shaking her head. "There's no food, no decorations and the DJ's probably the lamest person on earth. I saw his playlist lying around on the stage. The first song's 'Sweet Caroline'."

"Yikes," she said, feeling a tiny bit gleeful about that last part.

"So. You have to do something. You have to fix this."

"Me?" she sputtered. "I got *fired*, remember? And if I get one more deathstare from Ava's minions, I'm going to keel over from hate vibes."

Hudson tugged Carina closer. "Once people see what a disaster this is, they're all gonna leave and I don't want my debut to be to an empty room, OK? I'm stressed out about this enough as it is."

From the wild look in her eye and the colour in her cheeks, Carina believed her.

"I totally would, but Ava wants me to pay her back and I can't. Plus, she didn't like any of the things I was gonna do anyway. Why would she this time around?"

"Just get that DJ back," Hudson pressed. "She'll be thrilled to get him after the guy they got. Believe me."

"He's not speaking to me," she admitted.

Hudson folded her arms and gave Carina a long, thoughtful look. "Then this gives you the perfect reason to make up with him. Just try, C. We need you."

Carina thought about this. Maybe Hudson was right. Carina had almost certainly blown any chance of a romance between them, but she couldn't stand to think that someone out there as cool as Alex Suarez disliked her so much. At least if she went to see him today, and apologized up and down, and pleaded with him to do the dance, then she would have done everything she could to get him to see that she wasn't a terrible human being. Hopefully.

"C? You still with me?" Hudson asked, twisting a strand of black hair between her fingers.

"Fine," she sighed. "I'll do it. But if it's terrible and he hates me and I completely humiliate myself, it's all your fault."

"No, then we'll be even for you forcing me to do this show," Hudson said. "Oh, come on. You're *Carina*. He's gonna flip when you walk in that door."

"Thanks, H," she said, giving her friend a hug. Carina highly doubted that Hudson was right, but it felt nice to hear it anyway.

They reached the stairs and saw Ava, dressed in her final exam outfit of leather trousers and cashmere sweater coat, chatting with Ken Clayman and Eli Blackman. Hudson nudged her forward.

"Just go talk to her now," she whispered. "Come on. Get it over with."

"What am I supposed to say again?" Carina asked.

"That you can fix things," Hudson said. "Come on, C. You can do this."

Carina wasn't sure any more what she could do, but the old part of her – the part that could never resist a dare – flared up again. With a toss of her shoulder-length hair, she sauntered over to Ava and her crew.

"Hey, Ava, can I talk to you for a sec?"

Ava turned around and studied her with extreme distaste, as if she were a life-size roach. "Yeah?" she asked.

"I just wanted to ask how the dance is going."

Ava stepped away from the guys. "Great," she chirped, showing her bright white teeth. "We're all set for tomorrow night. It's gonna be awesome." She cleared her throat. "Just awesome."

Carina wasn't sure, but the way she repeated this sounded more like she was trying to convince herself.

"Cool," Carina said. "Well, I just wanted to say how sorry I am that everything worked out the way it did."

Ava stared at her, fingering her diamond A. "Me too," she said sulkily.

"And I'm sure you already have everything set, but if I can get that DJ to play for you guys tomorrow night, I'd be happy to do it," she went on. "He really is very talented. And I'd hate for you guys to miss out on him."

Ava was quiet for a few moments as she turned the A backwards and forwards in her hand. "Do you think you could get him?" she finally asked.

"I think so. I know he was really into playing the event."

Ava flicked a wayward curl off her face. "Well, we already have someone amazing," she said haughtily, "but it would be interesting to know if he was still available. Just so we have some options. That's all."

Yep, she's really desperate, Carina thought.

"No problem," Carina said. "And how are you guys doing on decorations? And food?"

Ava looked down and swallowed. "We're OK," she muttered. "Where'd you get that food again?"

"How about this?" Carina asked. "What if I just pick up where I left off and finish the job? The food, the music, the decorations. I really want this event to be as cool as it was supposed to be. And obviously you won't have to pay me a cent."

Ava put her hands on her hips. "What about that two hundred dollars you still owe me?"

Carina bit her lip. "I'm still working on that. And I promise I'll get it to you. But for now, just let me get back to work." She pulled her hair back from her face with her hands. "That sound OK?"

Her hands still on her hips, Ava tapped her foot. "Fine. You're rehired. But think of this as more of an unpaid internship." She belted her sweater coat and headed towards the stairs. "And don't forget those pastry bites. Those were awesome."

"I won't."

Ava walked into the stairwell and Carina could swear that she heard her sing a little under her breath as she clip-clopped down the steps.

Hudson reappeared by her side. "I watched the whole thing," she said. "Looks like it went well."

"You were right," Carina said. "It sounds like the dance was gonna be a disaster."

"Whatever you do, get that DJ," Hudson said as they walked into the stairwell. "If my first show is to an empty room, my mom's gonna kill me."

Chapter 30

At seven-thirty Carina climbed up out of the subway station and found herself back on the same bleak stretch of East Broadway she'd seen a month before. It looked even shabbier tonight, with nary a Christmas decoration in sight and an icy wind blowing in off the East River. She couldn't remember how to find the entrance to Club Neshka, but when she saw the sad, blinking neon sign that read JOLLY CHAN's she remembered the secret door. *Please, God, let him at least smile when he sees me,* she thought as she crossed the street. *Or at least not be mad.*

She pulled open the heavy iron door and walked into the club. Unlike the last time she'd been here, it was almost empty. Without a sea of hipsters blocking the entrance she only had to wait a few seconds to adjust to the darkness and the twinkle of blue and white Christmas lights before she saw Alex, standing behind his turntables and nodding to the beat as he held a headphone up to one ear. *It's not about me, it's about the party,* she thought as she took a deep breath and headed over to him. Still, the lump in her throat was so big she was afraid she wouldn't be able to speak.

"Hey," she asked as she came to stand in front of him. "You take requests?"

His big brown eyes lit up just for a moment and then turned cold. "Hey," he said, lowering his headphone. "What are you doing here?"

"Saying hi in person. Since it doesn't seem to work over the phone."

Alex fidgeted with his headphones. "I've just been really busy. What do you want?"

"Your help," she said, deciding to cut right to the point. "The dance is going to be a complete disaster. Ava's had the charity people plan it themselves and the DJ they got thinks Neil Diamond is hip. They need you. Desperately. Can you still do it?"

Alex blinked. "It's tomorrow night, Carina. And the last day of school before break. I have plans."

"He's playing 'Sweet Caroline' as the first song," she countered. "This is serious."

"And why should I care?" he asked as he pulled a Donna Summer album out of the milk crate.

"Look, I know you're mad at me," she said, stepping behind the turntables. "And I don't blame you. I was wrong. I screwed up. And I was a total coward on top of it. But now everyone at school knows I'm not who they thought. And I couldn't care less."

Alex looked up at her. "You don't?"

"You were right. It was lame of me not to come clean to Ava. I mean, the girl wears leather jeans. Why should I care what she thinks?"

Alex gave her a sceptical look.

"Look. I'm so sorry. I didn't mean to ruin everything. I really didn't. For you or Marisol. You're one of the coolest people I've ever met, Alex. You really are. But even if you don't want to be my friend again, please, please, *please* help us out. And if your sister can still loan us her artwork, that would be even better."

Alex dropped the needle on to Donna Summer. "Jeez. You really don't beat around the bush." He put down the album cover and looked right at her. "OK. I'll do it."

"You *will*?" she asked.

"Yeah." He shifted his weight from foot to foot. "I mean, what choice do I have? Neil Diamond?"

"Thank you," she said, clutching his arm. "Thank you *so much*. Really. You're the best."

Alex glanced down at her hand on his arm. She let him go. She had to be careful with him now.

"Well, I'm beat from exams," she said, feeling her stomach growl. "But I'll email you the details and then see you tomorrow night. And thank you. Again."

"You're welcome," he said evenly.

There was a pause as he looked at her in the dim light and he seemed about to say something more. But then he slid his headphones back over his head. "See you tomorrow night," he said.

She walked to the door, feeling a strange mixture of pride and sadness. She'd done it. Everything was back on track. But there was something even more awkward between her and Alex now. As if there were still things left to say. She shook off the feeling as she opened the door. They'd had their chance to start something. But she'd blown it and now she just had to get used to it.

Chapter 31

By the time she got home, she was so hungry she barely gave Otto a wave before making a beeline to the kitchen. She pushed through the swinging door, ready to devour the contents of the fridge, when she saw something that made her stop dead in her tracks.

There, elegantly placed on a cake stand, was a collection of the most beautiful cupcakes she'd ever seen in her life. Decadent-looking red velvet, chocolate with vanilla icing, carrot cake and more flavours than she could even begin to guess. She had no idea where they'd come from until she saw the pink box sitting just to the side of the espresso machine. *SUGARBABIES*, read the girly scroll lettering on top. Then she opened the fridge. Crammed on to every shelf were more pink boxes. There had to be three hundred cupcakes in their kitchen.

The door swung open and in walked Ed Bracken, wearing a charcoal double-breasted suit and a surprisingly genuine smile. "Hello, Carina." He nodded towards the open fridge. "So, what do you think?"

"Who ... who ordered these?" she asked.

"Your dad," he said. "Well, actually, my assistant. But your father must have reminded her about eight times."

She stared back at the pink boxes, momentarily speechless.

"He mentioned that you were trying to make some yourself, and there was no way he was going to let that happen." Ed smiled at her, and this time it wasn't a sneer. "I just brought them over. Your father loves you very much. I know you probably don't realize that."

"At least he shows it with cupcakes," she said, a little dazed. She let her bag fall to the floor. "I just don't get him sometimes. Does he confuse you as much as he confuses me?"

"Sometimes." Ed chuckled. "But I know more about him than you do. Things that would probably change your perception of him."

"Like what?" she asked. "How he runs a board meeting?"

He ran a hand over his vanishing hair. "No. Other things. Like what happened with your mother," Ed said carefully. "Those kinds of things. The things that make him a little more relatable, you could say."

Carina felt her skin start to get prickly. She didn't want to talk about her mother. But she was curious. And it bugged her that Ed was dangling information in front of her. "What sort of things?" she asked.

"Well, the fact that she broke his heart, for one thing," he said. "And he's never got over it."

"She broke his heart?" Carina almost laughed. "What? Are you kidding me?"

Ed just looked at her with his watery blue eyes.

"That's not true," she said. "He left *her*."

"Because she was in love with someone else," he said calmly. "She married your father for his money. He found out. That's why it ended." He looked straight at her, as if daring her to respond. "That's the whole story."

"That's a lie," she said heatedly. "My dad was the one who cheated on *her*. I know that for a fact. I was in this house. I heard them talking about it. She cried about it every night. You weren't here. Of course he would make up some story for you to make himself look better."

Ed shook his head somberly. "No, he never cheated on Mimi. Not once. He loved her too much. He didn't even want to end the marriage. But when he realized that she couldn't give this man up, he knew that he had to end things. He was too proud to go on like that. That was why *he* wanted to raise you," he said. "He didn't want you to grow up with the kind of values your mother had. Putting money ahead of everything else. He didn't want you to end up making the same choices she did."

Carina tried to grab hold of Ed's words and absorb them

288

but her head was spinning. It was too much to believe. Too much to accept.

But maybe, she thought, there was some truth in it. Why was it always so hard to reach her mom? And when she did, why was it so hard to have an actual conversation with her? Mimi would pick up the phone, but then she could never really talk for some reason. And when they would talk, they didn't *really* talk. Carina hadn't even wanted to tell her about being cut off. She knew that if she told her mom about it, she'd get nothing back, except for a lot of well-meaning words. It was as if her mom had let go of Carina after the divorce, little by little, first physically, and then mentally. Maybe if her mom hadn't felt guilty about something, she would have fought harder to keep her.

She picked up her bag and turned towards the door. "I think I need to go upstairs now," she said.

"Carina? Are you OK? Maybe I shouldn't have told you," he said.

"No, no. I'm just … tired. Goodbye, Ed," she muttered, feeling lost, and walked out of the room.

She climbed the stairs up to her room and lay down on her bed, curled up on her side. The space inside her head felt like a merry-go-round. She shut her eyes, trying to calm the spinning feeling, trying to listen to the sound of her breathing. But she couldn't. Every time she tried to clear her mind she went back to that night, the night she'd crouched in front of the closed door, listening to her parents fight.

Maybe if you actually had feelings, maybe if you could be a person for a few minutes, I wouldn't have to...

She squeezed her eyes shut. This whole time, maybe she'd been wrong. Maybe her mother had wandered through the apartment with bloodshot eyes and cried in her bathroom not because of her father's cruelty, but because she loved another man. Maybe she'd sacrificed love for security and then she'd regretted it. Maybe the end of her parents' marriage had been her mom's fault. And all this time, she'd never known.

She lay on her bed for a long time, thinking. Until there was a knock on her door.

"Carina?" said her father through the door. "Can I come in?"

She hoisted herself up. "Yeah!" she called out, trying to sound normal.

The door opened and her dad stood in the doorway. For a moment she thought back to that night just seven weeks ago, the night she'd posted that item online, when he'd burst through the door, out of breath and furious, his eyes like glittering dark coals. Now his eyes were gentle, his face soft and when he got to the side of the bed he knelt on the floor beside it.

"Ed told me he had a conversation with you," he said stiffly. "I thought I should come in and try to discuss some of it with you."

"Why didn't you tell me?"

"I've tried," he said gently. "So many times. That day in the kitchen, but you didn't want me to." He sighed. "And I never wanted to affect the way you thought of your mother. I know you still have a relationship with her."

"I wish I'd known," she whispered, looking down. "I'm sorry I had the wrong idea."

"It's OK, honey. You didn't know. There was no way you could know. Not many people do."

Carina twisted the fringe on her pale blue throw pillow. "Did you really want me to live with you here?" she asked quietly. "Or did you just not want her to have me?"

"Of course I wanted you," he replied.

"Then why don't you look at me?" she asked.

Her father blinked at her. "What?"

"You don't ever look at me. It's like you forget I'm around. Or you don't even want to remember."

His eyes got watery. "Oh, honey," he said, his voice catching. "It's just that you look so much like her. You're the spitting image of your mother. It's just hard for me sometimes."

The gentle tone of his voice was the only trigger she needed. Before she knew it, the burning in the back of her throat and behind her eyes gave way to sobs.

She leaned into her dad, crying into his sleeve. It was as if all the years of *not* crying had built up inside of her into an unstoppable wave of tears. Strangely, she wasn't even that embarrassed. He put his arms around her and she leaned against his suit, pressing her nose against his jacket.

"You OK?" he asked.

She brushed the back of her hand across her nose and nodded.

"We're gonna be OK, C," he said, tousling her hair. "I promise. We're gonna be just fine."

There was still pain in her dad's eyes but she knew that he was telling the truth. He was going to be OK. And she would be, too.

He let her go and stood up. "By the way, there's something else I want to talk to you about," he said, steepling his hands. "I think it's time we increased your allowance."

She sat up straighter. Despite her crying fit, she was definitely interested in this topic.

"You've shown me that you can handle money. So let's figure out an amount that sounds reasonable. But the Amex card stays with me."

"OK," she said.

"And one last thing. You might want to go in and talk to the *Princess* people," he said. "Give them all your thoughts. I think you could really do them all some good."

"Dad, she's totally in love with you."

"Who's in love with me?" asked her dad, slightly alarmed.

"Barb Willis. She's totally got the hots for you. Just don't break her heart too badly, OK?"

The Jurg blushed. Carina was pretty sure she hadn't seen that happen for years. "Uh, no. She does have the hots for someone. But not for me. For Ed."

"*Ed?*" she asked.

Her dad nodded. "They started dating a couple of weeks ago. I've got to hand it to him. He came right out and called her up. Something's got into him the past few weeks. He's got much more ... confident," he said.

Carina instantly remembered her love notes and fought the urge to crack up. "I guess it had to happen sooner or later," she said.

"You shouldn't be so hard on him, you know," her dad said. "He really does like you a lot."

"I'll keep that in mind," she said. "And I'll call Barb. But only on one condition."

Her father raised an eyebrow. "Yes?"

"That you're fine with the fact that I may never work for you," she said evenly. "And that I may not ever go to Wharton. Or even get an MBA."

A small smile crept across his face. "You realize that you already have what it takes to be a ruthless businesswoman," he said.

"Dad."

"OK, it's a deal," he said.

"And thanks for the cupcakes," she said. "I got rehired today, so they'll definitely come in handy. That was very cool of you."

"You're welcome," he said. "And if you need help with anything else, just ask me. Oh, I almost forgot." He reached into his jacket pocket and pulled out an envelope. "Open it," he said, handing it to her.

Holding her breath, she slid her finger along the crease and opened it. Inside were two tickets to the Silver Snowflake Ball. Two hundred dollars each. Already paid for.

"Dad," she said, stunned. "You really didn't have to—"

"I know." Her dad shook his head. "You earned it. You worked harder for that than anyone else who's going."

She gulped again. "Thanks," she said simply. "But I don't know who to take."

Her dad wagged his finger at her. "Just promise me it won't be that Carter kid."

She rolled her eyes. "That's so over with."

"Good," he said, and smiled just before he walked out.

Carina sat on her bed staring at the tickets in her hand for a long time. It was just a dance and there was no Prince Charming in sight, but she felt like Cinderella. And as she sat there holding the tickets, she knew exactly who she would take.

Maybe there really were happy endings in real life, she thought. Or at least new beginnings.

Chapter 32

"OK, this is good," Carina said as Max glided to a stop at the kerb. "Just wait here."

"Take your time," Max said, winking at her in the rearview mirror.

"Thanks, Max. Wish me luck."

She stepped out of the car on to the pavement, carefully avoiding a patch of ice in her four-inch heels. The wind blew up underneath her coat and across her bare shoulders and the freesia perfume she'd sprayed on her neck wafted up from under her scarf. There'd been only a few times she'd got this dressed up before, and now as she walked past the usual flock of paparazzi into the apartment building, teetering on her heels, she felt them watching her. It didn't matter that she was wearing a dress that she'd rocked a few times before and jewellery and a bag she'd borrowed from Hudson. She knew she looked pretty, and after the past several weeks of wearing turtlenecks and jeans, it felt wonderful.

Inside the cosy lobby, a doorman looked up from his desk. "She'll be right down," he announced.

"Cool," she said, taking a seat on the couch near a tall, skinny Christmas tree. She tapped her foot nervously and scratched at a shaving cut on her knee. Of all of the people she'd disappointed and alienated over the past few weeks, Lizzie was the only one she hadn't made up with yet, so it made sense to ask Lizzie to go with her. The drive down to the ball would be the most time they'd spent together in weeks. But the fact that she'd responded so quickly to her text about the dance had to mean that Lizzie wasn't mad at her any more, and that was a relief. Going to this dance without having Lizzie there would be like not even going to it at all. And of course, Hudson was already at the Pierre right now, preparing for her debut appearance.

Down the hall, the elevator door opened and Carina heard her footsteps approaching. Along with someone else's, too.

"Hey, C!" she heard Lizzie yell. "I'm coming!"

Carina leaped off the couch and turned the corner. Lizzie was walking down the hall, stunning in a seasmoke blue strapless gown, with her red curls twisted up in a knot. And beside her, bopping along on her All-Stars and holding a silver camera, was Andrea Sidwell, the photographer who had "discovered" Lizzie.

"Hey, Carina!" she said, waving her arms. "What's up?!"

Carina ran to Andrea and gave her a hug. She hadn't seen

her since the shoot in Central Park all those weeks ago, when she and Hudson had taken turns holding the camera. Seeing her now, with her familiar blonde ponytail and black hoodie, made Carina break into a smile.

"I thought Andrea could take some shots of us looking all pretty," Lizzie said. "Since it's kind of a rare occasion."

"Great idea," Carina said as she took off her coat to reveal her emerald green minidress.

"OK you guys, stand next to each other," Andrea directed. "And give me a big smile."

Lizzie leaned into Carina's ear. "I can't believe we're going to Ava's dance," she said.

"Me neither," Carina muttered, and then they both laughed.

Andrea clicked the shutter. "That was perfect, you guys! Let's do another one!"

"I just hope she doesn't attack me for not showing up with my mom," Lizzie quipped.

"No, she'll just attack *me*," Carina said, and they laughed again.

Andrea took another picture. "*That's* the one," she said. "You guys look beautiful!"

In that moment, Carina knew that everything with Lizzie was going to be OK. And in the car on the way down to the hotel, they laughed so hard about what Ava was probably going to wear that they didn't even have a moment to talk about their fight.

"So I'm excited to see what you've done with the party," Lizzie said.

"I don't want to build it up too much," Carina said. "But I think I might have a knack for this."

"So Ava's not mad at you?" she asked.

"Well, she is a little," she said. "She keeps hinting that I still owe her two hundred bucks."

"What are you gonna do about that?" Lizzie asked.

Carina shrugged. "Just try to pay her back as soon as I can. My dad said he's going to up my allowance a little bit. So hopefully it'll be pretty soon."

Lizzie gazed out of the window. "You really kicked butt with that whole twenty-dollars-a-week thing, just so you know."

"Thanks."

"Hudson, Todd and I could definitely learn from you a little."

Carina realized that now was the time to bring up Todd. "You know, I think Todd's awesome, Lizbutt. And I'm sorry if I freaked out about stuff. I guess it's just weird for me to know that he's that important to you. You know, as important as we are."

Lizzie grabbed Carina's hand. "It'll never be the same thing as what the three of us have. Never, ever, ever."

Carina smiled back at her. "OK."

"And hey, is that guy gonna be there? The DJ guy?" Lizzie asked with a smile.

"Only because I begged him to be," Carina said. "Don't get your hopes up for us."

"Just promise me one thing," she said. "Whatever happens tonight, I want you to have a good time. Because this party is as much yours as Ava's."

Carina realized that Lizzie was right. It was her party, too. "OK. I promise."

Max finally pulled up in front of the Pierre and they saw a knot of girls with long blonde hair in tight black dresses walk through the revolving doors. "Here we go," Lizzie said. "Into the land of the blue bloods."

They followed the blondes down the long carpeted hallway and up a flight of stairs to the ballroom. When they walked through the doors, Lizzie and Carina both gasped. "Nicely done," Lizzie managed to say, nudging Carina in the arm. And Carina had to agree.

People milled around on a dance floor the size of a football field, underneath a series of crystal chandeliers. Soft pink and purple lighting dappled the walls. Marisol's beautiful flowers lined the banquet tables to the side, where platters of colourful cupcakes and Trader Joe's hors d'oeuvres were being gobbled up by hungry ninth-graders. Votive candles covered every square inch of table surface. And on the stage, above the dance floor, was Alex in a red spotlight, standing behind his turntables like a magician, fully immersed in the music that was flooding the room.

"What's that music?" Lizzie asked.

"Sharon Jones and the Dap-Kings," Carina said. "They're amazing."

"Huh?" asked Lizzie.

"I'll play them for you sometime," she said.

They moved into the room, staying close to each other in the dim light. It seemed like people were having a good time, but she couldn't tell yet.

"Nobody's dancing," Carina murmured.

Lizzie patted her on the shoulder. "Don't worry. They will. At least it doesn't look like anyone's leaving."

"Hey, Carina!" said a bubbly voice. A girl with a purple stripe in her hair emerged from the shadows.

"Hey, Marisol!" Carina said, running over to give her a hug. "The flowers look gorgeous!"

"Thanks so much," she said, her brown eyes shining. She tugged at the piece of striped hair. "And thanks again for getting me a ticket."

"Oh my God, *what* are you wearing?" Lizzie asked her. "That is the coolest dress!"

"Oh, this?" Marisol held out the edges of her T-shirt dress. It was black and white and red stripes, with fake epaulets at the shoulders and a distressed hem. "I made this myself."

"You did?" Lizzie circled around her.

"Honestly, I just kind of copied it from this store on the Lower East Side where I saw something like it," she said. She twirled around. "But I love how girly it is."

"Wait a minute," Carina said, her mind clicking into

gear. "Would you ever want to be a trend scout for *Princess* magazine?"

"A what scout?" Marisol asked.

"They're looking for real-life teenagers who have great style and know what's happening before everyone else. Would you want to do it? I think you'd be great for it."

Marisol beamed. "Sure. I love *Princess* magazine."

"You *do*?" Carina asked, mildly stunned.

"Yeah," Marisol said. "It's kind of a guilty pleasure. I've been reading it since I was six. How do you know the people there?"

Carina paused. Alex still hadn't told anyone about her. Now she liked him even more. "I'll tell you later," she said. "But I'll email you with their information."

"OK, cool," Marisol said, bubbling with excitement. "Hey, go say hi to my brother. He's been waiting for you to show up." She covered her mouth with her hand. "Whoops. I'm not supposed to have told you that."

Hearing this sent a shiver right down her spine, but as she looked over at the stage, she saw the unmistakable silhouette of Ava in the electric purple dress, striding over to her with her hands on her hips. "Carina? Can I talk to you?"

Carina steeled herself. "Hey, Ava," she said. "Good to see you."

"What took you so long to get here?" she demanded, crossing her arms in front of her cleavage. "I've been texting you."

301

Carina's heart sank. "Why? What's the problem?" she asked.

"There's no problem," Ava said innocently. "I just wanted to tell you that five people have come up to me and said that this is the best Silver Snowflake Ball they've ever been to," she said. "Even people from *Exeter*," she added. "I have to admit, you did an amazing job."

"That's great," Carina said. She couldn't believe how thrilled she was to hear this.

"And I'm not sure how it happened, but there's a photographer here from the *Times*," Ava said, pointing to a young man with credentials taking pictures of some kids on the dance floor. "Did you do that?"

Carina smiled to herself. Her dad really was pretty awesome sometimes. "Listen, Ava, about the two hundred dollars I still owe you, I just want you to know that I'm gonna be able to get it to you really soon, like, as soon as break is done—"

"Oh, don't worry about that," Ava said.

"What?" she asked.

"It's fine if you keep it," she said. "You earned it. You did." Ava put her hand on Carina's shoulder and glanced at her outfit. "And nice dress, by the way."

"Thanks," Carina said, overwhelmed.

"Do you think my hair looks all right?" Ava asked, turning around so Carina could admire her complicated upsweep. "I can't really tell."

Carina sighed to herself. Maybe Ava wasn't a terrible person to the core, but she was certainly never going to change. "It looks gorgeous," she said.

Ava turned around and pulled at one stray curl. "Thanks," she said. "I went to Fekkai."

She strutted off and Carina moved closer to the stage. She felt something pulling her towards Alex. She just wanted to be with him.

She climbed the steps to the stage and walked over to his turntables. He wore a cool black scarf around his neck and a thin red T-shirt, grey skinny jeans and his scruffy Stan Smiths. She loved that he looked so different from all the boys here in dark suits and ties. Once again, he was completely focused on the turning records, a hand holding his headphones to one ear.

He looked up at her. "'Bout time you showed up. Aren't you throwing this thing?" he asked.

"I'm just trying to be fashionably late." She could see now that his T-shirt had a familiar image on it. It was the same image of the couple from the DVD he'd showed her. "Looks like you're *In the Mood for Love*," she teased, gesturing to his shirt.

He looked down at it and grinned. "Thought it might give me the guts to do what I've been thinking about for days," he said.

"And what was that?" she asked.

He took her by the hand and led her away to the side of the stage. "This," he whispered, leaning in.

She closed her eyes and held her breath. The music was swirling around them, and in her mind she pictured it as a lush, tropical landscape, full of swaying palm trees and gently lapping waves. Her eyes still closed, she stepped closer to him, and he put his arms around her waist. As his lips touched hers, she felt her knees go rubbery. She'd never thought in a million years that a boy who was a friend could be such a good kisser. Now she was thrilled to find out that she'd been wrong.

They stood there for what seemed like hours, until Carina felt someone tap her on her shoulder.

Carina opened her eyes. It was Hudson standing in front of her. "Sorry to interrupt, but I think I'm supposed to go on now."

"Oh my God, you look gorgeous!" Carina shrieked.

It was true. For the first time ever, Hudson looked like a real star. Her hair had been straightened and then curled into soft, romantic waves and her eyes were beautifully lined with purple kohl pencil. She wore a black halter dress that showed off her toned arms and narrow waist, and long gold earrings made of intersecting hoops.

"Oh my God, I'm so happy I made you do this," Carina said, jumping up and down. "Oh, and by the way, this is Alex," she said, holding Alex's hand.

"Hey, it's nice to meet you," said Hudson. "I've heard a lot about you."

"Hi there," Alex said, shaking her hand. "Um, sorry to

change the subject," he said, "but is that Holla Jones standing back there?"

He pointed backstage, where, sure enough, Carina could make out the petite frame and muscled arms of Holla Jones. "Holla's Hudson's mom," Carina told him.

Alex did a discreet double-take and then caught himself. "Wow," he said. "This is some school you go to."

"How're you feeling?" Carina asked Hudson. "Are you psyched?"

Hudson swallowed and nodded. "I guess you could say that," she said vaguely.

"Just go out there and kill," Carina said. She grabbed Hudson's hand. "No fear."

"C, I'm not about to surf a monster wave or anything," Hudson wisecracked.

Carina laughed out loud. Hudson could be sarcastic when she wanted to be. "OK, fine, break a leg."

She waited for Alex to finish his set and then they walked down to the dance floor. Lizzie and Todd walked up to them in the dark as Hudson's tech guys set up for her performance.

"Is she coming out soon?" Lizzie asked Carina.

"Any minute," Carina said. "Oh, and this is Alex. The DJ I told you about."

"Oh yeah, nice to meet you," Lizzie said, shaking his hand.

"Same here," Alex said.

When Alex wasn't looking, Lizzie gave Carina a wink.

Alex whispered into Carina's ear. "Why does she look so familiar?"

"She's a model," Carina said, her chest swelling with pride.

Suddenly Ava walked out onstage to the microphone stand that one of Hudson's tech guys had placed there. "Thanks, everyone, for coming!" she yelled into the mic. "And now I'd like to introduce to you the next huge pop music sensation, in her debut performance, the daughter of Holla Jones and my really good friend, Hudson Jones!"

The lights dimmed and the crowd clapped. Lizzie and Carina traded looks over the applause. Leave it to Ava to include herself in someone's introduction, Carina thought.

At last Hudson appeared on the stage. She looked scared but determined to get this over with, and as she crossed to the mic a narrow spotlight followed her all the way. Amid the applause were a few whistles and screams of "You're hot!" When she finally got to the stand, Hudson reached for the mic.

"Hi, everyone," she said softly. "It's great to see you all here."

The room became deafeningly quiet.

"This is a song off my first album," she said. "It's called 'Heartbeat.'"

Hudson bowed her head. A music track began to play, something fast and up-tempo that sounded more like Holla's kind of music than Hudson's.

Hudson kept her head down, listening to the track, until

it was her cue to start singing. She raised her head and turned to face the audience, bringing the mic to her lips … and then, nothing happened.

In the dark, Lizzie grabbed Carina's arm.

Hudson swallowed and seemed to collect herself, bringing the mic to her lips once more. This time, she opened her mouth, ready to start … and no sound came out.

Lizzie's hand tightened around Carina's arm.

Onstage, Hudson stood paralysed in the spotlight and started to tremble. The track continued to play mercilessly. And then, as if in slow motion, Hudson dropped the mic. A loud *BOOM!* echoed through the room. And then she ran off stage.

"Oh my God," Carina whispered.

"She has stage fright," said Lizzie.

"It's all my fault," said Carina. "All of this."

"Stop, it's OK," Lizzie said, grabbing her arm to console her. "We just need to find her."

Carina followed Lizzie as they elbowed past tech guys and roadies. *I'm sorry, Hudson*, she thought. *I had no idea. I'm so, so sorry.*

And as she set off towards the stage, Carina wondered if Hudson's career might have just ended before it even started.

Acknowledgements

Huge thanks go to Becka Oliver, Elizabeth Bewley, Kate Sullivan, Cindy Eagan, Amanda Hong, David Ramm, Fionn Davenport, Jay Tidmarsh, Jill Cargerman and Ido Ostrowsky.

Enormous thanks go to JJ Philbin. Sister, best friend *and* favourite writer.

And Costco-size thanks go to Adam Brown and Edie, who came on the scene while I was writing this book and changed my life. I love you.

About the author

Joanna Philbin was born in Los Angeles and grew up in New York City. She is the daughter of television host Regis Philbin. Joanna now lives in Santa Barbara, California.

www.joannaphilbin.com

Twitter: joannaphilbin

Look out for the first
CELEBRITEENS books

They didn't ask for fame, they were born with it

CELEBRITEENS

In the Spotlight

Joanna Philbin

They didn't ask for fame, they were born with it

Lizzie Summers is used to living in her supermodel mother's shadow. But after a photographer spots Lizzie's unique look, she becomes the "It girl" of New York's fashion scene.

But is fame all it's cracked up to be?